To Lola,

Get ready for the journey with Wanda

BOOKSTORE DISTRIBUTION
Contact:
INDEPENDENT VISIONS
PO BOX 2991
RICHMOND HILL, GA 31324-4120
Laharris4books@yahoo.com
Order online: www.LisaDumasHarris.com

ISBN: 13-digit 978-0-9785119-3-7
Library of Congress Control Number: 2010911111

Cover Design: Kelvin Carr- www.newmediadezigns.biz

Model: Roni Zormelo-http://www.modelmayhem.com/razb2555
Email: razzormelo@yahoo.com
Maureen Smith

Editor: Chandra Sparks Taylor-www.cstedits.com

Printed in the United States of America

This novel is dedicated to my loving grandmother,
the Late Ada Beatrice Bryant.
Thanks for all of the wonderful years, Ma. You will be missed.
I love you

Acknowledgments:

First, I give thanks to God for the gift of writing. I'm truly grateful for the patience and perseverance to complete my fourth novel.

Much love to my husband, Al, and my daughters Brittany and Alisha for your continued patience. I couldn't do this without your support and understanding. To my son, D'Andre. I love you, too.

To family and friends: my parents, Andrew Dumas and Martha Bryant; my grandmothers, Ada Bryant and Mary Dumas; Angela Bryant, Gwendolyn Bryant, Winsome Hudson Bingham, Cherrell Lindsey Cook, JoAnn Durm, Erin Emanuel, Joseph Fagan, Man and Yolanda Foreman, Ihsan "Esa" Frazier, Roy and Cynthia Frazier, Melvin Gilchrist, Joy Graydon, Gregory and Victoria Green, Inell Green, Keith Hayes, Alfred Haywood, Leonard Howard, Rickey Hurt, Vincent "Maurice" Jenkins, Danett "Candy" Jones, Shantelle Kuykendall, Sheryl Lewis, Mark Lloyd, Roosevelt McCray, Felton Mitchell, Antaeveon Payne, Schartess "Tasha" Robinson, Shonta Russell, Ray Thomas, Shannon Tolbert, Tracy Tolbert, Paul and Vickie Williams, and Victoria Williams. Also, the Dumas family of Fort Myers, Florida; the Frazier family of Lamont, Florida; Ruth Cooper, and my in-laws—the Jones and Harris families. I appreciate all of your love and support.

Jennifer "Kaye" Benyard. You have been such a blessing. Thanks for everything.

Sheriff Ron R. Robinson and Diane Robinson, your time and assistance are greatly appreciated.

A congratulatory shout-out to my supporters and military retirees: SFC R. Christopher Brown, SFC Valsaria Bynum, SSG Tyrone Darby, MSG Brian K. Davis, SFC Erin Felecia Emanuel, SFC Stacy Ferguson, SFC Pamela Franklin, SFC James "Mike" Frazier, BMC Chucky Fulwood, SSG Sharon Gainer, SFC Dennis T. Garrett, SFC Tamika Gatling, 1SG Karl J. Hall, COL Gwendolyn Boney Harris, 1SG Joseph A Henry, SFC Trina Hinds, SFC Dorene Hollins, SFC Lucinda Jackson, SSG Melissa Jackson, MGySgt Daryl Johnson, SSG John Kelly, SFC Darrick Lewis, SFC Sheryl Lewis, MSG Derrick Loney, MSG Eric S. Magee, HM1/USN Pamela Maloney, SFC Terry Mercer, SFC Tony O'Neal, LTC John R. Platt, SMSGT David Prince, MSGT Marsha Prince, SSG Charles Robinson, SFC Keith Sirmans, SFC Shon Swift, 1SG Cynthia Ann Whitfield, SFC Randy Wright. We appreciate your service!

To Chandra Sparks Taylor: I'm so happy to have you on my team. Best wishes to you for continued success. For your editorial needs, visit cstedits.com. Also, check out Chandra's young adult novels, *Spin It Like That, The Pledge,* and *The Promise.*

Kevin Carr, once again, I love the book cover. For your graphic design needs, visit www.newmediadezigns.biz.

A special thanks to my fabulous model, Roni Zormelo. To view more photos visit http://www.modelmayhem.com/razb2555. If interested in working with Roni email razzormelo@yahoo.com.

Lastly, I give a tremendous thanks to my readers. Words can't express how very much your support means to me. Continue to send the emails and feedback. I love you all, especially the ones who harassed and pushed me to complete this book. Thanks and God bless.

Trouble In My Way

Finding My Way Series, Book 3

Chapter 1

Wanda Boyd strutted through the Savannah/Hilton Head Airport refreshed after a much-needed getaway. She wore a V-neck, backless maxi dress offering a view of her cleavage, and the silk fabric rested perfectly against her firm backside. Wanda hid behind dark shades, gloating as lustful stares attested to her undeniable beauty.

She and her lover, Ron Phelps, had just returned from a weekend rendezvous in Las Vegas, Nevada. Ron's best friend, Pete Myers, and his fiancé, Casey Howard, had vacationed with them. Although Wanda was skeptical of them coming along, the couples had a blast. Ron and Pete splurged, making the trip unforgettable. They lodged at the luxurious Venetian Hotel, and the ladies were pampered with a personal masseuse and gourmet meals, and they spent hundreds of dollars at the gambling casinos.

The trip was intended for Wanda to escape family problems. Two weeks earlier, she'd learned her parents were getting a divorce. Wanda was devastated by the news. She'd never fathomed that after twenty-nine years of marriage her mother and father would call it quits. She was hopeful they'd reconsider and begged them not to choose such an extreme resolution. However, they informed her, the decision was final. Knowing her parents as well as she did, Wanda realized their issue was serious. She assumed it was infidelity. Wanda wasn't sure who did what, but she couldn't think of anything else that could shatter such a grounded relationship.

After learning their fate, tears burned her eyes every time she thought about her parents living separate lives. Wanda had always known them to be such a great team. Their marriage was a testament of opposites attract—her mother was loving, soft spoken, and kind while her father was dominate, opinionated, and bold, yet they complemented each other.

Wanda remembered admiring them while growing up. No matter how hard she or her siblings tried to divide and conquer, their efforts failed. There were occasional arguments as with any other couple, but her parents had always seemed to be on one accord.

As Wanda approached the baggage claim area she noticed the luggage hadn't arrived. In the meantime, she turned on her cell to check for new messages. There were three, but she focused on the one from her mother saying to come over once she'd arrived back in town. Wanda dialed her number, curious what was going on. The phone rang until she was prompted to leave a message at the beep. Instead she hung up, dropping the BlackBerry in her purse with intentions to try again later.

Then she looked up, making eye contact with Ron who was standing across the room with Pete and Casey. They shared a smile. Although Wanda had traveled with him, while in Savannah they were cautious of being seen together because Ron was still a married man—even if his wife was missing.

Before long, the luggage appeared. Wanda stepped closer to the carousel and waited. After grabbing her suitcase, she headed for the parking garage. Once inside her car she started the engine then dialed her mother's cell number before trying the home phone. Again her calls went to voicemail. *Why isn't she picking up? She normally always answers,* Wanda thought.

In the mood for easy listening, she slid in Anita Baker's *Rapture* CD. The sounds of "Sweet Love" filled the air. Moving to the beat, Wanda proceeded to pay her parking fee. When she veered onto I-95 South she increased the volume and accelerated up to eighty miles per hour within a matter of seconds.

Twenty minutes later, she parked in her parents' driveway, baffled that both cars were there yet no one had answered the telephone. "Oh, Lord. I hope Daddy hasn't done something crazy," Wanda said, feeling nervous. Her heart rate quickened as she raced toward the house. Wanda banged on the door, calling out for her parents, wishing she had a spare key. She prayed, pleading with God not to discover a murder-suicide crime scene.

Finally, her father answered.

Wanda sighed. "Thank God. What's wrong, Dad? Why didn't someone answer the phone?" Wanda fussed, walking inside.

"Everything's fine," he replied, closing the door. "Your mother and I were having a discussion so we ignored the telephones."

"What if it was an emergency?" Wanda complained.

Then she took in a deep breath and slowly exhaled, calming herself. When she looked in her father's eyes, she saw his pain. "Dad, is there any way you and Mom can work this out? What happened?" Wanda questioned, wanting specifics.

"I'm afraid not," he replied, sadly. "Honestly, I was just as shocked as you to learn your mother didn't want to be married anymore."

Wanda pitied her dad. She lowered her head, pursing her lips, trying to remain composed. "I'm so sorry," she said, consoling him.

"Don't be," he replied, forcing a smile.

They continued into the den. "How are you doing, Momma?" Wanda asked, walking in her direction. She was sitting on the sofa.

"I'm okay. Your father's moving out," she said.

"How do you feel about him leaving?" Wanda asked.

"Well, I'm not proud of it. I hope one day you'll find it in your heart to forgive me, Travis. I really am sorry," she said to her husband.

"So am I," he replied. "I have everything. I'm going to take off now so you two can talk."

"Don't leave, Dad," Wanda insisted.

"I think I'd better. Call me later," he said.

Wanda nodded before following him to the front door. When she returned, Joyce was wiping tears away. "Don't cry, Momma," she said in a comforting tone. It was tearing Wanda up to see her parents so broken.

"I never intended to hurt your father," Joyce said. "It kills me to see him so sad."

"What's the problem, Momma? I didn't see any of this coming," Wanda replied.

"I've strived to be a good wife and mother, but now I'm in a different place. It's time for me to enjoy myself and do the things I want to do," Joyce said.

"Why can't you enjoy yourself with Dad? I thought this was the time in life people lived for," Wanda stated.

"Yeah, that sounds good. Realistically, your father has grown to be old and boring. We've argued about it for months."

"Momma, y'all can fix this. I think counseling would be better than a divorce."

Joyce lowered her head. "It's too late," she said.

"It's never too late, Momma," Wanda replied.

"Yes, it is. I have a boyfriend. I'm in love with another man," Joyce said.

Wanda gasped, trying to process what she'd just heard. "A boyfriend?" she questioned. She hopped off the sofa and paced the floor, refusing to look at her mother.

"Sit down, Wanda," Joyce ordered.

"Naw, Momma. What have you done? What have you done to our family?" she rambled, continuing to pace.

Joyce got up and stood in her path. She looked Wanda directly in the eye. "I said sit down," she repeated authoritatively.

"How could you?" Wanda asked her, frowning.

"This is my life," Joyce shouted.

Wanda stepped away, facing the opposite direction. "I can't believe what I'm hearing," she mumbled, getting angrier by the second. Wanda became so frustrated she didn't know what to do.

"I've planned a cookout for Saturday, here at the house," Joyce continued, demanding her attention. "I've already told your sister and brother. I'd like to introduce Michael to all of you at once. Will you come?"

Wanda turned around in slow motion. "You're bringing another man into my father's home? Momma, you're not even divorced yet," she complained. "I never thought I'd have a conversation like this with you."

"You're absolutely right, Wanda, I'm not divorced yet," Joyce snapped, "but I have moved on. You need to accept that fact and deal with it."

"I see. Well, let me be perfectly clear. I don't approve of what you're doing and I will not be at the cookout. I couldn't care less about meeting Michael," Wanda sassed.

"Get over it," Joyce said. "The sooner, the better."

Wanda rolled her eyes and shook her head in utter disbelief. "I'm done," she said before storming out of the room.

Once in her car, she sat weakened by disappointment. Before driving off, she dialed her father's number. "What's gotten into Momma? Do you know she has a boyfriend?"

"Unfortunately," Travis replied.

"Who is this person? How long have y'all had all of this drama going on?" Wanda questioned.

"For months. We kept our problems kinda quiet, trying to work through them ourselves. When I found out Joyce had an affair, that was it for me. The marriage was over."

"Oh, my God," Wanda whined. "I can't even imagine how this has happened."

"Our relationship took a turn for the worst after she joined that women's social group," Travis pointed out.

"Why? I thought mingling with women her age was a good thing," Wanda said.

"I did, too, at first," Travis replied, "but, you know how ladies talk. She probably learned about the other women's lives and felt she was missing out on something in her own. I don't know."

"Wow. I guess that's possible," Wanda said sadly.

"She told me she's in love with the guy. Apparently, he's giving her the attention she wasn't getting from me. Your mother did attempt to get me out more, but we're older now. We can't do all that stuff we used to."

Wanda held the phone in silence, searching for the right words to say. "Well, Dad," she began, "just because you're older, that doesn't mean you can't add spice to your life. It was just you and Momma. Y'all could've been chasing each other around the house butt naked if you wanted or had date night once a week or once a month. Man, I wish I would've known what was going on. I could've helped you plan a trip or do something to let Momma know she's special. There's no doubt about it, Dad, women want to feel loved. Without that connection a relationship is doomed."

"If I could do it all over, I'd definitely make some changes. I love my wife," Travis admitted.

"Would you take her back?" Wanda asked.

"I can't. Not knowing she's been with another man. It's over. She made her choice," Travis replied regretfully.

"No one could've ever told me my parents would be getting a divorce. Never," Wanda repeated, thinking out loud.

It was hard for her to accept what was happening, but clearly there was nothing she could do about it.

"We'll get past this," Travis encouraged. "Let it go for now. We'll talk soon. I love you."

"I love you, too," Wanda replied.

When she made it home, she unpacked her bags and took a long, hot shower. After speaking with Ron for a short while, she dialed her boyfriend, Malcolm's number.

"Hey, baby. How was the trip? Do you feel better?" he asked.

"I did," Wanda replied. "Leaving Savannah for a few days was just what I needed. Now, I'm back to reality. My parents are definitely going through with the divorce."

"I'm sorry to hear that," Malcolm said. "I'm not too far from your house. Do you mind if I come over?"

"Of course not," Wanda replied. She realized it was necessary to make time for Malcolm to keep him happy.

Moments after she hung up with him, she received a picture message from Michelle showing off her pregnant belly. *She's getting big,* Wanda thought, staring at the photo. She closed the flip phone, excited to share Michelle's joy.

While she waited for Malcolm to arrive, she selected an outfit to wear to work the next day. Afterward, Wanda walked into the living room and noticed headlights in the driveway. She peeked out of the window, making sure it was Malcolm before disarming the security alarm.

"Hey, it's good to see you," he said once she'd let him in. "Are you okay?"

"I will be," Wanda replied, accepting his embrace.

Malcolm kissed her.

"I'm happy you stopped by. Where are you coming from?" Wanda asked, following him to the sofa.

"I just left the sports bar. I played a couple games of pool with a guy from work. Tell me about your weekend," Malcolm said, putting his arm around her.

"There's nothing to tell," Wanda lied.

"You didn't do anything exciting?" Malcolm inquired.

"No. I just needed relaxation and a change of scenery."

"Well, I'm glad you're back at home. Do you think you'll be up for dinner tomorrow after work?" Malcolm asked.

"Sure," Wanda replied.

"Great." Malcolm kissed her on the forehead. "I know you're tired and you have a lot on your mind so I'll go and let you get some rest. Call me tomorrow," he said, standing. Malcolm pulled Wanda to her feet and pressed his lips against hers. "Don't worry yourself too much. Everything is going to be fine. I love you."

"I love you, too," Wanda said.

She walked Malcolm to the door. After seeing him out, she reset the security alarm then returned to her room and snuggled in bed. Wanda regretted cheating on Malcolm because he was such a sweet person. However, he didn't fulfill her needs. He was romantic in spurts, and his sex drive didn't compare to hers. Wanda had tried, but found it nearly impossible to be faithful.

Next, her mind drifted to her parents. She remembered her father saying he couldn't take her mother back because she'd slept with another man. She wondered how Malcolm would react if he learned about her and Ron's affair. Wanda believed he'd forgive her but understood why her father felt so betrayed. Her parents had been together for more than thirty years. They'd dated for almost two years prior to marriage.

Finally, Wanda drifted off to sleep. At 1:40 the telephone rang, waking her. "Who in the hell is this?" she complained, reaching for the receiver. She was shocked to see her mother's name and number on the ID screen. Her intuition said something was wrong. "Hello," Wanda answered, hesitantly.

"Wanda, your father's been rushed to the hospital," Joyce managed to say between sniffles.

"What? What happened? Which one?" she asked, frantic.

"He had a heart attack. He's undergoing emergency surgery at Candler," Joyce replied.

"Oh, my God. I'm on my way," Wanda said. She threw down the phone, hopped out of bed, and scrambled around the room trying to get dressed.

Wanda hurried to the hospital, joining her mother, younger brother, Tony, and sister Tina, in the waiting room. She spoke and accepted an embrace from her siblings, then started in on her mother. "This is all your fault," she lashed out with a pointed finger.

"Come on, Wanda, let's not start the blame game," Tony said, calmly pushing her away.

"She's responsible. Are you happy now?" Wanda blurted in her mother's direction.

Joyce didn't respond.

Tony forced Wanda into a seat at the other end of the room. "Calm down, sis. We have to stick together. Trust me this is just as hard for Momma as it is for us. Leave her alone," he whispered.

Wanda frowned. She cut her eyes at her mother, pissed at all the confusion she'd caused the family. She pitied her father most. Although he'd put forth a macho image, Wanda knew his heart was aching.

During the lengthy wait, she impatiently anticipated an update while Joyce comforted Tina as she used an entire box of Kleenex and Tony sat quietly twiddling his thumbs. When the surgeon finally notified them that Travis was in recovery, they all exhaled a sigh of relief. The doctor said the nurse would allow a short visit once Travis was settled, but warned he needed to get plenty of rest.

At last, the family made it in to see him. Travis was sound asleep. They stayed for a few minutes, holding his hand and leaving kisses along his face, before heading home.

Later that morning, Wanda stopped by the hospital on the way to work. Her father was still resting. She continued on to her job at the Chatham County Courthouse, exhausted, but kept busy to keep from worrying so much.

Wanda and her siblings visited their father daily and his elder sister, Cathy, a registered nurse from West Palm Beach, Florida, took leave from her job to be with him. They were all very supportive and strived to keep Travis's spirits lifted during his recovery process.

Whenever Joyce showed up at the hospital, there was always a confrontation. Cathy also blamed her for Travis's condition. However, because they were still legally married, there was nothing she could do to keep Joyce away.

On Thursday evening, while visiting with her dad, Wanda was surprised to hear from Pete's fiancé, Casey. She stepped out of the room to take the call. Casey shared how much she enjoyed hanging out with her while they were in Las Vegas. Wanda assured her the feelings were mutual. When she asked to keep in touch or if they could get together sometime, Wanda invited her to the River Walk club the following night. Although she had a lot going on, partying allowed her to escape the pressures of the real world. Casey accepted Wanda's offer and they made plans to meet up before ending the call.

Wanda's mind drifted to Ron. They'd spoken on the telephone but hadn't seen each other since returning from the trip. Wanda smiled, remembering their adventure. "That was the best vacation ever. Ron, you're one hellava sugar daddy," she bragged.

Chapter 2

The alarm clock buzzed at 6:30 A.M. waking Kim from a deep sleep. After quieting the noise, her first thought was, *Thank God it's Friday.* She'd worked her full-time clinical psychology and part-time New York & Company jobs from Monday through Thursday. Finally, after the day shift at the hospital she'd be off for the weekend.

Kim stepped out of bed and made her way into the bathroom. While showering, she remembered the meeting with her friends that evening for girls' night out. Kim looked forward to the gathering. She'd eaten Ramen noodles for lunch and dinner the entire week to afford her meal.

After getting dressed in navy blue scrubs, she made her way into to the kitchen. She brewed a cup of coffee while she packed her lunch. Minutes later, she grabbed her purse from the sofa and scurried out the door.

Once at the office, the stack of folders piled on her desk made Kim want to do an about-face. The constant worry of finances and being exhausted while at work had affected her job performance. She'd fallen behind, but the goal for that day was to catch up so she could start the following week on the right track.

Kim realized instead of taking her responsibilities lightly she needed to excel so if a higher position became available she'd be considered. She sat down, ready to make progress. Kim worked without interruption until noon. Then, she took a short lunch before continuing where she'd left off. Around 3:30, her cell phone rang, distracting her. Kim picked it up to press Ignore Call but AL THE REALTOR was displayed across the screen. She quickly answered and smiled when Al scheduled a ten and two o'clock showing for her home the next day. Kim happily confirmed the times. She hung up, hopeful for good results.

"Maybe there's light at the end of this tunnel after all," she said, optimistic.

Kim had begun to feel helpless because her home was so nice, yet it had been on the market for over a month with only one showing. She was just as concerned about selling her SUV. The vehicle was advertised in the *Savannah Morning News,* the *Pennysaver,* and Kim had flyers posted around the city, however, she'd only received a few inquiries, but nothing serious.

She continued to pray for a breakthrough. Kim was on the verge of financial ruin and remained uneasy being in such a vulnerable position. Although working two jobs had kept her afloat, she wasn't getting enough rest or eating well.

Finally, around 5:30 she finished her last file. Kim cleaned off her desk before packing up her things. She hurried home to get ready for girls' night out.

The meeting place was Applebee's. Kim was the first person to arrive. She was in dire need of a social life. Wanda and Lynn showed up about ten minutes later, and Michelle wasn't far behind. Angel walked in as they were about to be seated. The ladies greeted one another with smiles and hugs, and everyone touched Michelle's pregnant stomach.

Once at the table they ordered drinks. The conversation began with an update about Wanda's father. She told them he was doing well. "The nurses love him," Wanda said. "Daddy might leave the hospital with a new wife." Then she reiterated her disappointment in her mother.

"It's hard to believe your parents aren't together anymore," Lynn said.

"I know. It seemed like Mr. Travis and Mrs. Joyce were made for each other," Michelle added.

"Momma had the nerve to invite us—her children," Wanda clarified, "to a cookout tomorrow to introduce us to her new man. Has she lost her mind? I am not going."

"Maybe you should stop by just to show your face," Michelle suggested.

"Hell no," Wanda exclaimed. She put her hand up, signaling to the girls not to try and persuade her. "I am not going. End of conversation."

"Although you don't agree with her action, that's still your mother," Kim said.

"I know that," Wanda replied. "I'm done talking about Momma. I came here to unwind and to have a good time."

The waitress approached the table, interrupting the conversation. She placed a drink in front of each of them, then the girls ordered dinner before she walked away.

Kim watched Wanda slurped down almost half of her strawberry daiquiri within seconds.

"Now, let me tell y'all about my Las Vegas trip," Wanda said, resuming the conversation. "We had a ball. Ron's best friend, Pete, and his girl, Casey, went with us. Casey is my new friend. I'm telling you, this chick is the coolest white girl I know. She's going to the club with me tonight."

"Wanda, we're glad you had a safe trip and all, but we really don't care to hear about you and Ron," Lynn said. "Did he mention his wife? Y'all better be careful. One day that lady might slip up on you."

"Whatever. When she's ready to come back home she will," Wanda said. "I'm not trying to keep her husband—I only borrow him from time to time."

"What's up with Malcolm?" Michelle questioned. "Where was he while you and Ron were gallivanting in Vegas?"

"Here in Savannah. Malcolm knows I'm having a hard time dealing with my parents' divorce, so I led him to believe I was going to Atlanta for the weekend to spend time alone."

"Wanda, you ought to be ashamed of yourself," Lynn said.

"You know, for some reason I'm not. Trust me, a break from my family was necessary. I wanted to choke Momma. I still can't believe her. Hell, I need another vacation," Wanda said, pouting.

"You need prayer," Kim said.

"Don't start, Missionary. I don't feel like hearing that mess," Wanda replied.

"Let it go, Kim. How's the home selling process going? Any hits on your house," Lynn asked, redirecting the conversation.

"Well, nothing much has happened at this point, but Al called today and scheduled two viewings for tomorrow. He's bringing a couple by and an agent with a different company is showing the house to someone else. Pray for me, y'all. I really need an offer. Trying to make ends meet until I sell can be overwhelming."

"Are you current on your bills?" Angel asked Kim.

"Pretty much. Between both jobs, I make enough money to pay everything, but I don't have much left. Occasionally I make a partial payment on the light bill or something in order to buy food, but I'm okay," she said. "Selling the house or truck would definitely lift a big burden."

"Don't default on your mortgage, Kim. If necessary, we'll help you pay the note so you won't ruin your credit," Lynn said.

"We who?" Wanda asked.

"I'm good for now, but thanks, Lynn," Kim replied.

"Kim, I have a question. I thought the Lord wanted you to have the best of the best. What happened?" Wanda asked sarcastically.

"I am not going there with you tonight," Kim replied.

Wanda laughed. "On a serious note, have you considered having a garage sale?" she asked. "You can make extra money by getting rid of stuff you don't use. What about Darius' things? Have you sorted through his belongings yet? He might have some items you can sell to pay a bill or two."

Kim shook her head. "I don't want to do that," she insisted.

"Why not?" Wanda asked. "Keep the sentimental items, of course, but cash in on the rest."

"That is something to consider," Lynn said.

"It makes sense to me, Kim, especially what you can't use," Michelle agreed.

"I don't know. I'm not over Darius' death yet. Having his possessions is my way of staying connected to him," she replied.

"I understand. However, getting rid of it all will probably help you heal. He'll always be in your heart," Angel said.

"I've got an idea. We can come to your house and help you go through Darius' stuff. Better yet, we can probably add to it. I'm sure we each have items we can donate to your sale," Lynn continued.

"Wait a minute. Who authorized you to volunteer our services all of a sudden?" Wanda asked Lynn.

"Who's in and who's out?" she replied.

"I'm in," Angel and Michelle said.

"I'm in," Wanda followed up seconds later.

"That's what I thought. Now shut the hell up, Wanda. What's a good day for us to come over, Kim?" Lynn continued.

"Um, next Friday will work," she said, snickering. "I can have the garage sale on Saturday."

"We'll be there," Lynn replied.

Then there was a brief silence.

"Michelle, are you and Kelvin ready for the baby to come?" Kim asked.

"Yes, we are. Especially Kelvin. He is so excited. I have about a month and half left," she said.

"Are you still having morning sickness?" Wanda asked.

"Girl, no. That usually happens during the first few months of pregnancy," Michelle said.

"Oh. What I keep track of is when you get pregnant so I can ask why, and once you give birth so I can see what the baby looks like. If it's cute, you're good, if not I'm gonna talk about the li'l ugly thing."

The girls giggled.

"Speaking of babies, I need to visit my godson," Kim said, looking across the table at Angel.

"Don't worry about it. You have a lot going on, Kim," Angel replied. "Maybe one day when you're off from your second job I can bring him by to see you."

"Would you? I'd like that," Kim said.

The waitress walked up. After she'd served the meals, Wanda ordered another daiquiri. When the waitress walked off, Kim said grace and they began to eat.

"Have you heard from the deacon guy you use to date? What was his name?" Michelle asked Kim.

"Leon. No, I last talked to him right after Darius got shot. He called to give his condolences. I'll probably reach out to him some day, but I'm not trying to relight old flames right now," Kim said. "Plus, I'm so busy I barely have time for myself."

"Well I'll be…I just thought of something. Kim is without a man. I can't believe it," Wanda said.

"Wanda, why are you messing with folk?" Angel asked.

"She can't help it. Are you still celibate?" Michelle asked Kim.

"Yes, ma'am," she replied with a huge smile. "It's been nine months. Isn't that great?"

"No, it's a miracle. J-K—just kidding," Wanda said, trying to be hip.

The girls laughed.

"You should try it," Kim told her.

"I'm good," Wanda replied.

"Hold up. Are you saying you and the love of your life, Darius, didn't have sex when y'all got back together?" Michelle asked Kim.

"Not once. It was a discipline thing. We agreed to wait until after marriage," she replied.

"Now, that took willpower," Michelle said.

"You ain't lying. You know how attracted I was to Darius. During our premarital counseling the pastor asked us to refrain from sex as an act of obedience, so we took the challenge. I admit, at times it was extremely hard, but we managed."

"Wow, that's great," Lynn said. "I forgot to tell y'all, my husband—Savannah's top cop—may be getting a promotion soon. One of the lead detectives is retiring. He applied for the position and feels his chances are pretty good."

The girls expressed their excitement for Chris.

"I really hope he's chosen because it's a day-shift position. I'm tired of sleeping alone. I'm ready for my man to lie in bed with me at night," Lynn said.

"Why? You're tired of improvising?" Wanda asked.

"Oooohhh," the girls sang, laughing.

"I'm kidding, Lynn," Wanda said, smirking. "I couldn't resist."

"Don't worry. I'll get you," Lynn replied.

"How is our soldier doing?" Kim asked Angel, switching gears. "We haven't talked about him tonight."

"Derrick's fine. The life of a soldier is quite demanding these days. Lately, he's been putting in a lot of hours at work because of the deployments to Iraq. Derrick Jr. and I enjoy him when we see him."

"Is he going to war?" Wanda questioned.

"No. Derrick's getting out of the military in August," Angel replied.

"Really? His enlistment flew by," Lynn said.

"It sure did," Wanda agreed. "I remember Angel acting a fool when that man left. All that damn crying for nothing."

"Wanda, you're a mess," Angel said.

Once everyone had finished dinner, they paid the tab, then exited the restaurant.

"Good night. I'll talk to y'all later," Kim said, waving to her friends. She continued to her car then drove straight home. Soon after getting there, she crawled in bed, excited about her house being shown on the following day. Eventually, she fell asleep.

Early the next morning, Kim did last-minute dusting and filled the air with scented oil. At 9:30 she drove to the Kroger in the Berwick Lakes Plaza. She ordered a Mocha Latte from Starbuck's then settled at a table. Kim pulled out a stack of bills to see what was due and what she'd be able to pay. After tallying everything she was left with less than twenty dollars in the bank and two unpaid balances.

"I can't believe I'm in this predicament," she mumbled, regretful. "What in the world was I thinking? I'm tired of living this way, Lord. What do I do? If my financial world doesn't change soon, what do I do?"

Kim lowered her head, wondering if she'd ever get her money dilemma under control. Then, she began to ponder ways to make a bad situation better. While brainstorming, she contemplated renting out the bonus room over her garage. Kim wasn't thrilled about the idea, but felt compelled to weigh any reasonable option.

On her notepad, she jotted down possible avenues to market her property and wrote a reminder to ask Angel if she knew of a place to advertise on the military post.

Kim's phone rang, distracting her. It was Al. He told her the couple he'd shown her home to had narrowed their search to three houses and hers was one of them.

"Thank you, Al," she said, smiling.

"You're welcome," he replied. "They've decided to talk it over and make a decision by tomorrow."

"Great. Let me know as soon as you hear something," Kim said.

"Most definitely," Al replied.

Kim hung up. "Please, please, please buy it," she said wishfully. She daydreamed of how great it would feel if the buyers chose her home.

A few minutes later, she looked at the clock hanging on the wall. It was almost 11:15. Although the temperature was in the upper eighties, Kim decided to go to River's Street to waste time. She packed up, purchased a bottle of water, then drove downtown.

The ambience was vibrant. Kim strolled along the boardwalk enjoying the live sounds of jazz. She took in the positive energy as chatter and laughter filled the space around her. Suddenly, she became overwhelmingly grateful for the moment she was in. Kim sat down and began to pray. After looking up at the clear blue sky she watched the waves of the Savannah River. Tears filled her eyes as she saw beyond her struggles and thanked God for her existence. Darius' death, the burnout from working two jobs, and stress from bills and debt had caused her to forget about the natural priceless treasures in life.

As Kim wiped tears away, she noticed a tall man with a camera strapped around his neck staring at her. She pretended not to notice him. However, minutes later he came toward her. *Please, don't bother me, mister,* Kim thought.

"How are you doing today?" the man asked, stopping in front of her.

"Hi, I'm fine," Kim replied, looking up at him.

"My name is Keith Anderson," he said, extending his hand.

"I'm Kim," she replied, accepting the handshake.

"Are you okay? You appear to be dealing with something. I just wanted to say regardless of what you're going through, Jesus loves you."

Kim smiled. "Thank you," she said, standing.

"You're welcome," Keith replied. He extended a business card to her.

Kim read it, noticing Keith was a youth minister. "Wait a minute. You attend Fellowship Baptist Church?"

"Yes, I've been a member for years," he replied.

"I recognize you," Kim said. "Do you know Darius Price?"

"I'm very familiar with Darius. Okay, you're the young lady who was coming to church with him," Keith said.

"I am. Darius and I were engaged."

"I'm sorry for your loss. Darius truly had a testimony. I prayed and watched that young man for months, hoping he'd sincerely changed. I'm convinced he had. Before his passing I expressed my interest of writing a story about his deliverance in our magazine."

"He mentioned that to me," Kim said, remembering the conversation.

"How are you coping with everything?" Keith asked her.

Kim took a deep breath. "Honestly, it's been hard. But today is a good day. I feel the best I've felt since I lost Darius. I was just sitting here acknowledging how we take things for granted. In the midst of my storm, I'm extremely blessed."

"Amen. Yes, you are, sister. I'm a freelance writer for *Keepin' It Real* magazine," Keith said, giving her a different business card. "Perhaps I can share Darius' story through yours."

Kim read his information, then she thought about his offer. "I have your number," she said. "I'll get back with you, if that's okay."

"Sure," he replied. "I'm certain your testimony will help others dealing with similar circumstances."

"I definitely have a story to tell," Kim agreed. Although she didn't take Keith up on his offer at that moment, she was very interested. Then as she reflected, she recalled the look on Darius' face when he told her about the gentleman wanting to write an article about his old lifestyle and deliverance. Darius had hopes of helping young men in the streets find their way to Jesus, and he was really excited about the opportunity.

"I'll do it," Kim said to Keith.

"Are you sure?" he asked. "Take as much time as you need."

"I'll do it," Kim repeated. She smiled. "I'd love to do it—for Darius."

"Can I call you later this week so we can set up a day and time?" Keith questioned.

"Of course." Kim gave him her phone number. "I'm happy we had this opportunity to talk."

Lord knows I was hoping you'd keep walking, she thought.

"The pleasure is all mine," Keith said. "Enjoy the rest of your day."

"You do the same," Kim replied.

After Keith walked away, she sat down again taking in the scenery, thinking about what had just happened.

Later, when Kim checked the time, she was surprised to learn it was almost three o'clock. Tingles filled her stomach as her mind drifted to the second showing of her home. "I hope it went well," she said.

Kim stood and walked in the direction of her car. During the drive, she continued to think about Keith telling her story so she could share Darius' testimony.

Once at home, she checked the mailbox before going inside. On the kitchen counter was the agent's business card from DBA Realty Company.

"Okay, Kim, now wait and see what happens," she said, coaching herself to be calm. The anticipation and excitement had caused her to be on the verge of an anxiety attack. She prayed one of the couples would purchase her house.

Minutes later, the phone rang. Kim hurried to grab it, hoping it was Al with good news, but ANGEL was displayed across the ID screen.

"Hey, girl. What's up?" Kim answered.

"Hi, Kim, it's Angel and Lynn."

"How was your day? What are you doing?" Lynn asked.

"I just got home not too long ago. I'm about to fix a salad for dinner," Kim said.

"Are you on a diet?" Angel asked.

"No. Just eating light," Kim replied.

"Oh. Well, we were calling to see how things went with the showings," Lynn said. "Any news?"

"Not yet," Kim replied. "The first couple narrowed their search to three houses, and mine was one of them. They're supposed to make a decision and get back with Al by tomorrow."

"That's good. You have a really nice house, Kim. It'll sell," Angel encouraged.

"I need it sold ASAP," she replied. "Oh, that reminds me. Angel, if I want to advertise something on the military post, who do I contact?"

"What are you trying to advertise?" Angel asked.

"My first option is to sell the house, but if that doesn't happen within the next month or so, I came up with a back-up plan to rent out the room over my garage. I have to get some extra money coming in," Kim said.

"You've gotta do what you gotta do, but why not try someone we know first or perhaps a friend of a friend before you solicit strangers?" Lynn asked Kim.

"That's a good point," she replied.

"Yeah. We can help you spread the word. If we don't find someone, then try advertising," Angel suggested. "I can talk to Derrick and see if he knows of anyone in his unit looking for a place to live."

"I'd appreciate it," Kim said.

"I'll ask my parents at the day care as well. We'll find someone for you," Lynn said.

"Sounds good. That's why I love y'all, but anyway, I'll talk to you ladies later. I'm about to eat. I'm starving," Kim said.

Lynn and Angel said good-bye, then hung up.

After preparing her salad, Kim sat in front of the television.

An hour later, she received the anticipated call from Al. "Have some good news for me," she answered.

"Hi, Kim," he replied. "I followed up with the agent who showed your house this afternoon. Her clients made an offer on a different property. They like the other floor plan better."

"Really? Oh, well. Thanks for letting me know. I'll cross my fingers for your couple," she said.

"Do that. I'll give you a buzz as soon as I get the word," Al said.

Kim was disappointed, but she refused to be discouraged. She took the empty bowl into the kitchen and washed it before going upstairs. She filled her whirlpool tub with warm water, then lit candles around the bathroom. Next, she took her Bible and set it next to the tub before lowering herself into the bubbles. The water was soothing as Kim flipped through the book of Proverbs searching for where she'd stopped reading the night before.

After bathing, she crawled into bed. Kim tossed and turned for hours, eventually falling asleep.

The next morning, she woke up and glanced at the clock sitting on her nightstand. It read 7:10. Kim wondered at what time she'd finally fallen asleep. She'd last remembered checking the time at 3:35. Although she didn't get much rest, she got out of bed and started her day.

Kim attended the nine o'clock church service so she'd be back at home to receive Al's phone call. Just before noon, he informed her the couple had chosen a different house. She rested her head against the palms of her hands and cried.

Chapter 3

Wanda had spent the morning snuggled in bed watching Court TV. Although it was rare for her to lounge around looking at television, she actually enjoyed it. She was recuperating from the day before. After visiting with her dad, she and Lynn took an unplanned road trip to Jacksonville, Florida. Lynn was a shopaholic dying to get to the flea markets, and Wanda went along to avoid her mother's cookout. She was sure her siblings would call trying to convince her to come. Being out of town eliminated the possibility. Wanda wasn't ready to be around her mother with another man.

At noon, as she approached the hospital, her cell phone rang. It was her younger sister, Tina. Wanda turned down her stereo. "Hey, what's up? How was the cookout?" she asked.

"Strange," Tina replied.

"What did I miss? Did Tony show up?" Wanda questioned.

"Yep. Momma begged him to come. I'm sure she regretted it though."

"Why?" Wanda asked, whipping into a parking space.

"Girl, when Tony saw who Michael was, he broke Momma's coffee table and all the picture frames sitting on top, trying to get to him."

"Why?" Wanda questioned, confused.

"You're not going to believe this, Wanda, but Michael went to high school with you and Tony. His last name is Peterson. Do you know him?" Tina asked.

"Michael Peterson? You'd better stop lying, Tina," Wanda said.

"I kid you not. Honey, your mother is a cougar. She has a young man. I called yesterday to tell you about it, but I kept getting your voicemail," Tina said.

"Momma cannot be dating the Michael Peterson I know," Wanda insisted. "How does he look?"

"He's a nice-looking guy—tall, dark skinned, deep brown eyes, nice smile."

Wanda held the phone in silence. "I'm absolutely speechless," she finally said.

"You should've been there, Wanda."

"No, I'm glad I wasn't there. I would've helped Tony whoop Michael's ass."

Tina laughed. "Momma and I managed to keep them apart. Afterward, Tony left. I stayed so the evening wouldn't be a total disaster. Girl, Momma tripped me out. She couldn't keep her hands off the guy," Tina said.

"This is unreal," Wanda replied.

"I don't think Michael's on her level, but he's her choice. I support their relationship because she's my momma and I love her," Tina said. "Eventually, you'll have to accept it, too, Wanda."

"No, I won't. Are you crazy? You don't approve of someone's actions just because you love them. It wouldn't do me any good to see Momma or Michael. I know who he is," Wanda said. "He was a star athlete who flunked out of college. Where in the hell did she meet him?"

"I don't know," Tina said.

"I just can't stomach how Momma's living her life right now. Sex is the only reason I can come up with to justify her messing around with that boy," Wanda said. "Throwing away a lifelong partner to get it is simply unfortunate."

"Regardless of how we feel, the bottom line is, it's her decision," Tina stressed.

"Yes, it is, but our relationship will suffer because of it. Somewhere down the line Momma's going to have a rude awakening," Wanda fussed.

"We'll see," Tina said.

"Indeed. I have to go. I'll talk with you later," Wanda replied.

She hung up the phone, stunned by her mother's revelation. *What is she thinking?* Wanda wondered. She couldn't begin to justify her mother's actions.

Wanda dialed Angel's number as she walked toward the hospital entrance. "You'll never guess who Momma's new boyfriend is," she said.

"Who is he? Did you end up going over last night to meet him?" Angel questioned.

"No. I just talked to Tina. It's Michael Peterson. Does that name ring a bell?" Wanda asked.

"I don't think—Wanda, no. From high school?" Angel quizzed.

"Yep, that's him," she replied.

"Naw… Where in the world did Mrs. Joyce run into Michael?" Angel questioned.

"I have no clue. I'm disgusted with her. I can understand women dating younger men, but someone half of their age? Come on, that's a bit ridiculous," Wanda complained.

"Blame it on our society. Nowadays, the riskier, more immoral or unsafe behaviors are, they're being labeled exciting and gratifying—that's what people want. Nothing's off limits," Angel commented.

"Yeah, but Momma should know better. Why in the world would she fall for a guy the same age as her children? I can't believe she'd stoop so low. Daddy thinks her attitude changed after joining that woman's group," Wanda said. "They might be robbing the cradle, too."

"Wanda, you of all people should know sex is in. Everybody wants it and will go to new heights to get it. Look at all the swingers and open marriages we have now. What's up with that?" Angel said.

"You ain't lying. I'm not willing to share my man. I'll break Malcolm in half if I found out he was seeing someone else. I may step out on him, but he'd better not think about cheating on me."

"For the most part, I think all five of us are pretty grounded in regards to relationships. If there's a swinger in the group they're keeping quiet about it," Angel said.

"Kim and I are the only two you'd question about swinger tendencies. You, Michelle, or Lynn—I can't see it," Wanda replied.

"No, I ain't with it. So, have you talked to Mrs. Joyce about Michael?" Angel asked.

"Not yet, but I will. I have to cool off first. I'd send my soul straight to hell if I encountered her anytime soon. My parents were in a good place in life," Wanda said. "Momma ruined it, thinking she's missing out on something."

"Lord, have mercy," Angel mumbled. "I hate when this kind of stuff happens. Why can't we have love and happiness without all of the heartache and pain?"

"Please. Anyway, I have to go. I'm at the hospital. I'm going to sit with my dad for a little while then meet Casey at the bingo hall."

"Aren't you tired of throwing your money away?" Angel asked.

"I stopped doing that a long time ago," Wanda said. "Ron is my sponsor. Believe it or not, my social life is keeping me from cursing folk out."

"You're crazy, Wanda. Have fun," Angel said.

"I will. Thanks for listening," she replied.

Wanda entered her father's room with a smile. She spoke, then kissed him on the cheek before continuing over to her aunt Cathy. Wanda hugged her.

"How are you doing today, Daddy?" she asked, sitting down.

"I'm fine, baby. I took a walk earlier," he said.

"Yes, he did," Cathy reiterated. "He's definitely getting his strength back. I was more winded than him," she said, giggling.

"Daddy, you'd better stop showing out on Aunt Cathy. She's gonna leave you and go back to Florida," Wanda said.

Travis laughed. "I didn't mean to. I'm just ready to get out of this place," he said.

"I can imagine. Are you comfortable? Do you need anything?" Wanda asked.

"No. Everything's perfect," Travis replied.

Then the room fell quiet. Wanda refused to mention her mother or anything going on with her because she didn't want her dad to stress about it. She watched television with him and her aunt for a couple of hours before leaving to meet Casey at the bingo hall. They sat at the bar chatting with Ron while eating hot wings. Afterward, he slipped her two hundred dollars. Wanda gave Casey fifty. "Let's try our luck," she said.

Once the money was gone, Wanda gave Ron a cue she was leaving. He winked and nodded, acknowledging her.

"What are you about to get into?" she asked Casey as they exited the building.

"Nothing really. I'll probably go home and relax. Pete and his biker buddies won't be back in Savannah until later tonight."

"Did you hear about the free jazz concert at Forsyth Park?" Wanda asked. "I'm going to check it out. Would you like to come along? I have a couple of chairs in my trunk. We can stop for snacks and drinks on the way."

"Sure. Sounds like fun," Casey replied.

"Great." Wanda unlocked the car doors and they got in. When she started the engine, Marvin Sapp's "Never Could of Made It" spilled from the speakers.

"This is my song," Casey said. She began to sing along.

Wanda smiled. "I like it, too. I don't do the church thing too often, but I listen to gospel from time to time."

"I love church. My father has been a pastor for years," Casey said.

"Really? I never would've guessed you're a churchgoer," Wanda said.

"Oh, yes. Girl, God has brought me a long way. Trust me," Casey said.

"I have to be honest with you," Wanda replied. "It irritates me when people act holy on Sunday, but lead a totally different life the rest of the week."

"Don't get me wrong. I'm a work in progress. I'm flawed, and I know God is not pleased with a lot of my actions, but regardless I can't think of a better way to start my week. I feel if I attend church faithfully and pray diligently, one day the worldly desires I'm struggling with will be taken away from me."

Wanda shrugged. “I guess. So, how did you hook up with Pete?” she asked.

“I met him at the club on his birthday. We’ve been dating for almost three years now,” Casey said. “How did you end up going out with Ron?”

“He used to flirt with me every time I went to the bingo hall, then he spoiled me by paying for everything while I was there. One night he put an out-of-order sign on the employee restroom door and pulled me inside. That was the first time we kissed. Our relationship has been physical every since. I love Ron’s excitement. I’m a chance taker, and he keeps the relationship interesting. I have a steady boyfriend named Malcolm, but he doesn’t provide the rush I need to keep me from straying,” Wanda said.

“Do you know Ron’s wife is missing? She has been for a few months now,” Casey said.

“Yes, I’m aware of that,” Wanda replied.

“Are you nervous about seeing him?” Casey questioned.

“Should I be? What do you think happened?” Wanda asked.

“I don’t know,” Casey replied.

“No, I’m not nervous. At times I do wonder why she ran off. I have a feeling she knew about Ron and me. What do you think of her? Are you two friends?”

“Naw. Sheila’s not sociable. She’s one of those high-class wannabes,” Casey said.

Wanda laughed.

“That’s why I enjoyed being around you while we were in Vegas,” Casey said.

“I had a wonderful time there. We must go back,” Wanda said, whipping into the convenience store parking lot.

Twenty minutes later, as she approached East Park Avenue she spotted a large stage and speakers set up at the north end of the field. After parking, Casey helped her carry the items from the car and they searched for a place to sit.

“Thanks for hanging out with me,” Wanda told her after they’d settled down.

“Oh, please. I’m enjoying this already,” Casey said.

“So, where were we with our conversation about Ron and his wife? Has Pete confided in you about the two of them? He and Ron are best friends, I'm sure he knows something," Wanda said, taking a sip of Dr. Pepper.

"If so, he hasn't said anything. I'm curious, too. I've asked questions, but Pete won't touch that subject," Casey said.

"I see. Well, at first I wasn't sure, but now I really don't think Ron would hurt Sheila. It is weird that no one, including her relatives, has heard from her though," Wanda admitted.

"She's left him a couple of times in the past, but they always end up getting back together," Casey said.

"Oh, really? I wasn't aware of that. I hope she comes back this time. I had no intentions of destroying a marriage. I'm just having fun," Wanda stressed.

"Has Ron mentioned their relationship to you?" Casey asked.

"Nope, not one word," Wanda replied.

"Testing, testing. Savannah… Are you ready?" a voice sang through the loudspeakers, interrupting their conversation.

The crowd cheered and applauded. Minutes later, local entertainers blended the sounds of instruments, creating an inspirational melody. Wanda and Casey enjoyed their performances for nearly two hours before packing up to leave.

"I can try to get some info out of Pete about Ron and his wife," Casey said, picking up their earlier conversation.

"No, don't mention it," Wanda insisted. "Not unless he brings up the subject. Pete knows you and I have been talking. If you start asking questions, he'll know why."

"You're right," Casey said.

"Have you two set a wedding date?" Wanda questioned, changing the subject.

"Yes, we're getting married next year on April first," Casey replied.

"On April Fool's Day? Are you sure Pete's not playing a prank on you?" Wanda asked.

Casey giggled. "No. We've planned a small, private ceremony," she responded.

"Three of my best friends are married. I'm not sure I can do it. Although I love sex and male companionship, I don't think I can handle the eternity aspect of marriage," Wanda said. "I like my freedom."

"Did you say three of your best friends? How many do you have?" Casey asked.

"Four. I'll introduce you to them one day. The five of us are like sisters. We bonded back in our school days," Wanda said.

"That's cool. I look forward to meeting them. I like having a steady man, and I look forward to marriage," Casey said. "The excitement has been taken out of dating these days. The last few guys I went out with before Pete were too cheap to buy dinner. One of them actually wanted me to pay for the meal."

"Oh, no. Honey, I don't date that type of man," Wanda stated. "I make it clear from the beginning, I'm a woman and I will be treated as such. If they can't handle that, I don't waste my time. Even my conversation has a price tag."

Casey snickered.

"Men are a trip. Malcolm and I have been together for nine years, so I haven't done the dating thing in a while. Not as far as searching for a steady boyfriend," Wanda said. "Malcolm's just not as sexual as I'd like him to be. Lately, I've conveniently distanced myself from him to be with Ron. Now that man knows how to make love," Wanda bragged.

"I know," Casey said.

"You know?" Wanda asked, staring at Casey, driving off the road. "Oh, shit." She narrowly missed a cement curb.

"Oh, um, not personally," Casey said. "I've heard that before. Sheila told me. I think that's the reason she goes back to him."

Wanda detected Casey's nervousness. She sat looking at her suspiciously, wondering if she was trustworthy. Her statement didn't set well with Wanda at all. She decided from that point forward she needed to be mindful of what was said around her.

"If I'm able to get any information from Pete, I'll call you," Casey said, breaking the silence.

"Do me a favor: Don't mention it," Wanda replied. "Like I said earlier, I don't want him to get suspicious of you asking questions."

"I can probe without being obvious," Casey insisted.

"I'd rather you not," Wanda insisted.

She drove into the bingo hall's parking lot and stopped behind Casey's car. "Thanks for hanging out with me," she said.

"Thank you. I can't wait to meet your friends," Casey replied, opening the car door.

"We'll get together soon," Wanda promised.

She waved as she drove off. Wanda immediately thought back to Casey's response to her saying Ron was good in bed. She also remembered her statement that Sheila wasn't sociable. "If that's true, why in the hell would she confide in you about her husband's performance?" Wanda shook her head, thinking, *Something ain't right.*

Chapter 4

Later that Sunday night, Kim sipped tea, dreading another exhausting week. Attending church was the highlight of her day, but after Al's phone call she laid around in her pajamas defeated by self-pity. The optimism and hope of selling her home had dwindled almost to nothing. Kim began to wonder if it were smarter to fight what appeared to be a losing battle or cut her losses and walk away, allowing the house to go into foreclosure.

Finally, she decided against giving up. Instead of letting the night end with no results, she chose to move forward with the plan of renting the bonus room. Kim grabbed her laptop and sat on the bed. She logged onto the Internet and emailed her friends, updating them on the showings and asked their help to spread the word about needing a roommate.

A couple of days later, she'd spoken to three prospective tenants. Kim was excited to get such timely responses and had arranged to interview them on the following Sunday. Anticipation of the meetings provided the motivation she needed to endure her long, tiring days. Still, by Friday, Kim was drained. Once she'd made it home, her first thought was to climb in bed, but she had a lot to accomplish prior to the garage sale the next day.

Kim headed upstairs. She went into the master bedroom and entered the closet, ready to clear out Darius' things. She paused, staring at his wardrobe, missing him again. She fought back her tears, searching for the strength to move.

Once she'd composed herself, as she took Darius' clothing from the hangers, she reminisced, remembering what he looked like wearing each piece. Suddenly, Kim fell to the floor, clinging to his favorite red shirt. "Why? Why did this have to happen?" she cried out, looking up toward heaven.

Kim leaned against the wall, reliving the pain of Darius' untimely death. Knowing he'd turned his life around and was ready to provide service to his church and community troubled her in the flesh. However, in the spiritual realm she rejoiced because he was covered by the blood of Jesus. "Praise the Lord," Kim whispered, lifting her hands into the air. Her sadness was quickly overcome by a sense of peace.

Minutes later, Darius' murderer, Greg, came to her mind. Kim hated the crime he'd committed as much as the probability he'd spend the rest of his life in prison. Although she felt the punishment was just, it reminded her of typical behaviors crippling black American communities. *How can we stop this vicious cycle of violence?* she wondered.

She reflected on the attitude and conduct of the youth. She shook her head, disappointed, thinking of the young men wearing pants below their backside and their lack of respect and motivation.

"We have work to do," she concluded.

The chime of the doorbell interrupted her thoughts. She hurried in the bathroom and freshened up before answering. It was her friends making good on the promise to come over and help sort through Darius' belongings. The girls walked in with bags and boxes filled with items they were donating to the sale.

"Oh, my goodness. Look at all of this stuff. Thank you," Kim said.

The girls expressed their appreciation as well. Their positive energy sparked Kim's excitement. She was ready to work.

"The majority of Darius' clothes are in my room. Someone can help me finish gathering those, and everyone else can start in the spare bedroom where he kept the rest of his stuff. It's a lot," Kim warned.

"I'll help you, Kim," Angel said.

"Okay. Cool," she replied

"Kim, have you eaten?" Lynn asked as they headed upstairs.

"No. Not yet. Why?"

"I told you," Wanda said, then smirked. "Go ahead and place the order."

"You told her what?" Kim asked.

"To buy pizza," Wanda replied.

"I know things are tight for you financially, Kim, but I didn't want to show up with food to find out you already had something for us to eat," Lynn explained. "I didn't call and ask you about it because I didn't want you to feel obligated to feed us, or feel bad if you couldn't."

"Oh. Well, I would've loved to provide dinner, but um... Anyway, pizza sounds great. Come on, Angel, we have work to do. There are racks for the clothes on hangers and tables for everything else, all in the garage," Kim said seconds before she and Angel disappeared into her bedroom.

They made several trips downstairs until the closet was emptied of Darius' possessions. As they coordinated the clothing and displayed accessories on the tables, Lynn, Michelle, and Wanda added more items from the room they were clearing out.

"I found a briefcase underneath the bed. Do you have the key?" Wanda asked Kim.

"No. Is it locked? Did you try to open it," she questioned.

"Of course I tried to open it," Wanda replied.

"I'll check it out in a few," Kim said.

After she and Angel had finished setting up, they joined their friends upstairs. Kim used a hammer and flat-head screwdriver as Wanda assisted her in prying open the briefcase. The other girls watched. They were all shocked when Kim opened it, revealing wads of money, handheld electronics, and jewelry stashed inside.

"Oh, my God," Kim said, scanning the faces of her friends. She covered her mouth with both hands.

"Dammnnn," Wanda sang. "Now you can pay for the pizza."

"I sure can," Kim said, tossing two twenty-dollar bills in Wanda's direction. "Should I turn this stuff in to the police or keep it?"

"You'd better keep it," Wanda said. "Darius died months ago. If the police haven't raided your house by now, they aren't.

"We hope not, anyway," Lynn said.

Michelle agreed with Wanda. "You got lucky, Kim. Spend it," she said.

"Help me count it, y'all." Kim gave each of her friends a bundle of money.

When the doorbell rang Lynn gave her stack to Angel. "I'll get it. It's probably the pizza guy," she said.

Kim and the others kept counting. She ended up with over twenty-five thousand dollars in cash, three iPods, a digital camera, and a variety of gold and silver jewelry.

"Knowing I have this much money in my house makes me nervous," she said. "I think turning it all in is the best thing to do. What if it belongs to somebody and they come looking for it?"

"Trust me they would've been here already. That's a lot of dough," Wanda said.

"You don't have to make a decision right now. Let's go eat," Michelle said.

Kim and her friends walked downstairs and she told Lynn how much money they'd counted.

"What are you going to do with it?" Lynn asked.

"Not sure yet," Kim replied.

"I have to fill y'all in on the latest," Wanda said after they'd settled around the table. I found out who my momma's guy friend is—Michael Peterson. Yes, the one we went to high school with."

The girls sat with their mouths open. Everyone was shocked, except for Angel who already knew.

"Now, that has got to be awkward," Lynn finally said.

"It really is," Wanda admitted. "I can't believe she's divorcing my dad to be with him. I'm still trying to figure out how in the hell they hooked up."

"Have you talked to her yet?" Angel questioned.

"No. I haven't seen or spoken to Momma since the night my dad was admitted to the hospital. It's been almost two weeks," Wanda said.

Kim shook her head. "I hope everything works out for you and Mrs. Joyce," she said.

"So do I, but at this moment I am pissed. My daddy's in the hospital recovering from a heart attack because of this bullshit."

Everyone fell quiet.

"Kim, can I get a loan?" Angel asked, redirecting the conversation.

"Sure, you can," she said with a smile. "Ain't God good? He'll make a way out of no way."

"Don't do it, Kim," Wanda said.

"What?" she replied.

"Thank Darius for that dirty money, not God," Wanda said.

"Please. I know where my help comes from," Kim stated.

"Darius was a drug dealer. I'm sure that's drug money. God had nothing to do with it, Kim. Just take the cash and use it," Wanda suggested.

"I don't care what you say, Wanda," Kim said rolling her neck. "This is God's favor, baby."

Wanda laughed. "Lord, have mercy. Why do you go to church, Kim? I don't think you've learned a damn thing," she complained.

"Excuse me. Who are you talking to, Wanda?" Kim asked.

Angel, Lynn, and Michelle sat back and listened.

"I'm talking to you," Wanda said. "Pay attention to the things you say, especially when God is concerned. When you wanted this house and that truck, your claim was God wants His people to have the best of the best. Now you're whining because you can't afford the crap and you're buried in debt. Why would God put you in a predicament like this? You can't enjoy the blessings you say He wanted you to have, because you work two jobs to pay for them? That's just stupid."

"Well, sometimes He allows up to deal with difficult situations so we can lean on Him. You wouldn't know anything about that," Kim replied.

"Yeah, then He'll rescue you with a bag of drug money, right? I understand where you're going with that, Kim, but I don't agree. He gives us free will. You're broke and hungry because of it. Not because of Him, but because of you," Wanda clarified with a pointed finger.

"Can we change the subject?" Angel slid in.

"Oh, hell naw. Who are you to give advice? When you stop screwing that woman's husband, maybe we can talk," Kim said.

"I'm not trying to advise you. I'm trying to help you get past your mental block. When God was blessing folks with common sense, where were you?" Wanda asked.

Kim grabbed a slice of pizza, then swung as hard as she could, slapping Wanda across the face with it.

Without hesitation, Wanda leaped across the table, spilling food and drinks, landing on top of her. They both threw punches as Angel and Lynn scrambled over to them. Michelle stood off to the side pleading with them to stop fighting.

The room became loud and chaotic as the five women spoke in high-pitched voices trying to gain control of the situation. Once Angel and Lynn had finally separated Kim and Wanda, they slowly loosened the grip on each other's hair.

Kim sat at the table, wiping tears from her eyes as she and the girls watched Wanda wet a paper towel and clean her face with it. After raking her hair with her fingers she walked past them. "I'm out of here," Wanda said. Angel followed her outside.

In the meantime, Lynn comforted Kim. "I cannot believe what just happened," she said.

"I know. Wanda makes me sick. She swears she has all the answers," Kim complained. "It's like she gets a thrill out of provoking me."

"Are you okay?" Michelle asked.

"I am," Kim said, "but I'm done talking about this."

She got up and left the room. When she returned, Angel, Lynn, and Michelle had finished cleaning the kitchen and were preparing to leave. Kim thanked the ladies for helping and hugged them on the way out. She set the security alarm then headed upstairs.

While running bath water Kim stood staring at her reflection in the mirror, rubbing the back of her head. She believed she'd hit it against the floor when she fell. There was slight swelling in the area, but Kim figured it was nothing serious. As she commenced to straightening her weaved micro-plaits, preparing to pin them up for her bath she caught a glimpse of a bald spot. Kim took a closer look and became furious with Wanda all over again. She'd snatched a patch of her hair out about the size of a golf ball.

"I hate that girl," Kim complained.

Wanda had always been the agitator among the group, but Kim never thought she'd get under her skin enough to provoke a fist fight.

She sighed. Finally, she undressed and stepped into the tub of bubbles. Kim laid back and closed her eyes, trying to calm herself.

After bathing, she went into the guest bedroom and emptied everything out of the briefcase except for the money, then she stored it on the top shelf of her walk-in closet. Kim wasn't sure what to do with the cash. She climbed in bed, contemplating whether to turn the money in to the police or use it to pay bills. Eventually she fell asleep with no solution.

The next morning, Kim woke up feeling horrible. Her body ached all over. She remembered the brawl with Wanda the night before and frowned. Tears burned her eyes. She was upset with herself and disappointed in Wanda for allowing their discussion to spiral out of control.

Moments later, Kim thought about the garage sale and hopped out of bed. After freshening up, she got dressed. While styling her hair, she ran her fingertips across the bald spot. Kim conditioned the skin with oil before pulling the plaits into a ponytail, hiding the baldness.

Next, she went downstairs and lifted the garage door. Kim dragged the big items outside along the driveway and set the racks of clothing at the entrance of her garage. There were five tables with items displayed on top. She put prices on everything and waited for her first customer.

Angel, Lynn, and Michelle stopped by later that afternoon to help out.

At five o'clock, the sale was over. Kim was pleased with the turnout. She had consistent traffic throughout the day and earned more than three hundred dollars.

The girls helped her store the remaining items in the garage. After putting everything away, they settled inside.

Kim served iced tea. As they sat in the living room chatting she noticed no one brought up what had happened the evening before. "I feel really bad that things went as far as they did last night," she said. "Y'all know how Wanda is. I guess she pushed me to my breaking point. My question is where do we go from here."

"Don't worry, Kim. Everything is going to work out. We'll let time pass and see what happens," Lynn said. "I believe you and Wanda will forgive each other and move on."

"I'm not so sure about that," Kim said. "For one reason or another she's always targeting me."

"Wanda is the same with all of us," Michelle said. "Any opportunity that girl sees to take a jab at us, she usually does. She's always been that way."

"Well, I'm not sure I want to continue to deal with her," Kim said.

"It's completely up to you," Lynn replied.

"You're upset, Kim. That's understandable, but I'm hoping we can get past this," Angel said.

"What kind of friend is she to pull out a handful of my hair?" Kim complained.

"Be fair. You attacked Wanda and she responded," Lynn said.

Kim lowered her head. "I guess I was wrong," she replied.

"So, how was the garage sale? Did it work out for you?" Angel asked moments later.

"Yes. The turnout was much better than I expected. I can donate what didn't sale to a nonprofit organization. I meet with the ladies interested in being my roommate tomorrow," Kim said.

"Good luck with that," Michelle said.

"Thanks. Oh, tell Derrick I appreciate the two soldiers he referred," Kim told Angel.

"I will. Let us know how it goes," she replied.

After finishing the tea, the girls left and Kim tidied up. When she was done she ran to Mom and Nikki's restaurant to get her favorite dish—smothered shrimp and grits. She hadn't had the meal recently because of her financial situation. She couldn't resist treating herself.

Kim took the food home. Shortly after eating, she fell asleep on the sofa. Around 4:00 A.M., she woke up and went to bed where she slept until it was time to get ready for church.

When she returned home, she changed clothes and waited for her potential roommates to show up. Kim had scheduled the appointments one hour apart.

The first two ladies were the soldiers Derrick had recommended. Kim felt they were nice, but she liked the third prospect better. She was a female sheriff closer to her age.

Kim informed the women of the rent amount and the move-in date of July 1. She told them she'd be in touch ASAP with a decision. She felt candidate number three was her best pick. Kim already knew the possibility of the soldiers being deployed. She didn't want to end up back at square one if they were ordered to leave.

"I got it," she said, coming up with another idea. "I can accommodate all three of them. The sheriff can have the bonus room and I can rent the soldiers a bedroom each, with access to the common areas. I wonder if they'd go for it."

Kim dialed Angel's number and ran the thought by her and Derrick.

They cheered her on. "That's a great way to get money coming in, Kim. I say give it a try," Angel said.

"Thanks. You know I value your opinion. Let me think on it some more," Kim replied.

Later that evening, she had a plan. The first thing on her agenda was to see if the ladies would agree to all three of them moving in. Kim made a mental note to call them the next day. She also decided to hang on to the money she'd found in Darius' briefcase instead of giving it to the cops or paying bills with it.

Kim walked up the stairs feeling a sense of accomplishment. She stopped by the room where Darius had stored his belongings and sat on the bed. All of a sudden it dawned on her, clearing everything out was a major step in her healing process. A huge smile spread across her face. For the first time in a long time, Kim was at peace.

Chapter 5

On Thursday evening, minutes after Wanda had arrived home for work, her mother showed up unannounced. Wanda was surprised by the visit, and butterflies tickled her stomach as she opened the door and invited her in.

"We need to talk," Joyce said.

"Okay. Have a seat. Would you like something to drink?" Wanda offered.

"No, thank you," Joyce replied, sitting on the sofa.

Wanda stepped out of her pumps and sat in the chair across from her.

"I want to start by saying, I'm sorry I've disappointed you, Wanda. I really miss the closeness we shared. If I could undo some mistakes I've made, I would," Joyce confessed.

"What mistakes are we talking about, Momma?" Wanda asked.

"Mainly, being more open with you about what was going on with your dad and me. I'd even work harder to save my marriage," Joyce admitted.

"Why didn't you tell me you and Dad were having problems?" Wanda questioned.

"We tried to deal with our challenges without involving you kids. Honestly, your dad didn't do anything. I take full responsibility for the breakup. I allowed another man to steal my heart," Joyce said.

"How did Michael get the opportunity to steal your heart, Momma?" Wanda asked. "Where did you meet him?"

"One of the ladies in the women's group had a gathering at her house. I invited your dad to go but he wasn't interested. We argued about it, then I went alone. Michael was there that night. The hostess of the party dates his friend."

"Let me guess, her boyfriend is a younger man, too," Wanda said.

"Yes, but what does that have to do with anything?" Joyce replied.

"Do you know Michael's only a year older than me? We went to school together, Momma," Wanda said.

"He told me," Joyce said.

"What else did he tell you about me?" Wanda asked.

"That was it. Although there's a significant age difference, I'm happy, Wanda," Joyce said. "That's what's important."

"Momma, I had sex with Michael," Wanda confessed.

"What?" Joyce sat with a dazed expression. "You're a liar," she finally said. "I will not allow you to play games with my life, Wanda Boyd."

"Ask Michael," Wanda suggested, outdone her mother had just called her a liar.

"You're an evil heifer," Joyce snapped.

"You're pathetic. There are too many men walking on this earth—or in this city for that fact—to settle with someone I've been intimate with. Come on. Not to mention, he's too young for you, Momma," Wanda stressed, trying to reason with her. "You need to break it off with him."

"That's what you want, isn't it? You're on your father's side," Joyce said. "You two are trying to sabotage my life so he and I can get back together. Forget about it, Wanda. It's not going to happen."

"Please. Don't flatter yourself. Daddy doesn't want you," Wanda replied bluntly.

Joyce hopped off the sofa and stormed over to Wanda, slapping her across the face. "Who do you think you're talking to?" she asked.

Wanda was shocked by her mother's behavior. Her cheek stung, but being respectful, she didn't hit her back. "Get away from me, Momma," she said, looking her in the eye.

"That smart mouth is going to get you in a lot trouble," she threatened, pointing.

"Don't take your frustration out on me. You did this," Wanda replied.

She watched Joyce snatch her purse from the sofa and head toward the front door. Moments later, it slammed shut. Wanda shook her head, disgusted, but also a bit sympathetic. She could only imagine Joyce's true emotions about the situation she'd put herself in. She'd destroyed her marriage and family for a man who'd slept with her daughter.

Damn. What happens now? Wanda wondered. Regardless of her understanding, she expected Joyce to end the relationship with Michael immediately. If she didn't break it off, Wanda had already decided not to be a part of her life.

"How in the hell did I manage to get attacked twice in a week? The next person who tries me better come correct. I've had enough. I'm ready to whoop some ass."

Wanda's mind drifted to Kim. Their fight had also affected her, but she didn't dwell on it. She hated the incident happened, but had no intentions of apologizing. In her opinion, she was simply defending herself.

Although Wanda's delivery wasn't always appropriate, she was a firm believer of saying what needed to be said. She loved Kim like a sister but refused to enable her. It irritated Wanda when she came across as shallow. That's why she felt so strongly about challenging her.

Admitting personal flaws was something Wanda lived by. Instead of finding ways to justify bad habits, she acknowledged them. Her perception of how Kim dealt with weaknesses was the exact opposite. Kim consistently found ways to make her wrongs seem right. Wanda had hopes she'd eventually learn to be truthful with herself.

As days had passed, she'd questioned whether the friendship was over. Despite Angel, Lynn, and Michelle's efforts to reconnect them, neither she nor Kim had taken the initial step. Wanda continued to stand her ground, refusing to call.

When Friday night came, she entered in the club leaving the pressures of a stressful week at the door. Wanda was ready to party. She also anticipated plans for an intimate evening with Ron.

While sitting at the bar, a tall and buffed gentleman walked up, asking her to dance. Wanda liked the way he looked, so she accepted. After taking the final sip of her amaretto sour, she led him to the dance floor, blending into the large crowd. With a sexy twirl, she faced her escort, moving to the beats thrusting from the oversized speakers. Wanda was careful not to exert too much energy. It was a habit to pay close attention to her appeal. She had to look and feel she was cute at all times.

At the end of the song, she declined an offer to slow dance. Wanda returned to the bar and consumed more drinks. Then around 1:00 A.M., she weaved through the packed room toward the VIP section. Once upstairs, she scanned the area looking for Ron. Realizing he wasn't there, she walked toward Pete's office.

When Wanda approached the door it was open, but not enough to see inside. As she raised her hand to knock, she overheard Ron saying, "A man's gotta do what a man's gotta do. She was crazy to think she'd get my money."

Wanda paused. She assumed Ron was talking about his wife, but wondered what he meant by his statement.

She eased over to the window. The blinds were closed, but there was a small gap at the bottom right corner. Wanda peeked in, finding a narrow view of Pete sitting behind his desk and Ron sitting across from him.

Pete rested his head against the back of his chair as he took puffs from a cigar. "I hope everything works out for you, man," Wanda heard him say, "but if it were me, I think I would've just given her the money and moved on with my life."

"I've worked too hard and too long for what I have. I'm not about to give it away just like that. I've encouraged Sheila to go to school or to start a business—many times. I shouldn't have to pay because she let life pass her by. Hell no," Ron said.

She watched as he leaned forward. Wanda couldn't believe her eyes when Ron sniffed a line of cocaine from Pete's desk.

She stood straight up. *What? Ron uses drugs? I can't believe this,* Wanda thought. She was very disappointed.

Once she'd gathered herself, she went to peek through the window again, but heard movement inside the office. As she scurried away, the door squeaked as it opened. Wanda could hear Pete tell Ron he wished there was a better way to handle his situation.

What situation? Wanda questioned. She was baffled. She turned around to walk back in their direction as if she'd just arrived.

"I weighed my options," Ron said as she emerged from around the corner.

"Weighed what options? Hey, Pete," Wanda sang, trying to blend into the conversation.

"Oh, nothing," Ron replied. "I was telling Pete my thought of increasing the prices at the bingo hall."

"Again?" Wanda questioned.

"I'm thinking about it. Are you ready to go?" Ron asked, changing the subject.

Wanda nodded.

"Alright, partner. I'll catch up with you later," Ron said, giving Pete dap. He put his arm around Wanda's neck, kissing the side of her head as they walked toward the exit.

Ron opened the car door for Wanda before letting himself in. She sat in the passenger seat, silent, still in shock about him using cocaine.

During the drive Wanda remained alert. She took note of how often Ron sniffed and nudged his nose. It all seemed so familiar. Before that night she'd associated the drainage with Ron's sinus problem. Now the reason seemed clearer. Responsible drinking was fine, but the use of an illegal substance wasn't something in which Wanda took a part. She knew firsthand some effects of cocaine. Her uncle Steve was addicted to the drug, and her aunt Vera and cousins suffered the consequences.

Wanda fidgeted with her hair and jewelry, fighting the urge to confront Ron. She'd never been good at hiding her feelings, but realized if she mentioned anything concerning what she believed to be his habit, she'd have to reveal details of learning about it. Admitting she had spied on him and Pete was not an option. Wanda didn't want Ron to become suspicious or cautious. She wanted him to slip up so she could find out what was going on in his life. Wanda was convinced the price excuse was a lie. He had just raised costs a few months earlier.

Her thoughts drifted back to Ron's statement about weighing his options. Wanda yearned to know to what he was referring. She preoccupied herself creating different scenarios, trying to connect snippets of the conversation.

"Why are you so quiet tonight?" Ron asked, interrupting her thoughts.

Wanda glanced his way, then back through the front window. "All of a sudden I'm not feeling so well," she replied. "Maybe I should've gone home tonight."

"Gone home?" Ron questioned. He whipped his Lexus into the Marriott parking lot. After turning off the engine, he made eye contact with Wanda. "Are you going to be okay?"

"I'll be fine," she replied, forcing a smile.

Ron moved closer to Wanda, initiating a kiss. He caressed her neck, moving down to her breasts, and ending at her thighs. "Let's go upstairs," he whispered.

Wanda reluctantly agreed. She knew they were too far into the evening to turn back. Although she remained unsettled, she decided to let the night happen as it would.

Once inside the hotel suite, Wanda showered while Ron put on some music. Afterward, she pampered herself before slipping into a red negligee. Each night she met Ron for an intimate evening, he'd have sexy lingerie picked out and waiting for her. She'd wear it for him, then take it home and pretend it was something she'd purchased for Malcolm.

Wanda stepped into her three-inch heels and stood in front of the large mirror, admiring how gorgeous she looked.

Moments later, she entered the room wrapped in a short silk bathrobe. Ron walked up to her, leaving a soft kiss on her lips. Without saying a word, Wanda began to unbutton his shirt. Next, she unbuckled his pants, allowing them to fall to the floor.

"Are you ready for this?" Ron asked.

"Ready and waiting," Wanda replied, smiling.

Ron licked his lips. When he attempted to pick up his pants and shirt, Wanda placed her foot on top of them.

"I'll get your clothes," she insisted. She untied the knot, loosening the belt to her robe, then stood with her hands on her hips, exposing the soft fabric resting against her smooth, caramel skin.

Ron grabbed his shaving bag and hurried toward the bathroom wearing boxer briefs and socks.

Once the door closed, Wanda waited for the shower to come on. She removed Ron's wallet from his pants and opened it without hesitation. She looked past the money and condoms to stare at his pictures before searching the hidden compartments. Wanda was disappointed again when she came across a small yellow bag of powdered cocaine.

She sat on the bed, staring across the room. "I don't get it," she said. "This dude has it going on. He's a retired army sergeant major, owns and manages a thriving business, and set standards when it comes to lovemaking. Why in the hell would he jeopardize his life and status by getting high?"

Wanda was curious to know how long and how often Ron used drugs and wondered if he was addicted. Regardless, she knew the result would be the same—a distraction and a complete turnoff.

Finding herself in such an unusual position annoyed Wanda. Her gut said to call a cab and leave, but she didn't want the relationship to end that way, so she stayed.

When Wanda heard the shower shut off, her adrenaline pumped as she hurried to put Ron's wallet away. She quickly unpacked her massage oils, placing them on the nightstand before hopping into bed.

Moments later, the bathroom door opened. "Wanda, will you bring me the pants I had on?" Ron called out to her.

"Sure." Wanda took the pants and handed them to Ron.

After he shut the door, she was tempted to put her ear against it but chose not to chance him hearing her or opening the door unexpectedly. Wanda felt being discreet with her suspicions would allow her to learn more.

She climbed back in bed, contemplating the next move regarding her and Ron's relationship. Wanda ruled out not seeing him. She needed answers, and to get them she decided to play along by acting as normal as she could. She wanted to feel in control of her and Ron's love affair as she had in the past, but at that point she didn't.

Minutes later, Ron distracted Wanda when he entered the room with a big grin. He winked, and she returned his smile, watching as he walked toward the bar. He prepared an apple martini for her and rum and Coke for himself.

They had consumed a few drinks when Ron began to seduce Wanda. She entertained his advances, allowing him to lay her back onto the bed. Next, he removed her negligee with his teeth and covered her body with oil.

Wanda shivered, savoring Ron's touch. She found it impossible to act normal and not enjoy his lovemaking. As usual, he drove her wild.

Afterward, they showered, and Wanda lay cuddled in Ron's embrace, staring into the darkness of the hotel suite. While he stroked her bare skin with his strong hand, Wanda questioned his character and integrity.

She struggled with the idea of Ron being involved with Sheila's disappearance. Months had passed since she'd vanished, and he'd shown no concern of her whereabouts. His conversation with Pete earlier that evening was the first time she'd heard him mention her, thus causing her speculation.

Wanda quickly acknowledged, even if Ron wanted to talk about his wife, she wasn't the person in whom he'd confide.

Is it possible? Could he be a part of Sheila's mystery? What kind of relationship did the two of them have? Wanda questioned.

As she tried to imagine details of Ron and his wife's life, she felt guilty for dating him. Wanda admitted the fact that Ron was married should've been her reason to stay away. Instead, she became involved and attached, and her selfish nature hadn't allowed her to break it off.

Wanda remembered Angel, Kim, Lynn, and Michelle chastising her about the decision to date Ron, especially after Sheila had been reported missing, but she wasn't ready to let go. Wanda enjoyed her and Ron's secret romance so much she had allowed it to cloud her judgment. All along, she'd given him the benefit of the doubt, convinced his wife would show up and things would return to normal. Not once had she considered foul play. Now, everything had changed. Wanda had some unanswered questions and an inquiring mind.

What? And why? she questioned, curious to know if Sheila had really run off or if something was wrong with her. Wanda went on to wonder if what had happened was a result of her and Ron's love affair.

I can't take this guessing crap anymore. Wanda turned to face Ron. "Can I ask you something?" she said.

"Yeah. What's on your mind?" he replied.

"Ron, your wife has been gone for months. How can you act as if nothing's wrong?"

There was a brief silence.

"This isn't the first time my wife has left," Ron finally said. "She'll be back."

"Did she leave because of us?" Wanda quizzed, recalling the day Sheila approached her at the bingo hall asking questions. She mentioned it to Ron.

"Look, my wife is a very jealous person and ridiculously insecure," he said. "Trust me, her decision to leave had nothing to do with you."

Wanda frowned. She wasn't sure if Ron's statement was a compliment or an insult. "Well, what's the problem?" she asked. "Why did she take off this time?"

"We got into an argument," Ron said. "I was tired of her complaining I'm not at home enough. I have a business to run. She doesn't seem to understand that."

"Are you saying you can't run a business and spend time with your wife?" Wanda questioned.

"Well I can, but…"

"You choose not to," Wanda replied, completing Ron's sentence.

"I can't sit around the house," he said.

"Is that what she's asking you to do? Just being at home more is probably all Sheila wants, Ron. Was she on board when you purchased the bingo hall?" Wanda asked.

"Yeah, she was. While I was on active duty, everything was fine because neither of us were hands-on with the business. Once I retired, I became more involved. I concluded some of the paperwork didn't coincide with the bank deposits. When I learned my manager had been stealing money, I fired him. Instead of hiring a replacement I decided to manage the business myself."

"I see. Have you thought about giving Sheila a role at the bingo hall? Maybe including her in the business will help the relationship, don't you think?"

"No. My marriage has run its course. The bottom line is it's cheaper to keep her."

Wanda didn't respond. She wasn't sure if Ron was telling the truth. Assuming at least some of his story was fact she realized he and his wife had issues to deal with other than her.

Ron feels the marriage has run its course, and Sheila took off because he's not around. That doesn't add up, Wanda concluded.

"Give your wife some attention," she told Ron to keep the conversation going. "I'm sure everything will work out."

"Wait a minute. What's up with all the questions? Why are you worried about my wife all of a sudden?" he asked.

"I'm just trying to understand what I'm involved in. I'm getting concerned because Sheila's been gone for so long," she admitted.

"If you were really concerned about Sheila, you wouldn't be sleeping with her husband," Ron said.

"What?" Wanda replied, shocked by his response.

"I'm done talking about her. I don't love her," Ron blurted. "I love you."

Wanda squinted. "Me?" she questioned. Her heart rate quickened as she sat at a loss for words. Unsure of how to respond to Ron's so-called confession, she didn't say anything at all. She looked away and up at the ceiling to avoid his stare.

"Why don't you get rid of that loser Malcolm so we can get married?" Ron continued.

"No thanks," Wanda replied. The words escaped her lips before she knew it.

"Ah, you're just saying that," Ron said, stroking his ego.

"No, I really mean it," Wanda clarified.

"Why not?" Ron asked, offended by her arrogance.

Wanda shrugged. "I'm not ready for that type of commitment. I'm sorry."

"So I'm good enough for you to sleep with but not to commit to? Why are you in my life, Wanda? Is it my money? Are you a whore?" Ron asked.

"Look-a-here, let's not do the name-calling thing, please. I'm in your life because we agreed to have a casual relationship. I had no clue you'd be suggesting marriage."

"Would you marry Malcolm?" Ron asked.

Wanda didn't respond.

"I thought so," Ron said.

Moments later, he broke the brief silence. "What happens now? Is this the end of our relationship?"

"I've said nothing about ending the relationship, Ron. What I am saying is, I'd feel better knowing your wife is okay," Wanda said.

Ron moved closer to her, looking Wanda directly in the eye. "You don't give a damn about my wife," he snapped. "Stop pretending you do."

Ron repositioned himself in bed with his back to her.

Wanda frowned. *I should've followed my mind and gone home. This relationship can never be the same after tonight. I've never depended on a man's money—and I never will,* she thought.

She remained awake, anxiously waiting for morning to come. Just before dawn, Ron woke up. When he climbed on top of Wanda, she cringed. Sex was the farthest thing from her mind. She allowed Ron to please himself, but lay completely disconnected, faking orgasms and outraged when he called her Sheila.

Chapter 6

Kim wasn't a morning person so she made a point to wake early to prepare for the meeting with Keith. After getting dressed, she snuggled under her plush, leopard-print blanket, sipping hot tea while watching the news. When her cell phone rang, she glanced at the clock, wondering who was calling her at 7:00 A.M. She was shocked to see Leon Hardy, the man she'd dated before reconciling with Darius, name displayed across the caller ID screen.

"Hi, Leon," Kim answered, smiling through the phone.

"Hello," he replied. "How are you?"

"Great. And you?" she asked.

"I'm doing well. I know you usually sleep in on Saturday, but I wanted to invite you to join me for breakfast this morning," Leon said.

"Thanks. I would love to," Kim replied, "but I have an eight o'clock appointment."

"Are you free afterward? I'd settle for lunch," Leon said.

"Sure. What do you have in mind?" Kim asked.

"The restaurant of your choice, or I can cook for you," he offered.

"No, I don't want to put you through any trouble," Kim replied. "We can go to Ruby Tuesday's at the Savannah Mall if that's okay."

"It is. How does eleven o'clock sound?" Leon asked.

"I'm not sure how long my interview will take, but if I need more time, I'll give you a buzz," Kim said.

"Okay. An interview?" Leon questioned.

"Yes, for a magazine article. I'll tell you more about it during lunch," Kim said.

"I can't wait to see you," Leon replied. "I'll talk to you later."

Kim hung up, thinking of how nice it was to hear his voice. She didn't consider having lunch with Leon a date, but something made her nervous about seeing him. She wasn't sure if the feelings were a result of excitement or guilt.

Refocused, she went from room to room, opening the shades, allowing sunshine to come through. Next, she poured another cup of tea. Then Kim waited for time to pass.

Keith showed up at 7:45. She invited him in and served him a glass of cold orange juice, then they settled in the living room. Kim gave Keith permission to record the session on his voice recorder. "Can you briefly tell me about yourself—background, education, and religious beliefs?" he began.

"Yes. I was born here in Savannah, the oldest of three children. I'm an army brat. I was reared in a Baptist home, but currently attend a non-dominational church. I'm employed at the Candler General Hospital as a clinical psychologist, educated at Savannah State University. I'm single, never been married, and no kids," Kim said.

"Good. Now tell me where you met Darius," Keith said.

The thought of Darius brought tears to Kim's eyes. "Excuse me," she said. "Um, Darius and I met in third grade. When I was younger we relocated quite often with the military. Then when I was eight years old we moved back to Savannah and stayed. Darius lived in our neighborhood, so we attended the same schools."

"What do you believe was the catalyst of Darius' change?" Keith asked.

"We weren't dating at the time, but from what he told me, he came to a point when he felt bad on the inside because of all the things he'd done and people he'd hurt, so he gradually ended friendships, began studying God's word, then he rejoined and became an active member in the church. I'll never forget the night he told me he'd been saved and baptized. I think I started shouting," Kim said with a big smile. "You have no idea, Keith. I had prayed and prayed for Darius to be delivered because I loved him so much. I saw his potential and wanted to be his wife. I just couldn't marry him while he was out in the streets, living life recklessly. With both of us striving to be God-fearing people, naturally we reconnected and became engaged. I was happier than ever. I felt my prayers had been answered."

Kim dabbed the tears from the corner of her eyes with her fingertips. "Then all of a sudden our dreams were shattered," she said.

"How did that make you feel?" Keith asked.

Kim sniffled. "Honestly, it caused me to have doubt, and I rebelled against God. I couldn't understand losing Darius at such a fulfilling peak, when everything had fallen into place for us, especially after we'd chosen to be obedient and pleasing Him with our ways. Darius and I enjoyed opening our Bible and helping each other grow. That short span was truly a phenomenal time," Kim said.

"If Darius was here, what do you think he'd like to share with our readers, or what would you like to say on his behalf?" Keith questioned.

"I'm sure his message would be about the dangers of the street life and how along with the quick money comes heartache, pain, and death. I can remember him saying how free he felt walking in God's light and how refreshing it was not to peek over his shoulder like he had to while he was in the drug game."

"What did it take for you to get over your loss?" Keith asked.

"I acknowledged my blessing in the midst of the pain."

"Amen," Keith sang. "Yes, sister, sometimes our faith is challenged, but I'm here to tell you God doesn't make mistakes."

Kim nodded as she wiped tears away. "Yes. It took some time, but I'm past the anger," she said. "I still love Darius, and I miss him, but I know he's not coming back. Now, I'm praying for the Lord to heal my heart so I can move on."

"He will," Keith said, patting her hand.

"What is it going to take to save our young black men?" Kim asked, taking the conversation in a different direction. "It's sad to see so many of them get caught up in the drug game, then they end up killing each other. One goes to the grave and another to prison. It's awful," Kim said.

"I agree. How did Darius end up selling drugs?" Keith asked.

"His uncles," Kim replied. "We have too many negative and not enough positive images in front of our boys, magnified by gangsta music and sagging pants. Everybody wants to be a thug. It's insane."

"Indeed. We have a lot of work to do. Thanks for telling this story, Kim," Keith said, extending his hand to her.

"Thank you," she replied.

"Darius is very well-known. I'm sure there's an audience interested in reading this article. Maybe it'll start dialogue in the home, which could help some of these young men headed in the wrong direction."

"I hope so," Kim said. "I pray those who need to receive his testimony will be blessed and inspired by it. That's my sole purpose of telling this story."

Keith nodded in agreement. Kim watched him press the stop button on his recorder. After writing a few more notes, he packed his bag. "I appreciate your time," he said.

"Same here," Kim replied.

"It's truly amazing how you were placed in my path on River Street last weekend. I've learned to follow my instincts," Keith said. "I'm sure as I came in your direction you hoped I'd keep walking and not bother you."

Kim smiled. "I can't lie. I did. I was having one of those moments where I just wanted to be left alone."

That thought took Kim all the way back to the day in high school when she'd met Angel in gym class. Angel was having a difficult time dealing with her mother. She had isolated herself from the rest of the students and was sitting on the bleachers with her head down. Although Angel wanted to be alone, Kim followed her instincts, offering to listen if she wanted talk. They'd been friends since that day. "Things do happen for a reason," Kim said.

"Truly. Your article will be in next month's publication," Keith said, standing.

"Can you set about six copies aside for me? I want to give my friends and my parents a copy," Kim said. "Is that too much to ask?"

"Of course not," Keith replied, "I'd be happy to. I'll save ten for you."

"Wonderful. I'll stop by your office and pick them up. Thanks again," Kim said, smiling.

She walked Keith to the door. Kim stood on the porch until he drove off, then she went back inside. She put the glasses they'd used and wiped the kitchen counters. Kim had an hour before she was due to meet with Leon, so she used the time to follow up with the three ladies she was considering as roommates. Both of the soldiers were fine with the idea of renting out a bedroom and sharing the common areas, but the sheriff was a little hesitant. She told Kim due to her divorce and needing a place to live ASAP, she'd be willing to give the arrangements a try, preferably on a month-to-month basis. Kim was skeptical so she insisted on a six-month lease. In the back of her mind, she prayed everything would work out so she'd remain at the house longer.

After the sheriff agreed to six-month term, Kim called Angel. She told her about the agreements and asked if she could have a copy of the lease she and Derrick used with their renters.

"Of course you can," Angel said. "I'll email it to you. Read over the terms carefully. You'll need to modify the draft to fit your specifications. Also, make sure everything you want to enforce is in writing. It's vital to be clear on your expectations from the beginning so there's no confusion down the line. For example, you may consider guidelines pertaining to guests. There'll be four of you living there so everyone needs to be considerate of the others. I already know you don't want people hanging out at your house all hours of the day or night, so be sure to make your rules known and understood beforehand. If you need help I'm here."

"Thanks, Angel. Guess what? I'm having lunch with Leon—"

"Whattt?" Angel sang.

"Yes. He called this morning, and I agreed to meet him," Kim said. "When I get back home, I'll print the lease and read over it. Oh yeah, the interview with Keith went well."

"Good. I can't wait to read the article," Angel said.

"It'll be in the July issue. I asked Keith to set aside some copies for me. I have to go now. I don't want to be late," Kim said.

"Okay. Enjoy lunch," Angel said.

"I will."

Kim hung up. Minutes later, she left for Ruby Tuesday's. She spotted Leon near the mall's entrance as she circled the lot looking for a place to park. Soon after, she walked toward him, and they greeted each other with a smile. When Leon embraced Kim, she didn't want him to let go. She hadn't felt a man's touch in months. When he held her as they entered the building she felt a little awkward, as if she was doing something wrong. She figured she was uncomfortable appearing as a couple with Leon because she'd just relived being with Darius, but she just went along with it.

After being seated, they ordered drinks. While Kim browsed the menu, she felt Leon watching her.

"So, how's life treating you, Kim?" he asked. "You've crossed my mind quite often."

"I'm doing pretty good. I've been working a lot, but that's about it. I had to put my house on the market. I can't afford to keep it," Kim said.

"Really. What happened?" Leon asked.

"I got in over my head. It was a mistake to buy a new house and a truck. I may have a temporary fix though," Kim said. "I've talked with a few ladies who are willing to be my roommates. At first I didn't want to share my space, but now I'm looking forward to the adjustment. Receiving rental income will allow me to quit my part-time job."

"You're working two jobs?" Leon asked.

"I had to. It was the only way to pay all of the bills I had coming in."

"If there's anything I do to help you, let me know," Leon said.

"I'll be fine. I appreciate the offer though," Kim replied.

The waitress interrupted the conversation when she approached the table. She placed their drinks in front of them then took their meal orders.

"How are your children?" Kim asked, resuming the conversation.

"Wonderful. They were here for spring break," Leon said with a smile. "Thanks for asking."

"You're welcome. So, what have you been up to lately?" she questioned.

"Oh, nothing much. I spend a lot of time at church. We've started a program for males getting ready to graduate from high school. Our goal is to help them focus and prepare for the transition to adulthood. Are you still attending church?" Leon asked.

"Yes, Lord. I have to," Kim replied. "Hearing and believing the Word of God is what gives me the strength to keep doing it all."

"Good for you. Consider visiting us sometime. I'm sure the members would love to see you," Leon said.

"Please. They're probably happy I'm not around anymore. It wasn't the same after everyone found out I got caught and went to jail for purchasing stolen clothes from Penny. Were you ashamed of me after that happened?" Kim asked.

"Ashamed, no. Disappointed, yes. If you couldn't afford to buy the clothes from the store, you should've done without having them. That's the bottom line," Leon said.

"You're absolutely right. Buying stolen property from Penny was more of a habit. I'd been doing it for so long I saw nothing wrong with it," Kim said.

"I understand. When we learn better we do better, right?" Leon questioned.

Kim smiled. "Yes. I haven't seen Penny," she assured him.

"Good. The only thing free in this world is salvation," Leon said.

"You've got that right," Kim agreed.

Then there was a brief silence.

"Are you dating anyone?" Leon asked, changing the subject.

"No, I'm not," Kim replied, looking away.

"Are you still grieving from the loss of your ex-boyfriend?" he asked.

The waitress arrived with two bowls of salad before Kim could respond. After she'd walked away Leon blessed the food.

"I think I'm finally letting go," Kim said, making eye contact with him. "Last weekend I cleaned out the house and got rid of most of his things. This morning, I was interviewed by Keith, a guy with *Keepin' It Real* magazine who had planned to interview Darius. He's the one I had the appointment with earlier. Anyway, he never had the opportunity to interview Darius, so the article will feature me, including Darius. Sharing with him the person Darius had become before he died helped me to release him even more. I'm at peace knowing he had accepted Jesus as his savior and repented for his sins. I believe he's in a better place."

Leon nodded.

"While we're on this subject, I'd like to apologize to you again. I didn't mean for our relationship to end so abruptly. I honestly tried to get over Darius. When he asked to stay at my house for a few days, it was completely innocent. I couldn't turn him down because he has helped me more than you'll ever know.

"When you called that night and Darius answered the phone, I felt horrible. I was upset with him for taking the call, but what could I do? The damage was done. Then as he and I talked, I learned Darius had changed his life and he was going to church regularly, which is something I constantly prayed and hoped for. As our conversation went on, he asked me to marry him, and I said yes. How could I not accept, you know? He had become the person I wanted him to be—on his own. Please don't think I tried to hurt you intentionally or didn't care for you. My situation was so much more complicated, Leon. I'm sorry for any heartache or disappointment I've caused. Will you forgive me?"

"I already forgave you, Kim," Leon replied.

"Thanks," she said with a smile. "I'll never understand why you're so patient with me."

"I know how it feels to love someone," Leon said. "When I saw you still loved Darius, there was nothing for me to do but let go."

"It's amazing how men can put their feelings aside so easily," Kim replied.

"Why would you think it was easy?" Leon asked.

Kim stared at him, but she didn't respond.

"I admit, when you told me there was nothing going on with you and your ex, I believed you," Leon said.

"How can you trust me now?" Kim asked. "I led you to believe he was an old boyfriend with no strings attached, knowing I was still in love with him. I embarrassed you at church when I was arrested. Why are you still willing to be my friend?"

"I see you striving to be a righteous person. I believe you have a good heart and good intentions, Kim. I want you in my life," Leon said. "Can we start rebuilding our relationship by calling each other and visiting from time to time and see where that leads us?"

"I'm okay with that," she said.

"Are you sure? I don't want to pressure you."

"I'm positive," Kim replied with a smile. She could tell by the look in Leon's eye that he was still in love with her.

He lifted her hand, gently kissing the back of it.

Chapter 7

Wanda couldn't believe how perfectly her night out began and how terribly it had ended. When she finally arrived home it was after twelve o'clock on Saturday afternoon. Wanda was livid. Usually, when she and Ron went to the hotel they wouldn't stay past 5:00 A.M., being somewhat respectful to his wife. Since she'd been missing they'd leave no later than 7:00 A.M. This time Ron had changed the rules, holding Wanda hostage until check-out at eleven o'clock. In the meantime, they had intercourse again, and Wanda noticed Ron was rougher than usual. As a result, her vulva was slightly swollen and a tad sore. Wanda believed he'd agitated her intentionally as a gesture of control or ownership. She didn't like how he'd handled her and was searching for a way to get even.

While bathing, Wanda covered herself with lather as the encounter with Ron replayed in her mind. She frowned at his audacity to propose marriage and for suggesting she was a whore. "Who in the hell do you think you are, Ron? And what have you gotten yourself into," Wanda questioned.

Next, she focused on Sheila. "Some chicks are just stupid," she concluded. "If Ron were my husband, I'd demand he hire a manager, especially if money isn't an issue—and I've spent enough to know money is not an issue.

"Then again, Sheila's probably one of those sistas with no clue of her financial status. This could be why Ron doesn't want her involved in the business. If that's the case, she's a dummy. I hate to see women depend on their man for everything."

"But what happened?" Wanda muttered, shifting her thoughts. "Did Sheila finally stand up for herself? If so, how did you react, Ron? Did you snap? Are you capable of harming your wife? If so, how far would you go? I need to know—and I shall find out."

Wanda rinsed the suds from her body, then grabbed a towel before stepping out of the tub. She dried off and moisturized her skin before slipping into her pajamas. She crawled in bed around one o'clock. Wanda was surprised Malcolm hadn't called. They had an understanding that on Friday and Saturday nights she partied, then after partying she slept in, so on the weekends Malcolm wouldn't bother her until at least noon. Wanda didn't call him, and she turned off her phones so no one could disturb her. She grabbed the remote from the nightstand and turned on the television, browsing through the channels, before quickly drifting off to sleep.

Hours later, she woke up starving. Wanda yawned and stretched, thinking of something to eat. When she remembered the leftover chicken salad in the refrigerator, she got out of bed and washed up before heading to the kitchen.

After eating, she grabbed the cordless phone, sat on the sofa, and dialed Angel's home number.

"Hey, chick. What's up?" she asked when Angel answered.

"Hi, Wanda. Nothing much. I just finished dinner. How are you?" she asked.

"I'm fine. What did you cook?" Wanda questioned.

"Baked chicken, pasta, spinach, and dinner rolls," Angel replied.

"I should've called before I ate that stale chicken salad. Are you up for company?" Wanda asked.

"Sure," Angel said. "What's going on?"

"Why do you ask?" Wanda quizzed.

"You sound low key. Is something wrong?" Angel inquired.

"I just woke up. Is Derrick home?" Wanda asked.

"No. He's out with Al looking at investment properties," Angel replied.

"Good. I don't want to get into it over the phone, but I have something to tell you. I'll be headed your way shortly," Wanda said.

"Oh, Lord. What is it now?" Angel asked.

"We'll talk when I get there," Wanda said.

"Okay. Hurry up," Angel replied.

Wanda got dressed, then took her keys and purse from the coffee table, walking out the door at four-thirty.

Once inside the car, she flipped through her organizer, searching for a CD to listen to. Wanda decided on Tupac. She cruised along Abercorn Street blasting the infamous rap "Hit 'Em Up." Tupac's dynamic flow allowed her to escape her thoughts as she moved to the rhythm, singing along.

At the end of the track she pressed repeat, listening to the same song the entire drive to Richmond Hill.

While sitting at the intersection of Highways 17 and 144, Wanda continued to enjoy her music. As she took in the scenery, she made eye contact with the driver sitting next to her in a Mercedes Benz. It was an older white guy with an expression that questioned how she could listen to music with such vulgar lyrics.

Wanda returned his stare. She wanted to send him a message that she listened to whatever she wanted. Although she agreed with the folks who said rap music was harsh, misleading, and ignorant, she actually enjoyed some of it.

The sound of a blaring horn startled Wanda. It was the car behind her signaling the traffic light had turned green. Wanda glanced into the rearview mirror. "Calm down, damn," she complained, driving off. She made a left turn, pulling into the far right lane. Wanda rolled down her window and drove slowly so the car could pass. The driver was an older lady who reminded Wanda of her grandmother, so she aborted the notion to stick up her middle finger and yell obscenities.

About ten minutes later, Wanda was standing on Angel's front porch. She rang the bell and pounded on the door. "Angel, it's me," she called out.

Angel greeted her with a smile. "I know it's you," she replied. She hugged Wanda and invited her in.

Wanda made her way over to Derrick Jr. She kissed his forehead and aggravated him by snatching the bottle out of his mouth, teasing him with it.

Angel watched Derrick Jr. get mad and kick his feet.

Just as he began to cry, Wanda gave him his bottle. "Okay, li'l man. I'm sorry," she said, smirking. She took a seat in Derrick's recliner.

Angel sat on the sofa. "So what's up?" she asked.

"Girrrrl," Wanda sang, "where do I begin? Well, first I'll share my good news. I've decided to go back to college to get a master's degree."

"Really? That's cool," Angel said.

"Yeah. I'm not sure what field I'm going to study yet, but I'm definitely looking to advance my career. I wouldn't mind starting a business," Wanda said, "but I really don't know what to do."

"What do you want to do? What do you like to do?" Angel asked.

"I'm trying to figure it out," Wanda replied. "Something exciting…"

"What's up with the sudden change? Did something happen at your job?" Angel questioned.

"No. Actually, I still enjoy working at the courthouse, but for some reason I don't feel I've accomplished enough. Now that I'm about to be thirty years old, I feel the need for a different direction."

"Oh, okay. Can you transfer to another department?" Angel asked.

"It's possible," Wanda said, "but I don't know if that's what I'm looking for."

"You'll figure it out," Angel encouraged.

"What frightens me about being an entrepreneur is customer service," Wanda said. "You know how I am. I don't have time for people and their crap."

"That's a good point. I do think it's important to be mindful of your personality when deciding on a business or service to provide."

"Honestly, I don't have a problem dealing with people," Wanda said. "I'm very sociable. It's the butt-kissing part I don't like. I ain't with it."

"If you have tact when dealing with consumers you'll do fine," Angel said. "Sometimes you tend to be too blunt, Wanda. You don't always have to say what's on your mind."

"Am I that bad?" Wanda questioned.

Angel looked at her and smiled. "I wouldn't say you're bad, but you're honest, and sometimes it's better to keep your opinion to yourself."

"I need a business I can run from behind the scenes. It'll come to me. Now let me tell you about Ron," Wanda said. "Angel, I think he may have been involved in his wife's disappearance."

"Why would you say that?" Angel asked.

"First of all, last night I found out that Ron snorts cocaine. Can you believe it? Now, you already know how I feel about that," Wanda said. "Anyway, I overheard a conversation between him and Pete. Ron made a statement that's been bugging me from the moment I heard him say it—talking 'bout, a man's gotta do what a man's gotta do. What in the hell is that supposed to mean?"

Angel shrugged.

"Kill her? Is that what he feels he had to do?" Wanda questioned.

Angel shook her head. "Don't start me lying. I don't know that man, Wanda."

"He went on to say Sheila was crazy to think she'd get his money. I'm telling you, Angel, he did something to her," Wanda continued.

"I think you should stay away from Ron," Angel suggested.

"I can't. I have to find out what's going on," Wanda replied.

"No, you don't," Angel said.

"Yes, I do. I'm not interested in a romantic relationship with him anymore, but I want to remain his friend so I can learn more about what he's done or is doing," Wanda said.

"You're insane. You suspect this man may have killed his wife and you still want to be in his life? How retarded is that?" Angel asked.

Wanda laughed. "I'll be careful," she said. "You're not going to believe what I'm about to tell you next: Ron called Malcolm a loser and told me to get rid of him so he and I could get married."

"That's crazy. If he's talking about marriage to you, he must know his wife's not coming back," Angel said.

"Exactly…I hate to say it, but Ron looks suspicious. I don't trust him anymore," Wanda confessed.

"Tell me why you're still willing to see him," Angel said. "This is the perfect time to end the relationship, Wanda."

"No. I gotta get 'im, Angel. A lot happened while we were together last night. I don't want to get into it, but I'm very upset with Ron. I have to find out what he's gotten himself into," Wanda stressed.

"It's none of your business. Have you lost your mind? Back off, Wanda. Let the police figure it out. You don't want to get caught up in whatever Ron is doing. Leave well enough alone and move on," Angel suggested.

Wanda sat quietly for a few seconds.

"Call Lynn," Angel continued. "Tell her what you told me so she can run it by Chris and see what he says."

"No, I can't. I don't want to draw any attention to Ron. If the police start snooping around, he'll cover his tracks. If he doesn't think anyone is looking, he may slip up," Wanda concluded.

"As a friend, I'm asking you to leave that man alone. You don't know what he's capable of," Angel stressed. "If he finds you meddling in his affairs, trust me, there'll be consequences."

"I'll be alright. I work at the courthouse. I know a lot about criminals and how they think. Hey, maybe I should get my master's degree in criminal law. I think I'd be good at it."

Angel didn't reply.

"I got it," Wanda blurted, "I can open up a private investigation firm. What do you think?"

"I guess." Angel was distracted when Derrick Jr. began to cry. She picked him up, patting him on his back. "That's kinda dangerous, Wanda," she said, sitting down again.

"It is, but girl, I can see me now, spying on somebody's cheating spouse. You know your girl likes to get down to the nitty-gritty. Oh yeah, I would love that," Wanda concluded.

"I'm not so sure," Angel replied.

"Why? I want excitement. I'm sure that business would give me plenty of it."

Wanda watched as Angel laid Derrick Jr. back in his crib. "What are you thinking?" she asked Angel.

"You know exactly what I'm thinking. Leave that man alone, Wanda Boyd, and move on with your life. You have a boyfriend. Give Malcolm some of that attention you're giving Ron."

"I do give Malcolm attention. You don't hear him complaining, do you?" Wanda said.

"Whatever," Angel replied.

"Wanda Boyd, private investigator, bringing liars and cheaters to their knees." Wanda laughed. "Oh, yeah," she sang, "that has a nice ring to it."

"Look who's talking. You have a lot of nerve," Angel said. "You're all hyped to expose someone for cheating when you're guilty of it yourself."

"Yeah, because I'll be the accuser, not the accused," Wanda stated. "Besides, I'm not breaking any law."

"So you have no regard for the law of marriage?" Angel asked.

"I'm not married," Wanda said sarcastically. "I hear you, Angel, but like I said earlier, the romance with Ron is over. Now I want to know if he's capable of murder."

"Of course he is. Ron served twenty years in the military. He's been trained to kill," Angel said.

"Well, you'd better be careful," Wanda replied. "Derrick's received the same training."

"Stop talking crazy. My husband is a lover not a fighter," Angel stated, smiling.

Wanda laughed. "I'm kidding, but seriously, Ron has messed with the wrong one. If he has harmed his wife, I want his ass sentenced to death. I like this detective stuff. I'll definitely research careers and opportunities in the criminal justice field. In the meantime, I'll practice with Ron," Wanda said.

Angel shook her head. "Would you like something to drink?" she asked Wanda.

"Yes. Can I have a daiquiri, please?" she replied.

"Of course. What about something to eat?" Angel asked.

"Not now. I'll take some food with me when I leave," Wanda said.

She followed Angel into the kitchen and sat at the counter while she prepared two strawberry daiquiris.

"Stop being stingy and hook me up," Wanda said, noticing the small amount of alcohol Angel put in her drink.

"Only if you're staying here tonight," she replied. "I refuse to be responsible for you drinking and driving. These Richmond Hill police don't play. You're wild enough as it is. I will not set you up for failure."

"Angel, please. You can make the drink a little stronger than that. I can handle it," Wanda said.

"The devil is a lie," she replied, and they both laughed.

The sound of the garage door lifting interrupted their conversation. Moments later, Derrick walked in, joining them in the kitchen. He spoke, then Wanda watched him kiss Angel.

She stood and greeted Derrick with a hug. "How are you?" Wanda asked.

"I'm good," he replied. "And you?"

"Wonderful," Wanda said with a smile.

"How did it go out there?" Angel asked Derrick.

"Great. Tomorrow I want to take you to see the sixteen units I'm interested in," he said. "I think you'll like them."

"Sixteen? Are they in different locations?" Angel asked.

"No, it's four four-unit buildings sitting next to each other," Derrick replied.

"Oh, okay. Are you ready for dinner?" Angel asked.

"A little later," Derrick replied. "Where's my son?"

"He's in his crib, taking a nap," Angel said.

"I'll give my li'l man a kiss, then go upstairs and let you ladies enjoy your drinks," Derrick said.

Wanda smiled, noticing Angel watch him walk away. "Stop drooling," she teased.

Angel blushed. "Girl, I love my husband," she admitted.

"It's written all over your face. Quite sickening if you ask me," Wanda joked.

"I wish love were all it took to make a relationship work. It takes a lot more," Angel said. "We got into a big argument yesterday."

"About what?" Wanda asked.

"His co-workers calling so much, especially the females. I can't stand it," Angel said.

"Is it someone in particular?" Wanda pried.

"No, but I feel if there's no emergency, whatever they want to talk about can wait until the next day. I don't mind one or two calls, but Derrick's phone rings constantly," Angel complained.

"I've heard soldiers have a special bond. They go through a lot together. You have to admit, Angel, Derrick is a very likable guy, and he's easy to talk to," Wanda said.

"True, but if the tables were turned and I had coworkers calling me all the time, it would be an issue," Angel replied.

"You already know it's a double standard for men," Wanda said.

"Not in my house," Angel replied. "I don't mind Derrick having acquaintances, but his coworkers see him more than I do."

Wanda giggled. "Lighten up. Derrick's not going anywhere. After dealing with Grant saying he was the father of her child and all the drama y'all went through with that, I'd be very disappointed if he cheated on you. I believe he's just being sociable," Wanda said.

"I know. I guess Grant ruined it for all women."

"Do you trust Derrick?" Wanda asked, just as he reappeared. Angel was taking a sip of her daiquiri so she didn't see Wanda look up at him.

Derrick waited for her to respond.

"Yeah, I trust him. Enough to be happily married to him, anyway," Angel said, "but I can't say what he won't do."

"No one can say what their spouse will or won't do," Wanda replied. "It doesn't work that way. That's what trust is, believing in him to do the right thing."

"I do," Angel replied, "but at the same time I guess I'm trying to protect my heart."

"I won't let you down, Angel," Derrick said, startling her.

She looked up at Wanda, then turned around, making eye contact with Derrick.

"I can never undo what happened in the past," he said, approaching her, "but believe me, there's no place I'd rather be than here with you and my son. I know all about the trouble and temptation out in the streets—that's why I'm not out there. I pray for focus every day, Angel, and consciously try to do the right thing. I love you, and I never want to hurt you again.

"Like I told you yesterday, you can trust me to have female associates. Some women need strong male figures around. For one, they don't give up hope on men, and two, to help them better understand life and relationships. I enjoy sharing wisdom because I want to help build the ladies up. I also feel it's important to set a good example and represent the other faithful, loving and dedicated men. Although it's rarely mentioned and often overlooked, there are some out there."

Wanda smiled as Angel stood and embraced her husband. They shared several short kisses before Wanda cleared her throat. "That's my cue," she said, taking her empty glass to the kitchen sink.

Derrick and Angel smiled.

"You don't have to leave. I just came down to grab a beer," Derrick said just before his cell phone rang.

They all laughed.

"No, I'd better get going," Wanda replied.

"Give me a minute to fix you something to eat," Angel said.

Wanda watched her pack food in a Styrofoam to-go box.

"I'll walk you out," Angel said, handing it to her.

Wanda grabbed her small purse from the counter and gave Derrick Jr. a kiss before walking behind Angel toward the front door.

"I'm glad you came over," she said.

"Me, too," Wanda replied. "Now go turn Derrick's cell phone off so you can enjoy your husband."

"You'd better believe it," Angel replied.

Wanda continued to her car. "I'll call you later," she said before getting inside. She started the engine, backed out of the driveway, then sped off, squealing, leaving tire marks on the street.

Chapter 8

Kim pulled out her laptop and logged into her Yahoo account. She scanned the inbox, searching for the email from Angel. After locating the message, she downloaded the attachment, then printed the four-page lease. Glancing over the document reminded her of what was happening. Kim's heart pounded at the thought of receiving rental income exceeding the wages from her part-time job and a three-hundred-dollar profit. She took a pen and pad from her desk and did a preliminary monthly budget, assuming the plan worked out as-is. Kim anticipated using the excess cash to catch up on delinquent bills, which she'd listed by priority, then she intended to start saving.

"Thank you, Jesus," she sang, lifting her hand in the air. Kim prayed for God's favor and thanked him for a fantastic day. Finally, she felt she'd overcome some of her obstacles.

The moments of joy led to thoughts of Leon. Kim smiled, happy they'd reconnected. Although she had no intentions of rushing into a serious relationship, she was content with their agreement to keep in touch. She admired Leon. Without effort or consciousness, he'd always inspired her to be a better person. Because of him, Kim also realized wisdom and humbleness were a necessity for true growth in life. Reflecting, she focused on where she came from in regards to maturity. Remembering her young and naïve spirit was almost embarrassing to think about.

Kim went into the kitchen for a snack. While popping a bag of popcorn, she took a bottle of water from the refrigerator. Just as she'd gotten comfortable on the sofa in the den, the doorbell rang. Kim peeked through peephole, surprised to see Lynn standing on her porch wearing dark shades.

"Hey, girl," she said, swinging the door open. "Come in. I didn't know you were stopping by."

"I wanted to surprise you. What are you doing?" Lynn asked, stepping inside.

"Nothing much," Kim said, closing the door. "Angel sent me a copy of her and Derrick's rental agreement. I was getting ready to read over it. Would you like some popcorn?"

"Sure," Lynn said.

Kim led her into the kitchen.

"So what's up with the roommates?" Lynn asked her.

"They all agreed," Kim said with excitement. "Can you believe it? The soldiers didn't have a problem at all, but the sheriff was a little hesitant. Her lease will be for six months instead of a year, but that's okay."

"Honestly, with you finding all that money I was sure that roommate idea was out the window. Congratulations," Lynn said.

"Thank you, girl. Naw. I'm trying to be levelheaded while I decide what to do with it. I can't wait for the ladies to move in and get settled. I'm looking forward to quitting my part-time job. It's killing me. I'm tired of working so hard. I want my life back," Kim said.

"I'm sure. We were really worried about you," Lynn confessed.

Kim handed her the bag of popcorn and a bottle of water. "Oh, really? How bad did y'all talk about me?" she asked.

Lynn giggled. "Trust me, we didn't say anything behind your back not said directly to you. Yes, there were plenty of discussions because clearly you were taking on too much. However, because you're the decision maker for Kim, we had to step back and allow you to make the call."

Kim nodded as she led Lynn to the den. They sat on opposite ends of the sofa.

"I'm happy things are working out for you," Lynn said.

"Me, too. I was just thinking before you got here about how at times we make moves convinced it's the right one, then somewhere down the line we run into a snag and learn it wasn't such a good idea.

Instead of identifying the root of the problem so we can rectify it effectively, we're more prone to a temporary fix. Know what I mean?" Kim asked Lynn.

"Yeah, I understand," she replied.

"A prime example is when Angel offered to sell me her condo. Honestly, the condo would've been perfect for me. I made the mistake of thinking I needed something grand, so I purchased a house I couldn't afford. My inability to pay the mortgage was the snag. The reaction was finding another job to sustain, which triggered another snag—fatigue and a lack of nutrition. Now, I'm looking forward to having roommates as a mean of income so I can slow down and take better care of myself."

"Don't give up on selling the property, Kim," Lynn suggested.

"If all goes well with the tenants moving in, I'm taking the house off of the market," she replied.

"Do you think that's a good move?" Lynn asked.

"Yes, I do. If the property sells within the next couple of months it wouldn't be fair to my tenants. Plus, I'll be making good money from the living arrangement."

"That's all you're looking at. You should be happy as hell for the house to sell in a month or two," Lynn replied. "Like you just said, you're willing to accept a temporary fix rather than address the root of your problems. Selling will prevent future snags, Kim."

"Yeah, but I'm ready to quit my part-time job ASAP. I can't do it anymore, Lynn," she said.

"We've offered to help you, Kim. I believe you'd be better off leaving the house up for sale—even if you don't make a dime. Hell, throw in the furniture if that'll help you move it. Desperate times call for desperate measures. You have to be creative," Lynn encouraged.

"Yeah. This is so hard. I'm trying to figure it out without spending the cash I found."

"I hope you're not looking for me to co-sign you using it. My suggestion would be give it to authorities. It's drug money," Lynn said.

"I know. Guess who called me?" Kim said, changing the subject.

"Who?" Lynn asked.

"Leon. We went out for lunch," Kim said.

"Oh, really. "How was it?"

"I enjoyed seeing him," Kim admitted. "We've agreed to be friends."

"That's great. You already know how much I like Leon. He seems to be a genuinely nice guy," Lynn said.

"I believe so. I've learned a lot from Leon," Kim admitted. "Although I cared for him, Darius wouldn't allow our relationship to grow."

"That boy had a serious hold on you," Lynn said, shaking her head. "I still can't figure out why you were so crazy about him."

Kim smiled. "You have no idea. Behind that drug boy facade was a gentle and loving man. That's the reason I've always had hope for Darius." Kim lowered her head. "I still can't believe he's gone," she said.

"Come on, now," Lynn replied, taking her by the hand.

"I'm okay," Kim assured her. "Right now my mind-set is live one day at a time and let life happen."

"I'm so proud of you. You've come a long way in regards to relationships, Kim. When it's time to move on, you'll know it," Lynn encouraged.

"That's exactly how I feel. So what did you get into today?" Kim asked, changing the subject again.

"Well, instead of going out and spending money as planned, I stayed at home and did some things around the house that I'd been putting off for a while—like dusting," Lynn said.

She and Kim giggled.

"After cleaning and doing laundry, I showered, then you crossed my mind, so here I am. I called Michelle to see if she wanted to come, but Kelvin was massaging her feet. She said they went to the Keller's Flea Market earlier today and now her feet are swollen."

"That reminds me, what's up with Michelle selling you her interest in the day care?" Kim asked.

"Oh, it's in the works. Since she'd due to give birth next month, we plan to have the paperwork finalized by June 30, which is also her last day working. That's only days away."

"I know you're going to miss her," Kim said.

"Without a doubt. So, have you and Wanda had an opportunity to talk yet?" Lynn asked.

"Nope. I can't deal with her at the moment. I have too much other stuff going on," Kim said.

"I understand," Lynn replied. "Things really got out of hand that night."

"They sure did. I shouldn't have put my hands on Wanda, but I got fed up with her smart remarks. I slapped her across the face with that pizza before I knew it," Kim said.

"I'm hoping you guys will talk soon. If not, perhaps when we meet for girls' night out, all of us can engage in the conversation," Lynn said.

"I reckon. It really doesn't matter to me. Honestly, I'm not sure I want to work things out," Kim said.

"You don't mean that. We're friends because of our differences," Lynn said. "Wanda is our pain in the butt with a big mouth."

"True, but I don't have time for her drama. I have other priorities, like getting my life back on track," Kim said.

"You will," Lynn encouraged. "You're a survivor."

There was a brief silence.

"I can't lie. I did think about calling Wanda one day," Kim admitted.

"That's good. See, deep within is the desire to make things right. I love y'all girls," Lynn said. "I'd hate to see anything destroy our friendship. I need to plan another get-together at the house so we can mingle and have a good time. We haven't played cards in a while."

"Let me know when and I'll be there," Kim said.

Lynn finished eating her popcorn and left around 7:30. Soon after, Kim received a call from her realtor, Al. He was happy to say the couple he'd shown her property to the week prior had made an offer on her home.

Kim was confused. "I thought they chose to buy another house," she said.

"Someone submitted a better offer on the same day and the homeowners accepted theirs. My customers ended up making a back-up offer because they liked the home so much, then they decided to withdraw it and move forward with purchasing your house, which was their second pick," Al said.

"Wow. Okay," Kim replied. "So what happens now?"

"I'd like to come over and review the paperwork with you," Al said.

"Sure," Kim replied, unsure of what she wanted to do. She'd taken a different direction because nothing had happened with selling her property, now all of a sudden she had buyers.

After hanging up the phone, she contemplated whether to sell. She suddenly liked the idea of renting out rooms and keeping her house, more.

She called Angel to get her thoughts.

"If it was me, I'd sell," Angel said. "The roommate thing is a good idea if you have no other options. Now, it looks like you have another option, Kim."

"I've already told the ladies they can move in on the first of next month. I did a budget, Angel, and I'd be making good money with them living here."

"Yeah, you probably will—while they're there. If the arrangement doesn't work, you'll be stuck with that high mortgage payment again. If you sell the house, the debt is gone and so is the liability. Ultimately, you're responsible," Angel stressed.

"I know," Kim replied.

"Talk to Al and see what he suggests. I recommend you sell," Angel said. "Let me know what you decide."

"I will," Kim agreed.

She sat staring across the room, trying to make up her mind. The rental income was really tempting.

"What should I do, Lord? What should I do?" Kim asked.

Then she remembered how desperate she was before coming up with the roommate idea and reality set in. "I don't need this big place," she said to herself, "and I really don't want to share my living space. The money is appealing, but I'd be better off selling. I can move into a smaller home and retain my privacy."

When Al arrived, Kim invited him to sit at the dining room table. She watched him pull out a folder with papers inside.

Al explained that the buyers had offered full price, but needed her to contribute toward their closing costs. "I've plugged the figures into this worksheet. Here's the breakdown of the costs and your net profit."

"I get one-hundred-eighty-two-dollars back? Is that all?" Kim asked.

"Yes. Remember when we first did the numbers before I listed the property, I told you it looked like you would barely break even or possibly end up bringing money to the closing," Al said.

"I'm okay with it," Kim replied moments later.

"Good. You actually lucked up because of what happened with the first house they tried to purchase. I believe they gave you a full-price offer to avoid someone else overbidding them. Anyway, the buyers would like to close on July 12. Is that day okay for you?" Al asked.

"Where do I need to sign?" Kim replied.

After Al left she did a praise dance, giving thanks to God, believing everything to work out.

Later Kim called and updated the ladies who were interested in renting from her. She apologized for inconveniences and promised to inform them of any changes, then she logged on to her laptop and searched for an apartment or condo to lease. Kim figured it would be best to rent a place for six months then purchase a more moderate-sized home.

"I really need this sale to happen," she said. "I'm tired of the rollercoaster ride."

Chapter 9

Wanda whipped into her neighborhood, still grooving to the raw, uncut lyrics of Tupac Shakur. While cruising through the community she lowered the volume, glancing at the clock on the dashboard. It read nine-fifteen. Moments later, Wanda approached her house, convinced her eyes were deceiving her. Ron's truck was in the driveway. "What the hell?" she questioned, pressing the garage door opener.

By the time Wanda parked and got out of the car, Ron was walking toward her. "What in the world are you doing here?" she asked, clearly agitated.

"I wanted to see you," Ron replied in a calm, persuasive tone.

"You saw me earlier. Coming to my home is off limits, Ron. You know that," Wanda complained, furious he'd shown up uninvited.

"Why haven't you returned any of my calls? I've left several messages," Ron explained.

"When? Why? What do you want?" Wanda questioned, flustered.

Then she remembered shutting her phone off earlier that day. "I forgot to turn my cell back on after I woke up from a nap. Did you need something?"

"Where have you been?" Ron asked.

"Excuse me?" Wanda replied, noting his boldness.

"Where were you?" Ron questioned.

"I ran some errands," Wanda said, avoiding a specific answer. She didn't feel it was Ron's business knowing her whereabouts. Meanwhile, she rifled through her purse, searching for her cell phone. When she turned it on, it whistled, alerting her of new messages.

"Can I come in?" Ron asked.

"No. It's not a good time. I've had a long day, and I have a headache. I'm going inside to take a pain reliever so I can lie down," Wanda said.

"Is something wrong?" Ron asked, just as her phone started to ring.

Wanda shook her head. "Everything is fine, Ron," she said, ignoring the incoming call. MALCOLM was displayed across the ID screen.

"Aren't you going to answer it?" Ron asked.

"No, I'm not. Um, Ron you need to leave, please. I'll call you tomorrow," Wanda said, changing the phone setting to vibrate.

Ron stood silent for a few seconds. "Okay," he finally said. He kissed Wanda on the cheek. "Go take something for your headache. Give me a buzz if you start to feel better."

"I'll call you tomorrow," Wanda repeated.

As Ron walked away, she mumbled profanities until her phone began to vibrate. It was Malcolm calling again. Wanda didn't answer. She stood waiting for Ron to get in his truck, then she walked back in her garage. After taking the to-go from her front seat, Wanda pressed the button and watched the garage door close.

Once inside, she placed her things on the counter, then dialed Malcolm's phone number. He answered after the first ring.

"Hey, baby. I'm outside. I was calling to let you know I was coming over," he said.

"You're at my house, now?" Wanda questioned.

"Yep. Come open the door," Malcolm replied. He hung up without giving her an opportunity to respond.

"Damn, he must've driven up as Ron pulled off," Wanda said out loud.

Dismissing her thought, she went to let Malcolm in. She opened the door as he turned off the engine, then she watched him get out of his car, set the alarm, and walk toward her.

"Hey," Malcolm said in a bubbly tone. He kissed Wanda on his way inside.

"Hi. Why are you in such a good mood?" she asked, watching him swagger by. She could clearly see he was excited about something.

"Why not be in a good mood? It's a beautiful day. I need to wash my hands," Malcolm continued, heading for the bathroom.

As Wanda went to shut the front door, she noticed Ron driving by her house. He rolled down the window, staring directly at her.

She frowned. Wanda slammed the door, irritated by him acting like a stalker.

"I'd better cut that fool completely off before I have to kill him," she said softly.

"What's wrong?" Malcolm asked, reentering the room. He sat on the sofa.

"Nothing." Wanda took a deep breath and started toward the kitchen. She warmed up her food, poured a glass of wine, and sat at the table and began to eat.

Five minutes later, Malcolm appeared. "You're being kinda rude, aren't you?"

"No," Wanda said bluntly.

"It would've been considerate to let me know you were eating dinner. You don't just leave me sitting in the next room."

"Malcolm, I'm eating," Wanda said.

"Please…don't let me disturb you. When you're done, I'd like a few minutes of your time," he replied. Malcolm shook his head and walked away.

Wanda wasn't fazed by him or his comments. She continued to eat, still annoyed by Ron. After consuming a glass of wine, she poured another. Once she'd finished dinner, she sipped on her drink while cleaning the area. Next, Wanda started a load of laundry.

Malcolm was waiting in the kitchen when she returned from the laundry room. "Is it possible for us to have a conversation?" he asked.

"What is it, Malcolm?" Wanda complained.

"Will you come have a seat so we can talk like adults?" he insisted.

Wanda rolled her eyes as she walked past him. She led Malcolm into the living room and plopped down on the sofa.

"Why are you such a hard woman to deal with?" he asked, sitting next to her.

"I'm not," Wanda said. "I don't feel like being bothered, but you're bothering me. You wanted my undivided attention, now you have it. How can I help you?"

"First, you can lose the sarcasm. And stop being so damn hateful," Malcolm demanded, cutting his eyes at her.

Wanda smiled within at his attempt to take charge. She was shocked. "I'm listening," she said.

"I think it's time we discuss our relationship. Are we going to continue this thing or what?" Malcolm asked. "I'm not sure what's wrong, but I'm beginning to feel I'm wasting my time. Have I done something wrong? Is there anything you need to say to me?"

"It's not what you've done, Malcolm. It's what you're not doing," Wanda stated.

"Are you being serious?" Malcolm asked.

"Do I look serious?" Wanda said, fixing her eyes on him.

"Okay. What am I not doing?" Malcolm asked.

"Are you really ready to have this conversation?" Wanda questioned. "I know y'all men have that ego thing going on, but I'm not in the mood to beat around the bush. If we're going to discuss what's wrong in our relationship, it needs to be real."

"Go for it. If I didn't want to talk about the problem, I wouldn't have brought it up," Malcolm said.

"Okay. Well for me, our problem is romance," Wanda said.

"Romance? Are we talking about romance as in sex or romance as in wine and dine?"

"Both," Wanda answered. "More so, sex. I'm not being satisfied."

"You're not being satisfied?" Malcolm repeated.

"That's what I said," Wanda replied.

"Can you be more specific?" Malcolm requested. "I don't understand. I'm not doing anything different now than I was when we first began to date."

"Exactly. I was settling then, and I'm settling now," Wanda blurted. "I was hoping our love life would get better with time, but it hasn't."

"I don't please you in bed?" Malcolm asked.

"Well…" Wanda shrugged. "I mean, it's alright, but I know it can be better, Malcolm. I like excitement and aggression. Instead of taking charge and making our intimacy about us, you'd rather rush right to intercourse—and I hate that shit."

"Why didn't you tell me how you felt?" Malcolm asked.

"Again? Did you forget after the last time I mentioned it? If I've said it once, I've said it a thousand times. What makes it so bad is I've tried to teach you about my body and what I like, but instead of taking note you act as if it's only for that one time. This complaint shouldn't be surprising," Wanda stated.

Malcolm lowered his head. "Are you seeing someone?" he asked. "I know you, Wanda. If you say you're not getting what you need from me, I'm willing to bet you're getting it from somewhere."

"No, I'm not," Wanda replied to keep the conversation simple. She had officially decided not to be intimate with Ron anymore.

"So, what's next? Do you love me?" Malcolm asked.

"Yes, I love you, Malcolm. That's why I'm still with you. You're a good person and a true friend," Wanda said. "Even if we do break up, you'll always be a part of my life."

"Is that what you want?" Malcolm asked.

"No. I want to be pleased. Good romance is vital for me. You need to loosen up, Malcolm, and have some fun. Be spontaneous from time to time. I'm your lady. You should be comfortable with me by now," Wanda said.

"I am," Malcolm replied.

"No, you're not," Wanda said.

"Okay. What do I have to do?" Malcolm asked.

Wanda didn't respond, but gave a devilish grin.

"What do you want me to do?" Malcolm asked again.

Seconds later, he shook his head. "Oh, no. I'm not licking your behind, Wanda. That's out."

Wanda burst out laughing.

"Not only is that disgusting. It's plain nasty," Malcolm said. "If that's what you're looking for, it's over. I'm not the one."

"I can deal with that," Wanda replied. She continued to giggle.

Malcolm's cell phone rang, interrupting their moment. Wanda sat back, listening to the one-sided conversation until he hung up the phone.

"Listen, baby, I have to get going," Malcolm said. "The guys are waiting on me so we can go to Uncle Bruce's bachelor party. Do you believe he's really going through with this wedding?"

"I think it's great," Wanda said. "He needs to settle down with one woman. Not to mention, Sharon is a nice person."

"Yeah. Is it okay for me to come back later?" Malcolm asked.

"Tonight? Who are you kidding? You know how your family is. You guys will be partying until morning," Wanda said. "If it does end at a decent hour, you're welcome to come over. Call me first."

"Why?" Malcolm asked.

"Who knows? I might go out tonight," Wanda said.

"Oh. Okay." Malcolm stood, pulling Wanda into his embrace, kissing her.

After he left, she thought about their conversation and laughed, wondering what it would be like the next time they made love, which reminded her, she wasn't sore anymore.

Her thoughts drifted to Ron. Wanda couldn't believe he had the nerve to watch her let Malcolm in. "What's up with that?" she wondered. "I don't have time for a clingy man. I hope he doesn't think I want him to be jealous. I'm the not one for that foolishness."

When Wanda first met Ron she was under the impression he was a settled and content man. Now, his life seemed to be unraveling quite quickly. Their relationship had taken a turn for the worst, his wife was missing, and he had a drug addiction. Wanda almost pitied Ron. Learning more about him allowed her to see he was one of many men living a reckless, self-fulfilling life.

"This is exactly why I'm not married," Wanda complained. "Men are too unstable. At Ron's age, he should have it together."

Wanda pondered ways to penetrate his life without dating him. Instead of being involved by remaining friends like she'd told Angel, she decided it was best to gain insight by following Ron and employing Pete's fiancée, Casey, to find out what she could from Pete. Although she didn't fully trust Casey, she was her best option for gathering personal information.

To clear her mind, Wanda went into the bedroom and browsed through her array of clothing as she toyed with the idea of going out. When she came across her black miniskirt she matched it with a sexy blouse. "It's Saturday night. I may as well hang out for a little while and have some fun. Ron is adding unnecessary stress to my life."

Wanda laid her outfit across the bed and assembled matching accessories, then she remembered to check her voicemail. She had six messages, all from Ron asking her to call him ASAP. "I get it. He's trying to act concerned because he's realized he messed up. Yes, you did mess up, Ron. It's over, homeboy. You can go on about your business. I am not your wife," Wanda said.

She tossed the phone on the bed before going into the bathroom. Although she and Ron used protection, Wanda cleansed the inside of her body with warm water. Then after showering, she lounged around until it was time to get dressed.

Once at the club, she strolled around trying to find a place to sit, eventually settling at the bar. Moments after she'd sat down, someone kissed the back of her neck. Wanda turned around, ready to swing. She was shocked to see Malcolm standing there, smiling. "Hey. What are you doing here?" she asked. "I thought you were at the bachelor's party."

"It ended already," he said.

"So soon? What happened?" Wanda asked. She found herself blushing as she took note of how fine he looked in his slacks and dress shirt.

Malcolm chuckled. "You're not going to believe this," he began. "The stripper we hired was married to one of the guys Uncle Bruce invited to the party. Apparently, he had no idea his girl was a dancer. She told dude she was a nurse, and she supposedly worked the night shift."

Wanda laughed. "You're lying. How in the world did he not know where his wife works?" she questioned.

"The way I heard it, the relationship is still pretty new. They met on the Internet and dated for a short while before getting married."

"That's crazy as hell." Wanda shook her head. "He deserved just what he got. How did y'all end up at the club?" she asked.

"When I saw there was going to be drama at the party, I left with a couple of guys who wanted to stop by and see what was going on here. I'm not trying to go to jail. Also, I called your house and when you didn't answer I knew I'd find you here. Come on. Let's dance," Malcolm said.

Wanda took his hand and followed him to the dance floor.

Malcolm added excitement with his dramatic moves. He gripped Wanda's backside, grinding his pelvis against hers, then he dipped, worming his body back up.

Wanda laughed as he joked around.

As the song came to an end, he pulled her close, gyrating seductively against her. Malcolm kissed Wanda on the lips. "You wanna stay at my place tonight?" he asked.

"Why don't you come to my house?" she replied.

"That'll work. Before we go, I need to catch up with the guys and tell them I'm leaving with you," Malcolm said.

Wanda nodded. She followed as he maneuvered the club, trying to locate his buddies.

Afterward, Malcolm offered to treat her to breakfast. Wanda wasn't ready to go, but he insisted. She was flattered by his persistence. They left the club and headed for the IHOP on Mall Boulevard.

Once at the restaurant, Wanda searched for a place to park. The lot was packed. As she drove behind the restaurant she spotted a vehicle backing out of the space farthest from the building. Wanda approached the car then waited until the driver drove off. She pulled in.

After she'd parked, Malcolm hopped out and walked around to the driver's side. He opened the door for Wanda. "I feel spontaneous tonight," he said, smiling.

"Spontaneous?" Wanda questioned.

"Yeah," Malcolm replied, scanning the area.

He closed the door, then led Wanda to the passenger side, sitting her on the hood.

Wanda couldn't believe what was happening as he positioned her buttocks on the edge of the car. When he stood between her legs, she felt his erection.

Oh, my goodness, Wanda thought as Malcolm layered kisses along her neck, then he found her lips, piercing them with his tongue.

As they kissed, heat filled her body.

Soon after, Malcolm unzipped his pants and pulled Wanda's thong to the side, penetrating her. She held him tightly, releasing soft moans.

In the midst of making love, a group of people emerged from around the building.

"Relax, baby," Malcolm said, trying to be discreet.

Wanda wrapped her arms around his neck, taking his earlobe into her mouth. "Don't stop," she whispered.

Malcolm gave short, quick strokes, trying to satisfy her as he watched the gang of people split up. One set approached a car a few spaces down and the other continued toward them. Seconds later, they surrounded the car parked next to Wanda's.

"How's it going?" Malcolm said because they were all looking in his direction.

They spoke.

"Is everything okay?" one of the gentlemen asked.

Malcolm stopped moving. "Yeah, man. Everything's fine," he managed to say.

Wanda stole Malcolm's attention when she tightened her vaginal muscles around his manhood, thrusting gently.

"Get a room—y'all nasty asses," one of the ladies yelled before slamming the door.

Although the windows were closed, Wanda and Malcolm could hear the roaring laughter spill from their vehicle as the driver started the car and drove away.

They both snickered before Malcolm reengaged. Moments later it was over. Malcolm had beaten her to the finish line. Although Wanda didn't reach her peak, she wasn't upset because he'd made a big step in the right direction.

She slid off the car onto her feet, embracing him. Malcolm took her completely by surprise when he began massaging her erogenous zone. Wanda closed her eyes and smiled within. "That's what I'm talking about. Work it."

Chapter 10

As rain pounded against the rooftop and lightning rippled across the dark skies, Kim lay with pillows over her head trying to evade the sounds of thunder. She'd tossed and turned for hours, unable to fall asleep. Finally, at 8:45 the next morning she got up and made her way into the bathroom. After getting dressed for church, she straightened the covers on her bed, displaying decorative pillows on top.

Kim had skipped early morning worship, hoping the weather would clear up. Although rain continued to fall, missing the eleven o'clock service was not an option. During altar call she preceded to the front of the sanctuary, requesting prayer for direction. The preacher dabbed her forehead with oil then began communicating with God on her behalf. Kim understood that along with praying, she had work to do. She was prepared to be faithful, more obedient, and vowed not to create unnecessary situations in life then expect God to bail her out.

On her way home she thought about Leon. Kim contemplated calling, but figured it would be best to let a couple days pass before reaching out to him. However, when she approached Leon's neighborhood she gave in to the urge of dialing his number. When he answered, she asked if it was okay to stop by. Leon welcomed Kim and offered her dinner once she arrived. She ate baked fish and a serving of broccoli with cheese.

Afterward, they settled on the sofa. Leon flipped though the television channels, tuning in to the news while Kim sat preoccupied.

When he put his arm around her, she rested her head against his chest, wondering if the time was right for them to resume a more serious relationship. She believed wholeheartedly had she not reconciled with Darius, it was likely they'd still been dating.

Although Kim wasn't completely over Darius, she realized he could never reciprocate her love. She persuaded herself to release him and give the feelings for Leon a chance to grow.

"You're kinda quiet. What's on your mind?" he asked, breaking her thoughts.

"I'm fine. I was just thinking," Kim said, looking up at him.

He massaged her shoulder. "Are you sure?" he questioned.

"I am. Can I kiss you?" Kim asked.

Leon's eyes widened. "Sure," he replied, surprised by her request.

Kim blushed, and her heart fluttered as she leaned toward him. They shared a gentle kiss.

"I'm ready for our relationship to be the way it used to," Kim said.

"Are you?" Leon asked.

"Yes, I am," she replied.

"I have to ask, is there anyone we need to discuss first?" Leon questioned.

Kim smiled. "No. This time it's just you and me. I promise," she said.

"Good, because I want you all to myself," Leon replied, pulling her close, initiating a more passionate kiss.

Afterward, they sat holding hands.

"There is something we need to discuss," Kim said, resuming the conversation, "starting with the magazine article I told you about yesterday. It's written about me, but includes my feelings for Darius. It's pretty deep, Leon. I expressed our love for each other and shared how we felt our reunion was a blessing.

"The issue comes out next month. I'm sure members of your congregation will read it and pass judgment. I want to date you, but I don't want to attend your church so soon," Kim said. "I think it'll be best to let some time pass."

"Our relationship is our business. We have to do what feels right to us," Leon stated.

"You're a well-respected deacon. I really don't want to jeopardize that or have members disrespect you because of me," Kim said.

"Everyone in that congregation is human just like you and me. We all have issues and tough decisions to make. They're on the outside looking in, Kim. Whatever we agree to do, they'll have to accept," Leon said.

"I'll stay at my church for now," Kim insisted.

"If that's what you want, I'm behind you. I do have a question," Leon said. "Is there a possibility of marriage in our future?"

"I don't know about that," Kim replied. "I'm trying to take things slow."

"I'll go as slow as you need me to," Leon said.

Kim's mind went straight to sex. She didn't know if that was Leon's intention so she didn't reply to the comment.

"I'm not proposing," he said. "I'm just curious to know if there's a possibility. Our relationship isn't something new—it's a continuance. I loved being married and I miss it."

"Your question is overwhelming me, Leon. If I say yes, I feel I'll jinx the relationship. I remember bragging how I'd never make a lifelong commitment to anyone, then I accepted Troy's proposal and our relationship went sour. I agreed to wed Darius and he was killed. I can't handle that thought," Kim said, shifting in her seat.

"Calm down, love. The third time is the charm," Leon said. "I'm not a young boy like those guys. I'm a man. I want to take care of you."

Kim smiled. "We'll have this conversation later, I promise," she said.

"Okay." Leon kissed the side of her face.

"Guess what," Kim said excitedly, changing the subject. "My realtor came by last night to discuss an offer on my house. I accepted it. We're supposed to close on July 12. "I'll be so happy if everything works out."

"Congratulations," Leon said. "What are your plans regarding housing? Will you make enough money from the sale to relocate?"

"Not quite, but I have money set aside to put with the proceeds. Once I find a place to live I'll know exactly how much my expenses are."

"I can help you move," Leon offered.

"Great. You'll get to see my friends. They've all been asking about you, trust me," Kim said. "Maybe I can treat everyone to a game of bowling afterward. You can give the guys another beat down."

Leon chuckled. "I'd love that. How are they?" he asked.

"Fine. I haven't spoken to Wanda in over a week. We had a fight," Kim said.

"A fight? Why?" Leon asked.

"Because of her smart mouth. I got tired of her sly remarks," Kim said. "I slapped her across the face with pizza and we ended up in a fist fight."

Leon shook his head.

"We haven't talked since then. I have plans to meet with her and the girls at Angel's mom's place later this evening. She and her husband had their home on Whitaker Street renovated. Angel invited us over for tea to celebrate, but we agreed to have a small housewarming party," Kim said.

"That's nice. I'm sure you and Wanda will work out your problems," Leon said.

"I'm sure we can be cordial, but I wonder how awkward it's going to feel being in the same room with her and not talking."

"Why wouldn't you talk to her?" Leon asked.

"I'll speak, but other than that I don't have much to say to Wanda."

"Go to the party with a positive attitude, Kim. Be the bigger person. You can do it," Leon said.

Kim looked away. "I'll try," she mumbled.

Leon shook his head again. "I'm thirsty. Would you like something to drink or more to eat?" he asked.

"No, thank you," Kim replied.

When Leon got up and headed toward the kitchen, she stretched out on the sofa. Kim woke up an hour later, underneath a blanket. Leon was sitting in his recliner watching TV.

"Oh my goodness. I can't believe I fell asleep," Kim said, yawning. "I didn't get much rest last night because of that nasty thunderstorm. I thought it would never end."

Leon looked at her and smiled. "Yeah, you were in a pretty deep sleep. You were snoring so loud I could barely hear the television," he teased.

Kim giggled. "Was I really?" she asked, sitting up.

"Naw, I'm kidding," Leon replied.

Kim folded the blanket, then placed it on the arm of the chair before going to the bathroom.

"I enjoyed the visit, but I'd better get going," she said when she returned.

"I'm glad you came by," Leon replied, standing.

Kim accepted his embrace.

"When can I see you again?" he asked.

"Anytime," Kim said. "I really believe our relationship is going to work this time, Leon."

"I hope so," he replied with a smile. "Let me know how things turn out with your friends tonight."

"I will," Kim said. Leon walked her to the front door. Before she could say good-bye, he kissed her.

Leon's affection made Kim yearn for him. She loved how special he made her feel. She had no idea the visit would end so wonderfully.

Twenty minutes later, Kim fussed as a car began to tailgate her SUV. She maintained the neighborhood speed limit of twenty-five miles per hour until she approached a stop sign. When she turned onto her street, the vehicle followed. Kim pulled along the edge of the road, going ten miles per hour, allowing the driver an opportunity to pass. When the Dodge Charger sped around and swerved in front of her, she slammed on her brakes. Kim watched as Darius' ex-girlfriend Janay hopped out and threw a can of soda against her windshield. "Slut," Janay yelled in her direction, sticking up her middle finger.

Kim's first instinct was to stomp the gas pedal and ram into the side of her car. Since Janay's passengers were children, she decided not to follow through, but shook her head as Janay hopped back into her vehicle and speed away.

After rinsing the soda from the windshield, Kim started toward her house again, wondering from where Janay came. She was curious if she'd finally learned where she lived or if they'd coincidentally crossed paths.

Kim pitied her kids, imagining all they'd seen as minors. She hoped for their sake, Janay would mature and start leading by example.

Once at home, she changed clothes before going into her office. Kim continued to think about the opportunity she missed with the roommate arrangement. She almost dreaded passing up the chance to keep her house while earning extra money, however, she was sure she'd chosen her best option.

Moments later, she unlocked the bottom drawer of her desk and pulled out a stack of journals she'd accrued over the years. As she thumbed through the pages of the one dated June 1995, it reminded her of some of the things she'd endured as a young adult. Kim found it quite intriguing to reconnect with feelings and emotions from past years. As she read, there were several pages she was tempted to rip out and shred.

It was almost two hours later when Kim noticed the time. As she replaced the notebooks in the desk she realized her stories were interesting. For just a moment she toyed with the idea of penning an autobiography. "Naw, there's no need of airing dirty laundry. Unless my stories can benefit someone… Could they?" Kim wondered.

She engaged in deeper contemplation about writing a memoir. Kim had always been a good storyteller. Her journals weren't only to capture life experiences but also to express her creativity by manipulating words.

Suddenly, she visualized becoming an author. Kim smiled, curious if she could put together a relevant piece of work. Because she was currently overwhelmed with everything else going on in her life, she stored the idea in the back of her mind with intentions of revisiting it later.

After placing the rest of her journals in the desk and locking it, it dawned on Kim that she'd just made a good decision by not taking on something else while already overextended, without going back and forth about it.

"I'm growing," she cheered. "Thank you, Lord."

She leaned back in her chair, then looked around the room. Kim became exhausted by the thought of packing. She had two large shelves filled with books and a variety of pictures and paintings hanging on the walls. She pushed aside all that had to be done and planned to sort through things along the way. During the weekend prior to her closing date she'd pack up her household items.

Kim prayed for everything to work out with selling the home. She'd learned with real estate anything could happen, so to prevent disappointment she remained mindful of taking one day at a time. Although she could hardly wait to get the sale behind her, she leaned on the Bible verse telling her to be anxious for nothing.

Her excitement stemmed from the desire to move beyond a horrible financial situation. She never again wanted to find herself in a position where she could barely afford food. Kim felt humiliated reliving the recent months of her life. She could clearly see she was her own problem. Now, she was prepared to be obedient.

Chapter 11

Wanda strolled along the tree-lined walkway of Ray and Mrs. Wesley's large Victorian-styled home. She admired the colorful plants and neatly trimmed shrubs creating fabulous curb appeal, then she continued up the steps and rang the doorbell. While waiting for someone to answer, she scanned the details of the spacious porch. Although Wanda wasn't a fan of historic houses, she was impressed at how nicely the property had been redone.

Angel distracted her when she swung open the front door. "Hey, girl, come on in," she sang, giving Wanda a hug.

"Hi, Angel." Wanda stepped inside, stopping in her tracks. The high ceiling and five-tier chandelier hanging in the foyer immediately caught her eye. "What an entrance. This is beautiful," she said.

"Thank you. Mama's going to show y'all around. Now we're waiting on Kim. Everyone is in the kitchen. Follow me," Angel said.

Wanda trailed her. "Greetings, all. Wanda's here," she bellowed moments later, entering the room with a smile, posing with one hand on her hip.

"So what," Lynn blurted.

The others giggled, then they spoke.

After placing a gift bag on the table, Wanda circled the room giving hugs. "From what I can see, the house is marvelous, darling," she said, approaching Ray and Mrs. Wesley. "I can't wait to view the rest of it."

They both thanked her.

Wanda sat in a chair next to Angel. She looked at her and smiled.

"What?" Angel questioned.

"Nothing. Did you go and see the apartments today?" Wanda asked.

"Yes. They're really nice. We made an offer," Angel said. "Now we're waiting to see if it's accepted."

"Cool deal," Wanda replied.

"I might need to invest in rental property," Lynn added.

"Derrick loves being a landlord. You know he's getting out of the military in a couple of months, so we're hoping to purchase a few more units before his income changes. It's likely he won't work a traditional nine-to-five after being discharged," Angel said.

Seconds later, the doorbell rang. "There's Kim." Angel hopped up, going to let her in.

The gang spoke almost in unison when they returned.

"Are y'all ready for the tour?" Mrs. Wesley asked.

Everyone agreed and gathered around her. As Mrs. Wesley showed off the spacious rooms on the first floor, Wanda fell in love with the contemporary shades of yellow, brown, and green. The colors gave a cozy, classy feel while the fixtures and lighting added pizzazz. The wooden floors and crown molding added the final touch.

Then the girls *ooh*ed and *aah*ed as they stepped up the wide staircase. The refurbished detail of the original wood was breathtaking, like something taken from a movie or a magazine. The bedrooms on the second level were huge also, each with a fireplace and mantle.

After the tour, Wanda and the girls offered to help Mrs. Wesley prepare hot tea, but she wouldn't hear of it and fussed until they settled in the sunroom. While waiting, Ray showed them pictures of the house before it had been renovated. They all agreed the transformation was incredible.

Once Ray left the room Wanda initiated a private conversation. "I have some bad news, good news, and great news to share," she said.

"Bad news first," Lynn replied.

"Okay. I finally told Momma about Michael and me," Wanda said.

The girls were all ears. No one said a word, waiting for her to continue. "That woman accused me of lying, called me evil, and she slapped me."

"Wanda, stop lying," Lynn said.

"I'm serious," she replied.

Angel, Kim, and Michelle sat in disbelief.

"What did you do?" Lynn asked.

"Nothing. I didn't hit her back," Wanda said.

"Oh my God. I'm sorry to hear that," Michelle said.

"I'm shocked," Lynn added.

"I'm speechless," Angel said.

Kim didn't comment.

"Momma's off the chain. I still can't believe how she has flipped out. Anyway… The great news is—"

"Wait a minute. When did all of this happen?" Angel asked Wanda.

"It was on Thursday after I got home from work. I had no idea she was coming over—supposedly to make peace," Wanda said.

"Wow. I can't see Mrs. Joyce acting the way you're describing," Lynn admitted.

"Imagine how I feel. I contemplated telling y'all about this because I didn't want to make her look bad. I'm not trying to make her look bad," Wanda said. "I just decided a few minutes ago to say something. Again, the altercation happened on Thursday—it's Sunday. I haven't told anyone, not even my sister or brother about the incident. I'd hate to see them lose respect for Momma, but if they do, I'd rather it be a result of something between them personally that doesn't involve me."

"Well, what's the good news?" Michelle asked.

"First, the great news. My dad's back at home," Wanda said, excited. "He was discharged earlier today and is recovering well."

The girls cheered.

Seconds later, Mrs. Wesley walked in the room. "What's going on?" she asked.

"Remember I told you Wanda's dad had a heart attack. He's out of the hospital," Angel said.

"Oh, that's great. Praise the Lord. Yes. Well, I'm almost done in the kitchen. I'll be back in a few minutes, okay?" Mrs. Wesley said before leaving.

"Now, the good news," Wanda said, resuming the conversation. "Malcolm is finally stepping up his game, girls. Y'all are not going to believe this. He and I made out in the parking lot at IHOP last night. Not in the car…on the hood."

"What? How in the hell did you get Malcolm to pull his drawers down in a parking lot?" Lynn asked.

The other girls laughed.

"Get this: It wasn't my idea," Wanda said. "He came by my house earlier to talk about what's wrong in our relationship, and I told him the truth."

"Can you be more specific?" Lynn asked.

"I let Malcolm know he's not getting it done in the bedroom. I probably wouldn't have been so blunt on a good day, but Ron had just pissed me off. That asshole showed up at my house. We agreed at the very beginning of our relationship not to cross that line. Anyway, I told him I had a headache and didn't feel like having company. He left literally seconds before Malcolm came, then drove back by to watch me let him in."

"Girl, Ron is a nut," Lynn blurted.

"Yes, he is. Guaranteed, baby," Wanda stated.

"You'd better stop playing and take that man seriously. Be careful with him, Wanda," Michelle suggested.

"Please. I'm not worried about Ron. He should be worried about me," she said.

"I don't want to talk about him anymore. Ron scares me. Tell us how Malcolm responded to what you told him," Angel insisted.

"I guess he heard me this time. After fooling around at IHOP we went to my place. Malcolm set the tone with the Boyz II Men's hit, 'I'll Make Love to You.' I wanted to holla. I'm telling you, it was a great experience. While we were lying in bed, I asked myself, *Why am I cheating?* Then I blamed Malcolm. I shouldn't have to beg to be loved the right way," Wanda complained. "But any way, it was after four o'clock this morning when we finally went to sleep, then I woke up to breakfast in bed."

"Go, Malcolm. Do your thang," Lynn said. "We told you, Wanda. If you would've spoke up earlier you'd have no need for that psycho, Ron."

"I'm not dating him anymore anyway," Wanda said. "I believe he's a man with many secrets and possibly involved in his wife's disappearance."

"What?" Michelle questioned.

"Why?" Lynn asked.

"For more reasons than one. Now, I need to prove he was involved," Wanda said.

"How do you plan to do that?" Lynn asked.

"By following him. Oh, I haven't told y'all my interest in becoming a private investigator, have I? Well, that's my plan," Wanda said. "I'll get all the hands-on experience by keeping tabs on Ron."

"Considering what's going on within your family, I can't believe you'd waste time with Ron," Michelle said.

"It's personal. You wouldn't understand. I can't let confusion slow me down," Wanda replied.

Mrs. Wesley interrupted their conversation when she appeared with a round tray. While she and the girls got things situated with the food, Angel grabbed gifts from the kitchen and set them in the sunroom.

Soon after, as they sipped tea and ate hors d'oeuvres, Mrs. Wesley opened the presents—Kim gave a crystal crucifix, Wanda provided stainless cookware, Michelle supplied washcloths and towels, and Lynn contributed decorative candles and a picture frame gift set. Lastly, Angel presented her gift, a *Sugar Shack* painting signed by the artist, Ernie Barnes.

Both Mrs. Wesley and Ray's eyes lit up. They smiled, admiring the painting before giving Angel a heartfelt embrace for the *Good Times*–inspired painting.

Later on as they prepared to leave, Kim, Lynn, and Michelle tidied up the sunroom, and Wanda and Angel assisted Mrs. Wesley with cleaning the kitchen.

"Mama disappeared on us," Angel said after they'd finished.

"She has been gone for a while," Wanda replied.

Within seconds, they watched Mrs. Wesley stumble out of the half-bath with a blank expression.

"Are you okay, Mama?" Angel questioned, rushing toward her.

"Yeah, baby. I'm fine," she replied, gripping the wall.

"Let me help you to a chair," Angel said, holding onto her. She braced Mrs. Wesley as she sat down at the kitchen table.

"Thanks. I'm okay now," she said. "I felt a little lightheaded. It's probably from not eating. I had toast and coffee for breakfast but that's all. I wanted everything to be perfect for you girls so I spent the entire day preparing for your visit."

"Mama, you have to take care of yourself," Angel said.

"I know," she replied.

"Well, my friends are getting ready to leave. Will you be okay sitting here for a few minutes while I walk them out?" Angel asked.

"Yes. Go ahead. Thanks for the gifts. It was nice seeing you ladies," Mrs. Wesley said on their way out.

Wanda latched onto Angel's arm as they gathered out front. "She'll be okay. I wanted to tell you, her and Ray look really happy together," she said.

"I know. I'm excited for them. You can't imagine how awesome it feels to finally see Mama move out of those projects and into a home. I pray Ray doesn't change now that they're in his house," Angel said.

"He won't. It's no secret he loves your mom. Did you see how he was touching on her?" Kim asked.

"You would be the one paying attention to that man touching his wife," Michelle said.

Kim sucked her teeth, and her friends giggled.

"Don't worry about Mrs. Wesley. She done whipped that thang on Ray. He's not going anywhere," Wanda said.

"I think growing old has its perks," Lynn said. "It seems to be the most settled part of life. No more chasing dreams or children to rear. I like it."

"All they do is go to church," Angel said.

"That's what you think," Wanda replied. "I'm outta here. I'll see you ladies later."

"Wait a minute, Wanda," Lynn said. "I'm having a get-together at the house next Saturday at four o'clock. Be there. More importantly, I was hoping you and Kim would talk tonight."

"Now's not the time," Kim said, ignoring Leon's advice to be the bigger person.

"Kim, you have been kinda quiet," Michelle said.

"I'm fine. Lynn, can I bring Leon to the cookout?" she asked, dodging the pressure to deal with Wanda.

"Of course you can," she replied.

Wanda approached Kim. "I apologize for pulling your hair out," she said, taking her by surprise, "but my opinion is the same. My comments weren't meant to hurt you. I was trying to help."

"I don't need your help. I'm not sure our friendship will recover from this," Kim said bluntly.

"So be it. We argue back and forth all the time. What set that night apart was you getting physical. Was I supposed to sit there and allow you to hit me? I don't think so. Either you can deal with me or you can't. It's really up to you, Kim."

Instead of addressing Wanda, Kim stepped away, diverting the conversation to Angel. "Don't worry about Mrs. Wesley," she said. "Your mother is happy, and with God's help she'll remain on the right path."

Angel nodded.

"I'll see you ladies later," Wanda repeated, walking off.

"Good night," her friends said to her.

Wanda hurried away. She already knew Kim was about to initiate prayer for Mrs. Wesley. When she made it to her car she looked back toward the house and saw her friends holding hands with their heads bowed. Wanda honked the horn as she sped away.

During the drive, she reflected on Mrs. Wesley, concerned with her being in the bathroom for so long, then coming out appearing disoriented. *I hope she's not smoking crack again,* Wanda thought, dreading the heartache she knew Angel would endure if her mom had relapsed.

Next, she picked up her cell phone and dialed voicemail. There were three new messages from Ron telling her to call him. Wanda sighed. "This man is getting on my nerves," she complained. She pecked in his number and called like she'd promised.

"Hey, baby," Ron answered.

"Hi," Wanda replied.

"What's going on? Why is it so hard for me to catch up with you all of a sudden?" Ron asked.

"I was hanging out with my friends today. Do you need something?" Wanda asked.

"Um, I wanted to apologize for what happened the other night. I really didn't mean to call you Sheila. She was the last person we talked about before I went to sleep. I guess that's why her name was on my mind. I'm under a lot of pressure, but the last thing I want is for my distractions to interfere with our relationship. I love you, and I don't want to lose you."

"Love is a powerful word, Ron."

"I know, and I mean it," he replied.

"You have a wife. I don't think it's appropriate for you to say you love me. Matter of fact, it's time to end this relationship. You're being a little too serious. That's not what I intended. I'm not in love with you, Ron," Wanda said. "I was just having fun."

Ron held the phone but didn't respond and Wanda sat quietly on the other end.

"You're not leaving me, Wanda," he finally said. "It doesn't work like that. Do you think you can spend all of my damn money then call it quits? Naw, you owe me."

"I don't owe you anything," Wanda rebutted. "What you've given me you gave freely, and what I've given you I gave freely."

"Oh, there's no comparison," Ron blurted.

"I'm not going to argue about this. If you feel I owe you, bill me," Wanda said. "Good-bye."

"If you hang up, I know something," Ron dared.

Wanda closed her flip phone, ending the call. "Who in the hell does he think he is? He almost made me curse his ass out," she complained.

She listened to her phone ring over and over. The palms of her hands began to sweat, and the adrenaline rushed through her body as she grew angrier by the second. Wanda forwarded Ron's call to voicemail ten times before he finally stopped calling.

Minutes later she approached her house, scanning the area to make sure he wasn't nearby waiting for her. After pulling into the garage, Wanda quickly lowered the door, watching as it closed. She grabbed her hand bag from the passenger seat and went inside, disarming the security alarm, then resetting it.

Wanda placed her keys and purse on the counter, then she leaned against it thinking of how crazy Ron had been acting. Her gut feeling led her to believe he'd show up that night. Wanda took a knife from the kitchen and a baseball bat from her spare bedroom. She placed the knife between the mattress and box spring with the handle barely exposed and slid the bat underneath the bed. Although the security system was activated Wanda felt more secure having accessible weapons.

Once an hour had passed, she calmed down. Wanda figured Ron found something else to do with his time other than harass her, so she began to prepare for work the next day, starting with a warm bath. Just as she stepped out of the tub, her home telephone rang. Wanda wrapped a towel around her and walked in the bedroom. She glanced at the caller ID and saw Malcolm's name on the screen. "Hi, Malcolm," she answered.

"Hey. What are you doing?" he asked.

"Drying off. I just got out of the tub," Wanda said.

"Man, I should've been knocking on the door instead of calling on the phone," Malcolm replied.

"Don't hurt yourself," Wanda teased. "We've had more sex within the last twenty-four hours than the last twenty-four months."

"Come on now. I'll make it up to you," Malcolm said.

"Is that a promise?" Wanda questioned. "Not tonight though. I'm tired as hell. We didn't get any rest, but I enjoyed your company."

"Same here," Malcolm replied. "I won't hold you up. I just wanted to make sure you made it home okay. How did the housewarming go?"

"It turned out really well," Wanda said. "Mrs. Wesley has a beautiful home. She gave us a tour, then we drank tea and ate hors d'oeuvres while she opened her gifts. I left Missionary Kim and the girls in the front yard praying."

Malcolm chuckled.

"She needs to hoard those prayers for herself," Wanda sassed. "We talked briefly about our altercation, but she's not over it yet."

"How do you feel about making up with her? Do you think the friendship will be the same?" Malcolm asked.

"I love Kim, but she gets on my nerves. She makes the simplest situations complicated, and that drives me crazy. If I can't say what's on my mind when she's around, I don't need to be around her. I'm trying not to be insensitive, but I keep thinking, if one of my friends whooped my ass I probably wouldn't want to hang out with them anymore either," Wanda said.

"Stop it," Malcolm said. "I hope you girls can work it out. I like all of your friends."

"We'll see," Wanda replied.

Shortly after, she hung up the telephone and cuddled underneath her covers. When the doorbell rang she sat straight up. Wanda knew it was Ron. She could feel it. She eased out of bed and grabbed her bat, then tiptoed in the living room. She peeked out of the front window and saw Ron standing at the door with a huge vase of roses.

She didn't say anything, hoping he'd go away. Seconds later, he rang the bell again. Then he knocked. "Wanda, I know you're in there," Ron called out. "Open the door, please."

Wanda stood there listening to him plead for nearly thirty minutes before she finally responded. "Ron, you need to leave or I'm calling the police," she said.

"Baby, let me in," he begged.

"Go home, Ron," Wanda replied.

She listened to him degrade himself a little while longer without answering before returning to her room and crawling back in bed. Eventually, Wanda fell asleep. She woke up at six o'clock the next morning when the alarm clock buzzed. Her first thought was Ron. She hurried in the living room and looked out of the window. There was no sign of him, so Wanda followed her morning routine, preparing for work.

Once inside her car she pressed the remote, lifting the garage door, then she put the gear in reverse and looked through her rearview mirror. Wanda jumped. Her heart pounded as Ron's tall frame charged toward her with something in his hand. She immediately thought it was a gun. Wanda stomped the gas pedal, barely missing him as she sped backward. Then she slammed on the brakes to prevent crashing into her neighbor's yard.

Wanda sat in the middle of the street, shaking. Finally, she managed to roll down her window. “Stay the hell away from me, Ron,” she yelled. “If you come here again, you’re going to jail. I’m filing a restraining order today.”

Moments later she lowered the garage door and drove off, noticing neighbors standing outside watching. Wanda had had it with Ron. She couldn’t believe how crazy he’d been acting. She really hated him for bringing drama to her community. Seeing that side of his personality triggered her ability to identify with his wife. She began to understand why Sheila may have run off without letting anyone—not even her family—know where she was going.

Wanda became anxious to find incriminating evidence against him, but she needed a strategy to outsmart him.

During her lunch break, she called Angel and filled her in on Ron’s showing up at her house the night before and the incident earlier that morning.

“Wanda, I don’t know what to tell you. I already gave you my advice, and it hasn’t changed. Leave that man alone,” Angel encouraged.

“I’m trying. Apparently that idiot hasn’t learned no means no. He won’t let go, Angel. I’ll figure something out,” Wanda said. “I have to find a way to deal with him popping up at my house whenever he gets ready. That’s not cool. I keep thinking about Malcolm. I would hate for the two of them to cross paths, especially since things are so much better between Malcolm and me.”

“How do you think he’d respond if he found out about you and Ron?” Angel asked.

“Um, I’m not sure. He’ll be pissed, but Malcolm loves me. I think he’d forgive me. If not, life goes on.”

“Wanda, you can be a cold person,” Angel said.

“I know,” she replied, “but honestly I love Malcolm, and I really like the direction our relationship is going in. Clearly, I’d rather he not learn about Ron. If he does, it’s his call. I’d be willing to accept the consequences for my actions, but I don’t want to make him bitter.”

“My, my, my. Behind all that tough talk is a little compassion. I like that,” Angel said.

"Whatever. If you still lived in Savannah, I could've crashed at your place to shake Ron off my tail," Wanda said, shifting the subject. "He doesn't know what any of my friends look like or where you live. That's a good thing. I need to change my routine so I can trail him instead of him stalking me. I thought about Lynn, but Mr. Policeman Chris would be all up in my business. Michelle and Kelvin are in love, so I don't want to impose on them. Staying with Kim is not an option. She doesn't like me anyway."

"You can stay here, Wanda. I'm sure Lynn and Michelle would welcome you, too. Kim is upset, but I'm willing to bet she's got your back," Angel continued.

"I'd sleep in my car before I ask to live with Kim. There's no way," Wanda stressed. "How's your mom, Angel? Is she okay?"

"Yeah. She was feeling a little lightheaded, that's all. She was fine when I left."

"Good. I was hoping it was nothing serious," Wanda said.

"Naw. Anyway, when you figure out what you're doing, let me know. If I can help, I'm here," Angel said.

"Thanks. I love you, girl," Wanda replied.

"I love you, too. Where'd that come from?" Angel asked.

"I appreciate that you're always willing to lend a hand. Knowing you're such a great friend makes me feel bad about how I dropped the ball at the club that night you asked me to watch your back because your ex-fling, Mike, was acting crazy. I allowed his buddies to distract me while he cornered you in the parking lot. A true friend would've taken the time to walk you to your car."

"Wanda, please don't go there," Angel said.

"I have to," she replied. "Although I let you down, you've remained true to me. Had the tables been turned, I would've been mad as hell. Mike could've beaten you to death and it would've been my fault. I apologize, Angel. I am so sorry. I should've been there to help you whoop his ass."

"Apology accepted. Now, forget about it," Angel insisted. "I don't want to talk about Mike. Getting involved with him was the worst mistake of my life, and I'd rather not relive any of it."

Wanda held the phone, regretful. She believed if she were with Angel, Mike wouldn't have put his hands on her. "I'll talk to you later," she finally said. She closed the flip phone and lowered her head, knowing no excuse was good enough.

Chapter 12

Kim submitted a two-week resignation to her part-time job at New York & Company. Although the sale of her home wasn't final, she felt confident about quitting because of the backup plan for roommates if the house didn't sell and her stash of cash. The thought of having more time for herself and to be with Leon was refreshing. Kim glowed with excitement. She was counting down the days for a social life.

On Wednesday night after work she stopped by the Walmart on Ogeechee Road, surprised to cross paths with Darius' mother, Victoria. Kim hadn't seen her since the funeral.

"How are you?" she asked, smiling.

"I'm blessed," Victoria replied.

"I've tried to contact you to see how everything was going," Kim said.

"I received the messages. Thanks for your concern," Victoria replied.

"No problem. Actually, I'm happy I ran into you. Be sure to pick up a copy of the July issue of *Keepin' It Real* magazine. There's an article in it about me, featuring Darius."

"Excuse me? Did you get permission to include Darius in this article? Who gets the proceeds?" Victoria asked.

"Proceeds? Get permission for what?" Kim questioned, shocked by her response.

"I'll be sure to pick up a copy," Victoria said. "If you've done something illegal, you'll hear from my lawyer."

"Lawyer? You've got it all wrong," Kim explained. "I don't need anyone's consent to tell my story. I included Darius' thoughts and inspirations to honor him."

"Be prepared to pay for those thoughts and inspirations because they belong to my son," Victoria snapped.

Kim stood looking at her in disbelief. "Is money all you think about when it comes to Darius?" she asked.

"Whatever he's entitled to passes on to me, and I want it," Victoria said.

"This conversation is so over," Kim replied, stepping away. She couldn't believe Victoria didn't see the significance of sharing Darius' story without expecting monetary gain.

Once she made it home, she continued to think about her remarks. Kim was saddened by the reality of countless family members who loved relatives beyond words as long as they had something to offer. Once they left the world, after the initial sadness and shock, they were merely a passing thought every now and then, unless there was still something to gain.

Kim sighed. She was torn but wondered if it were better to remove Darius from the article altogether. Her heart said to leave everything as-is, but she wasn't sure of the law regarding the situation and didn't want to chance Victoria suing or causing confusion.

While at work the next day, Kim had intentions of calling an attorney Lynn had suggested, but her workload didn't allow her to follow through. Friday during lunch she made time. Kim contacted the attorney and told him the scenario. He informed her based on the information she'd provided, Victoria didn't have a case. Kim was relieved. She thought about calling Lynn to tell her about the conversation but opted to wait until her cookout the next day.

Kim and Leon were the first couple to arrive.

Lynn welcomed them with a smile. "Hey, Leon. It's been too long. It's great seeing you again," she said, embracing him.

"The pleasure is all mine," he replied.

"Come on in. Make yourselves at home. Chris is out back tending to the grill," Lynn said.

Kim set her pasta salad on the island, then followed Leon outside to speak to Chris. She returned minutes later, leaving him behind.

"Do you need help with anything?" she asked Lynn.

"No, I'm almost done. Have a seat," she said, wiping off the stove. "What do you want to drink?"

"Nothing. I'll get something later," Kim said.

"Okay. So, what's up with Leon? How are things going for you two?" Lynn questioned.

"Really good," Kim replied, blushing.

"Wait a minute. What's this I see written all over your face?" Lynn asked, smiling.

"Am I glowing? Leon and I are officially dating again," Kim said.

"Ahhhh. She's moving on with her life. Thank you, Jesus," Lynn said.

"It's only been a week, but so far I'm happy with my decision. I really like Leon," Kim admitted. "He's wise, caring, and I'm very comfortable around him. Let me tell you, he asked if I saw marriage in our future and I freaked out. I wasn't ready for that question. Every time I get engaged the relationship explodes."

Lynn laughed. "Don't let that stop you. For someone who never wanted to be married, you have made quite a few attempts lately. This is it, though," Lynn said. "I can feel it. Leon is the right man at the right time."

Kim nodded. "What do you think about our age difference? Leon is eleven years older than me," she said.

"Normally, I'd say ten years max, but in this case I don't think one more year will hurt anything. You two seem to get along very well."

"We do. I admire Leon's contentment and his mind-set. He's settled, but still willing to learn," Kim said.

"That's a good thing. Some men carry the mentality from their teen years into their fifties. I guess it's the same for women. Have you spoken to your mom about Leon?" Lynn questioned.

"Not yet. I already know what the conversation will be like with me telling her I'm in a new relationship. Do you realize I've been engaged twice and now dating someone different, all within a three-year span." Kim sighed.

"It sounds bad, but I'm here with you and I know the details of those courtships. So, how's your family doing? When are they coming back to the states?" Lynn asked.

"No time soon," Kim replied. "They want me to come visit them in Germany."

"Are you? Sounds like a nice trip," Lynn said.

"Maybe once I get my finances in order. My parents don't know about my struggles or me selling the house. I'll tell them after everything's back on track," Kim said.

"Well, when we marry you off it'll be Wanda's turn," Lynn said.

"I don't know about that. Then again, from the sound of her conversation about Malcolm the other night, it may be possible."

The doorbell sounded, interrupting their conversation and rang over and over again until Lynn answered. "I knew it was you, Wanda," Kim heard Lynn say.

"Yes, it's me. Open this damn door and let me in," Wanda replied.

She smirked. *That girl is crazy,* she thought.

"What's going on in here?" Wanda asked as she and Lynn entered the kitchen.

Kim made eye contact with her and smiled, shaking her head.

"Hey," Wanda said, waving.

"Hi," Kim replied. She stood and walked over to Wanda. "Girl, you are one crazy chick. I can't even be mad at you right now."

They embraced and apologized.

"Wow, that was unexpected. When I think you're going to kiss and make up, you don't, then when I least expect it, you do. Where's Malcolm, Wanda?" Lynn asked.

"He's at his mom's house. He'll be here soon," Wanda replied.

"Kim is engaged," Lynn slid in.

"No, I'm not," Kim blurted.

"Lynn, you ain't right. We just made up and you're causing trouble already?" Wanda looked at Kim. "Are you engaged, again," she questioned.

"Technically, I'm not. I told Lynn, Leon asked if I see marriage in our future."

"Do you?" Wanda asked.

"I can't say at this point," Kim replied, fidgeting with her earring.

"I have a tip for you. Don't get engaged," Wanda suggested. "Just marry the man. You've had a rough history with fiancés."

"I know that's right," Kim replied.

"Look at the bright side and think positive. The third time is the charm," Lynn said.

"That's exactly what Leon said," Kim confessed.

"You may as well marry him, hell. Darius is gone," Wanda said.

"That's what I told her," Lynn added.

"He's settled, he has a home, and his children are adults, so he's probably not going back down that road. You don't want kids anyway, do you, Kim?" Wanda asked.

Kim hesitated.

"Oh, Lord. You've changed your mind about having kids, too?" Wanda questioned.

"Maybe. The way I see it, marriage and family go together. Before I didn't want either, but now I feel one justifies the other. What do you think?" Kim asked Lynn.

"Have you and Leon discussed having a family?" Lynn asked.

"No. Actually, we're getting way ahead of ourselves by having this conversation. I didn't agree to be Leon's wife yet, therefore we haven't had a conversation about babies."

The sound of the doorbell tore Lynn from the discussion. When she returned, Malcolm, Michelle, Kelvin, Angel, Derrick, and Derrick Jr. followed. The room grew loud with chatter and activity as they greeted one another.

Kim took Derrick Jr. from Derrick's arms, then she watched him, Malcolm, and Kelvin join Leon and Chris outside. She left the kitchen and sat on sofa, hugging and kissing her godson. Although he wiggled, trying to climb down from her lap, Kim held onto him. She stole his attention by jiggling the bracelets on her arm.

After playing patty cake for a while, Derrick Jr. began to yawn and rub his eyes. Kim cuddled him close, gently rocking him. Meanwhile, she reflected on Wanda's question about having children.

Do I want kids? Does Leon? Kim wondered. "I guess we really do need to talk about this. If I choose to have a child and he doesn't want any more, that could be a problem."

Kim looked down at Derrick Jr. just as he closed his eyes. She kissed him on the forehead.

Minutes later, Angel walked toward them wearing a smile. "Thanks for putting him to sleep," she said.

"Girl, I'm in love with your baby. It's funny, before y'all got here, Lynn, Wanda, and I were talking about family. Now, I can't stop thinking about it. Oh, I haven't told you the news. Leon and I are dating again," Kim said.

"Congratulations, Kim. Good for you. I thought you were bringing him," Angel said.

"He's here. He's out back with the guys. Anyway, Leon told me he enjoyed being married and wanted to know if I saw that type of commitment in our future. I couldn't answer the question then, but now I'm thinking past marriage and wondering if he'd want more children being the two he has are adults."

"Yeah, that's definitely something you need to discuss. Now is the time," Angel said. "Even if you haven't decided on marriage, knowing his position can only help the situation."

Kim agreed.

"I heard you and Wanda made up," Angel said.

"We did," Kim replied.

"That's great. Let me lay big man down so you can hang out with us," Angel said.

Kim nodded. She watched Angel wrap Derrick Jr. in a blanket and put him in his car seat. Afterward, they went into the kitchen.

"Wanda, have you spoken to Mrs. Joyce?" Lynn asked.

"Nope," she replied.

"How's your dad?" Lynn questioned.

"He's doing well," Wanda said.

"Good. Are you ready for something to drink now?" Lynn asked Kim.

"Yes, please. I'll take some juice. Any kind," she said.

Lynn took a glass from the cupboard, cranberry juice from the refrigerator and set them in front of Kim.

"What's up with the hospitality?" she complained.

"There is none. Does everybody know Kim's exciting news? Leon is back in the family," Lynn said.

"Ah, yeah. You've made the announcement how many times today?" Kim replied.

"I didn't know you two were dating again. Kim, have you gotten your groove back?" Michelle asked.

"No. Not yet, but that reminds me of something," Kim said. "When Leon and I were talking about getting back together, I told him I wanted to take things slow. His response was, 'I'll go as slow as you need me to.'

"Now y'all know how I think. I'm still a freak. It's by the grace of God that I've gone nine months without sex. Lawd, have mercy."

The girls burst into laughter.

"Watch out, Leon. Don't hurt him, Kim," Wanda said.

"I won't, but I have something else to share," she said.

"Dang. Are you trying to make up for being so quiet at the housewarming party?" Michelle asked.

"Whatever," Kim replied. "This is more serious. Long story short, I went to River's Street the day my house was being shown and met a guy who works for a magazine company. He introduced himself and we chatted, and he ended up being a minister at the church Darius attended.

"He told me he'd spoken to Darius about doing a story of his life. I remember Darius mentioning it. Anyway after we talked for awhile he offered to do a write-up about me, so he could tell Darius' story through mine. I agreed and I've already done the interview.

"Now, I have two problems. Tell me what y'all think. My first concern is the article itself because the story goes in-depth about my feelings for Darius and how much I love him, yada, yada. Even though what I've said is fact, now that I'm back with Leon I feel a little uncomfortable providing so much detail. The members at his church aren't fond of me as it is. Y'all remember how bad they treated me after I was locked up for purchasing stolen property from Penny. I'd hate for them to lose respect for Leon as a deacon because he and I are dating again. Should I leave the story as-is or change it?

"Next, I ran into Victoria, Darius' mom, at Walmart a couple of nights ago. I let her know about the magazine article and told her to be sure to get a copy. Well, she asked if I had permission to tell Darius' story, made it clear she's entitled to any money due to him, and even threatened to get an attorney if I've done something illegal. Do y'all know I had to walk away to keep from disrespecting that woman? Initially, I felt she was just being money hungry. Now, I've had a couple of days to think on it, and maybe she's trying to make sure I'm not taking advantage of the situation or capitalizing on Darius' death. What do you think?" Kim asked her friends.

"I'll go first. I have two questions," Wanda said. "Does Leon know about the article, and what was your purpose for doing it?"

"Yes, I told Leon. The reason I agreed to do the interview was to share Darius' testimony. That's it. He had plans to do it himself. He felt telling his story would benefit young men living his old lifestyle. Since he's not here, I told my version of his testimony. Darius wasn't getting paid, and neither am I," Kim said.

"If it were me and I'd confided in Leon about the situation and he understood and respects the truth, then I'd say to hell with the church members or whoever makes a negative judgment about the story or you as a person for that matter," Wanda said. "Some of those same folks have purchased stolen clothes themselves. I guarantee it. The bottom line is the article expresses your feelings, Kim, regardless of who likes or dislikes it. As for Darius' mom, tell her to get a damn job."

"Wanda, I couldn't have said it better myself," Lynn said.

Michelle and Angel agreed.

"Okay. Well I'll let it print. I appreciate your input," Kim said.

"Do you think about Darius a lot?" Michelle asked her.

"Um, yeah, especially when he first passed away," Kim said. "I still miss him, but not having him around anymore has become much easier to deal with. God is so good. He helps us through the mourning process, then as time passes our hearts heal."

"Yes, that's the cycle of life. It's not always easy, but we manage to get through," Michelle said.

Lynn, I'm ready for another daiquiri," Wanda said.

"So am I. Hook me up," Lynn said. "I'll go check on the guys. The meat should be done by now."

Soon after, everyone gathered around the dining room table. Leon blessed the food and they began to eat.

"It's really nice seeing you again," Michelle said to Leon, initiating the conversation.

"Thank you. I'm happy to be here," he replied. "Good food, great people. I can't think of a better place to be."

"I can. The Galaxy Lanes Bowling Alley," Chris said, smiling. "Derrick and I want revenge."

"We sure do," Derrick agreed.

"Anytime," Leon replied.

"If y'all help me move as promised, then on the following Saturday I'll treat everybody to a game of bowling. How does that sound?" Kim asked.

"Great. Look at that, Leon. Your woman is paying for us to beat you," Chris said.

"Bring it on," he replied.

"This is a highly anticipated rematch. I don't mean to tattle, but Chris and Derrick have been practicing, Leon. You stole their manhood when you beat 'em down the way you did," Lynn said.

Leon smiled.

"Yes, we've practiced. It's no secret. That's how Leon became so good," Derrick said.

"Hold up. Do you understand the repercussions of a snitch?" Chris asked Lynn.

She rolled her eyes at him.

"Check that out, Kelvin. They're polishing up their skills without us, man," Malcolm pointed out.

"What's up with that, fellas?" Kelvin asked.

"You two are hopeless. That's what's up," Wanda blurted.

"No, it's not like that. Don't listen to Wanda," Derrick said, shaking his head.

"Bring your A game, Leon. I want you to beat 'em again," Lynn said.

"We shall see," Chris replied.

"Angel told us you're going on leave next week," Lynn said to Derrick.

"Yep. My military days are almost over," he replied.

"Must be nice," Wanda said.

"Oh, yeah. More time to bowl," Derrick joked.

"I don't think so. You're getting a job," Angel said, shocking everyone at the table.

"Ooohh," they all sang.

Derrick laughed. "I'm glad you feel that way, baby. Now is the perfect time to tell you that I've reenlisted."

"Ha ha ha," Angel said sarcastically.

"Kim, I heard you hit the jackpot. Twenty-five thousand dollars is a lot of cash," Derrick said.

Everyone looked at Kim. "It is a lot," she replied.

"Did you keep it, turn it in the cops, what?" Derrick asked.

"I still have the money," Kim said.

"Wait a minute. What are we talking about here? Kim, you're not breaking the law, are you?" Chris asked.

"Of course not. Me and the girls were going through Darius' things and ran across a briefcase with money inside," she said.

"What? Ultimately it's your decision. I advise you to turn it in," Chris said.

"Why haven't you given it to authorities?" Leon asked Kim.

"Honestly, I was hanging on to the funds until everything works out for me financially. I may need to use some of it," she said.

"You need to take every dime of that money to the police station. It's drug money. Don't block your blessings, Kim. I'll help you," Leon said.

"Okay, I will." Kim was angry Angel had told Derrick her business and pissed he blurted it out in front of everyone. "I don't care what any of them think. I'm running this," she said.

Chapter 13

When Friday night came, instead of going to the club as usual Wanda borrowed her father's car and had staked out down the street from Ron's bingo hall. She looked through binoculars, snacking on vinegar-and-salt potato chips, waiting for him to leave. Wanda was anxious to learn details of Ron's private life, clues of Sheila's whereabouts, or proof he was involved in her disappearance.

She wanted a companion, but her partner in crime, Casey, was with Pete, and she knew her friends wouldn't participate in the scheme, so she didn't bother to ask. Instead, Wanda sat lonesome, watching as pedestrians passed. Her hopes of going unnoticed appeared to be working, which she credited to the dark but legal shade of window tint. However, she had a knife, brass knuckles, and Mace lying on the passenger seat just in case an incident occurred.

Finally, around 2:00 A.M. Wanda saw Ron's Lexus exit the parking lot and drive in the opposite direction. She quickly started her vehicle and followed him, leaving a moderate distance between them. Before long, she realized where he was headed. Wanda shook her head as Ron entered her housing community. She went straight, then turned around and waited for him to return.

Thirty minutes later, Ron still hadn't shown up. Wanda became restless. "What in the hell is he doing?" she complained.

Suddenly it occurred to her, he might be parked at her house believing she'd come home from the club soon. Wanda was tempted to cruise through the subdivision to confirm her suspicion, but didn't want to chance Ron seeing her father's car. There wasn't much activity going on at that hour so she was sure he'd notice.

As she pondered her next move, the phone rang. Wanda rolled her eyes when she saw Ron's name across the ID screen. She ignored his calls, but continued waiting for him to leave the neighborhood. After another thirty minutes she gave up. Since Chris worked the night shift, Wanda had made prior arrangements to stay overnight at his and Lynn's house. She arrived at approximately around 3:30 A.M. and used the spare key Lynn had given her.

Wanda showered then crawled in bed, focusing on her and Ron's courtship. She remembered the excitement when they began dating. Now he was stalking her and she was spying on him. Wanda was especially exhausted with Ron's carelessness of being seen at her home. She wondered what would happen if he and Malcolm crossed paths. Not being accustomed to the confusion Ron had added to her life or having patience to deal with it forced Wanda to consider a monogamous relationship with Malcolm.

Eventually, her thoughts subsided and she drifted off to sleep. The next morning, she washed her face and brushed her teeth before going downstairs. Wanda found a note on the kitchen counter informing her Lynn had gone shopping at garage sales.

She returned to the bedroom where she'd slept and texted Casey asking her to call when she got a chance before dialing Lynn's number. "Why didn't you tell me you were going to garage sales?" Wanda asked when she answered.

"Because I knew you wouldn't come with me. Did you sleep well?" Lynn asked.

"Yeah, I did. Thanks. Is Chris here?" Wanda questioned.

"Oh, no. You my girl and all, but you date married men. I can't leave you at home alone with my husband," Lynn replied.

"Lynn, I cannot believe you just said that. That is so messed up," Wanda said. "I hope you're kidding."

"Yeah, I'm teasing, but no, Chris isn't there. He's with me," Lynn replied.

"Damn. Why would you make a statement about me dating married men in front of him, Lynn?" Wanda complained.

"Calm down, chick," she replied. "Chris didn't hear me."

"Oh. Okay, cool. I really don't need Malcolm to find out about Ron right now. I'm stressed out as it is. You know I don't respond well when I'm aggravated. Anyway, I'm going home, but I'd like to stay at your place again."

"Sure. What happened last night?" Lynn questioned.

"Well, as far as me getting information, nothing. I did see and follow Ron, but that fool went into my subdivision and never came out.

Lynn laughed.

"I'm serious. I believe he sat at the house waiting for me to come home from the club. I hung around for more than an hour, then left. I'll try again," Wanda said.

"That's fine. As long as you don't bring Ron's drama to my house, you're welcome at any time," Lynn said.

"I won't. I promise. I'll talk to you later," Wanda said.

When she hung up she had a text message from Casey agreeing to contact her. An hour later, Wanda received the call. She filled Casey in on details of the night and shared plans to spy on Ron until she gained information. "I wish you could hang out with me," Wanda said.

"Sounds like fun, but it's almost impossible for me to get away from Pete during those hours. Please be careful out there, Wanda," Casey said.

"I will. Thanks, girl," she replied. "I'll keep you posted."

As planned, Wanda followed Ron again and he led her on the same route as before. "Why is he going by my house every night?" she grumbled, watching him enter the subdivision.

This time Ron surprised her. Within five minutes he reappeared. Wanda trailed him and ended up traveling west on Highway 204. She assumed Ron would exit at Highway 17 then go through the Berwick Plantation community to get to his Southbridge home. When he passed the road, she questioned his reasoning for taking the longer drive, via the interstate.

Wanda continued behind him, veering onto the I-95 northbound ramp, then she lagged behind on the high-speed journey. When Ron zoomed past I-16, she realized he wasn't headed home. Wanda's heart thumped. She became excited and hopeful he was about to reveal secrets of his mysterious life and provide answers to her questions. However, as they approached Exit 109, the last Georgia turn-off before entering South Carolina, she noticed Ron didn't slow down. Wanda hadn't anticipated him leaving the state. At the last minute she applied her brakes and whipped off the highway. "Damn," she shouted in frustration. "Where in the hell is he going?"

Moments later, she yielded back on Interstate 95 driving southbound. Wanda was clueless and more baffled than before. She coached herself to be encouraged. She knew the key to her success would be dedication and being prepared to reveal facts as they surfaced. It was evident something suspicious was happening with Ron, so there had to be proof. Wanda was confident he'd slip up at some point.

Although she'd arranged to stay at Lynn's house again, she went home. With Ron out of the area she felt more secure. Wanda armed her security alarm, then showered and slipped on her pajamas, then she lay restless, questioning Ron's whereabouts. She brainstormed trying to remember if he'd mentioned friends or family members living in South Carolina. Her mind was blank. She couldn't come up with anyone, but she knew Ron was well known wherever he'd gone at such a late hour.

The next morning, Wanda prepared a serving of hash browns, eggs, and two sausage patties then filled a glass with orange juice. She sat at the table nibbling on her food, trying to come up with different ways to intrude in Ron's life without his knowledge. She thought about sneaking into his home or office, hacking his computer, or tapping the phones, but preferred not to commit illegal acts. Wanda was terrified by the thought of going to jail.

She appreciated Casey for trying to get information from Pete, but wondered if she'd be more hands-on. "There's only one way to find out," Wanda said.

She called and gave Casey an update and asked if she knew of anyone close to Ron living in South Carolina.

"Um, no, I don't think so," Casey replied after moments of thought. "I'll keep my ears open and let you know if I find out anything."

"Sounds good. I have a question," Wanda continued. "Will you snoop around for me, if I need you to?"

"As long as getting what you need isn't too risky," Casey said. "Betraying Ron is like betraying Pete. I need to be really careful."

"I agree. I don't mean to put you in a bad situation, but you're the only person who's somewhat close to Ron that I can depend on," Wanda replied.

"I'll do what I can. Just let me know," Casey said.

"Thanks. I want to nail that bastard so bad. I can tell by how he's been harassing me, he's capable of anything," Wanda said before ending the call.

Once she'd hung up the phone she emptied the rest of her food in the garbage and cleaned the kitchen, then she turned on the television and lay watching Court TV, napping on and off. Around two o'clock Malcolm stopped by. Wanda invited him in and he snuggled behind her on the sofa. She closed her eyes when he slid his hand underneath her T-shirt, gently caressing her breast. She could feel Malcolm's erection pressing against her backside as he spread kisses along her shoulders and neck. Wanda moaned. She reached back, fondling his manhood as he slid off her shorts. When Malcolm removed his pants and entered her from behind, nothing else mattered.

Afterward, they showered and got snacks from the kitchen before cuddling on the couch again.

Later, when Malcolm went home, Wanda checked her cell for missed calls. Ron's name filled up the screen. Although Wanda had questions, she stayed firm on the decision not to deal with him anymore. She erased his voicemails and left the phone setting on silent, dropping it back in her purse.

The next morning was the beginning of a new work week. Wanda stepped inside the Chatham County Courthouse, shocked to learn of a woman's body discovered near the Georgia and South Carolina border. "Oh, my God. Is it Sheila? This can't be a coincidence," she said.

Wanda became weak in the knees, and the breakfast she'd eaten churned inside of her stomach, making her sick with anticipation. A coworker distracted her when she called out her name.

"Hi, Sherry," Wanda said.

"Did you hear about the news? They found a body last night," she said.

"I did," Wanda replied.

"Isn't that sad? I wonder who she is," Sherry said.

Wanda shook her head but didn't respond as they stood behind the crowd waiting for the elevator. Finally, the doors opened and the group poured inside. Once on the third floor, Wanda lost her train of thought. She nudged Sherry. "Who is that?" she asked, discreetly pointing at a brown complexioned gentleman wearing a long-sleeved white shirt with a sky blue satin tie and a pair of slacks. He looked like an athlete—tall, broad shoulders, large arms.

"Oh, he's a new criminal court judge," Sherry said.

"He's a judge?" Wanda questioned, taking note of his short, neat haircut and neatly trimmed mustache.

"Yep. I can't believe you're just seeing him. He's been around for a couple of weeks at least," Sherry said as they entered the office.

"How did a fine brother like him get past me? Dude is straight sexy," Wanda said.

Sherry smiled. "If I'm not mistaken, he's single. I heard some of the other ladies commenting," she said.

"I need a reason to go to criminal court so I can introduce myself. I hope he's not gay," Wanda said, continuing to her work station. As soon as she sat down, she overheard her supervisor on the telephone talking about the body they'd found.

Wanda refocused and the sickness soured her stomach once more. "If this turns out to be Sheila, it's over for Ron. He will be out of my life for good," she vowed.

Her cell phone vibrated, alerting her of an incoming text. She unlocked the keypad and read the message. It was Angel asking had she heard the news.

She replied yes and told Angel she'd call her during lunch.

Throughout the morning Wanda couldn't focus on her job. She kept glancing at the clock, but time seemed to stand still.

When 12:30 rolled around, she hurried outside the building and spent her entire lunch break talking on the telephone to friends, ending with Malcolm. He invited her out to dinner later that evening. Wanda agreed to go, but picked over the meal with her fork, taking small bites.

"Does your food taste okay? You haven't eaten much at all," Malcolm said.

"Yes, it's fine," Wanda replied. "I don't have much of an appetite tonight for some reason. I can take my leftovers home."

"Okay. I'll be on vacation during the week of August 18. Do you think you can take yours the same week? I'd like for us to travel somewhere together this year," Malcolm said.

"I need a vacation," Wanda replied. "Sure, I can check the calendar and see if someone has requested those days off. If not I will."

"Is there a specific place you'd like to visit? The trip is on me," Malcolm said.

"Let me think about it for a few days," Wanda replied. She was too preoccupied to focus.

Finally, on Friday afternoon the identity of the female body found earlier that week was announced. It wasn't Sheila. Wanda couldn't believe the news. She was discouraged and disappointed to be back at square one again. All day she'd been hopeful the fiasco with Ron would be over.

Later that night Wanda skipped the club scene again, trying to track Ron. She was amazed he drove to her community before taking her on the same chase across the South Carolina state line. This time she followed and ended up on Hilton Head Island. Wanda watched Ron park next to an SUV in front of a mid-sized home.

A house further up the street was completely dark so she pulled in the driveway and turned off her headlights, hoping the homeowners wouldn't notice her trespassing on their property. She quickly rolled down the window just enough to see out with her binoculars. Ron was alone. Wanda watched him step out of the car and walk toward the house. As he approached the door someone opened it, letting him in. "Who is that?" she questioned.

Wanda backed out and drove slowly, jotting down the address on the mailbox as she passed by, then she headed for Savannah. Once at home, she sat up until almost six o'clock searching for information about the property where Ron had gone. She learned it was owned by an LLC. She looked up the bingo hall and it was owned by the same company. Wanda's mind raced. She wondered if Ron had been leading a double life.

"I need to know who resides in that house," she concluded.

She wished she could talk with Sheila's family to find out if they knew about the property in South Carolina, but being Ron's previous other woman put her in an awkward position. Wanda felt

Sheila's family could get the wrong impression and assume she was somehow involved with Ron's scheme.

Moments later, she shut off the computer and went to bed so she could rest and drive back to Hilton Head the next day. When she woke up, she called Casey and asked her to ride along. Casey agreed. Wanda grabbed a wig from her closet and a pair of shades then she scurried out of the door. Seeing Jehovah's Witnesses in the neighborhood gave her another idea. Wanda asked one of the ladies for a couple of the magazines they were handing out.

She scooped up Casey, and they drove toward South Carolina. Once at the house, Wanda persuaded Casey to disguise herself with the wig and shades. "Here," she said, handing her the literature she'd gotten from the woman in her neighborhood. "Give this to whoever answers the door and act like you're a Jehovah's Witness."

Wanda waited in the car. She watched Casey knock several times after she rang the doorbell. No one answered, so she walked back in her direction. As she approached the car a teenager riding his bike stopped in the street. "Are you looking for Mr. Ron?" Wanda heard him ask Casey.

Casey glanced at her. "No, actually I'm trying to find a classmate named Tina," she said, making eye contact with the boy.

"That tall lady?" he asked.

"No, she's about my height. Maybe a little shorter," Casey said.

"Oh," the boy replied.

"When was the last time you saw the tall woman?" Casey asked.

"I see her every day. She lives here. There she is," the boy said, pointing at a black Cadillac Escalade coming up the road behind Wanda.

Casey looked in that direction. "I must have the wrong address," she said to the boy. "My friend drives a white car. Thanks for your help."

"You're welcome," he said before riding off.

Casey got in the car and Wanda went a little farther down the street and made a u-turn. She and Casey watched from a distance as the Escalade pulled into the driveway. A woman got out and took grocery bags from the backseat. "Wait a minute. She looks like one of the ladies who works at Ron's bingo hall. Do you recognize her?" Wanda asked Casey.

"That's Ron's cousin Sonya," she said.

"She lives here? Why would Ron come to his cousin's house during the wee hours of the morning?" Wanda questioned.

"I don't know," Casey replied.

After Sonya went inside, Wanda cruised by the house and headed back to Georgia. "This gets weirder by the minute, and it's really pissing me off," she complained. "I thought maybe Ron was hiding another woman over here. Now, I'm really confused. Why in the hell would he drive all the way to Hilton Head to his cousin's place at two o'clock in the morning instead of going to his Savannah home? It doesn't make sense."

"Man, I'm glad Sonya wasn't there to answer the door. Oh, my God, that could've been a disaster," Casey said. "I'm sure she would've told Pete and I'd have a lot of explaining to do. The wig and glasses weren't enough to keep her from recognizing me, Wanda."

"You're right. Damn. Gathering information about Ron is harder than I imagined, especially since I'm not connected to him anymore. If we were still dating, things would be a lot different. I could easily steal his keys, his wallet, or cell phone."

"I wish I could be of more help," Casey said.

"Don't worry about it. I'm not trying to get you caught up, Casey, but I can't give up," Wanda said. "I have to find a way to get Ron. That bastard cannot win."

Chapter 14

Time had dwindled. Kim had less than a week before her scheduled closing date. Al had done a great job of keeping her informed, and although there were still a few items pending, it appeared her home was going to sell. Finally, Kim developed a sense of urgency about finding a place to live. She and Leon viewed more than ten homes before deciding on a condo. Kim filled out an application and paid the non-refundable deposit without Leon's assistance. She scheduled her move-in date for the following Monday, July 9 so she'd have an opportunity to clean with a personal touch before moving her furniture inside.

On July 12 she sat next to Al with a huge smile on her face. Kim was relieved when Attorney Mason handed her a check for the proceeds of the sale. She thanked him and congratulated the buyers, then she provided a duplicate set of keys for the new homeowners and signed an agreement to have everything out of the property by 9:00 P.M. Kim hugged Al before leaving the room. As soon as she exited the building she called Leon, telling him the closing was a success. Once inside of the car, she sent her friends a text sharing the news with them as well.

Twenty minutes later, Kim parked along the street in front of the house. Not long after she'd arrived, she heard Leon backing up the truck in the driveway. As she looked out of the window Chris drove up. "Yes," Kim cheered.

She greeted the guys at the front door and they expressed excitement for her.

"Thank you," she sang with a big grin. She accepted Leon's embrace, and he kissed her on the lips.

Moments later, Kim watched him lead Chris upstairs. They loaded furniture from the spare bedrooms and items she'd set aside to be put in storage as she cleaned the bathrooms. By the time they'd finished Angel had shown up. She'd taken Derrick Jr. to Lynn at the day care so she could assist without worrying about him getting hurt or being in the way.

While Leon and Chris went to the storage unit and Angel vacuumed the rooms they'd emptied, Kim put Darius' briefcase in a duffle bag and hid it in her truck. She told Leon she'd turned the money in. She didn't know why she felt the need to hang on to it.

An hour later, all of her friends were at the house. The guys reloaded the truck and the ladies cleaned.

At last, the house was empty. Kim experienced sentimental moments as she did the final walkthrough. When she closed the door, locking her keys inside, it dawned on her she'd just ended a chapter in life and was about to begin another. She walked slowly along the driveway toward her car. Before getting inside she glanced at the house again. It was a bittersweet moment as she drove away. Kim was sad to leave her dream home behind but was relieved it had sold. She was ready to live a better and less stressful life.

With the help of Leon and her friends, the setup at the condo went smoothly. The men handled the large furniture and the ladies took care of the rest.

On the following Saturday night they all met up at the Galaxy Lanes Bowling Alley. Wanda brought Casey along and introduced her to the gang. As she'd suggested, Casey was fun to be around. Although she wasn't a great bowler, she blended in well.

Michelle didn't participate in the game because of her large stomach. She had less than a week before her anticipated delivery date.

Although Chris and Derrick had improved their bowling skills, Leon won all three games by at least twenty points. He didn't brag but smirked as they complained about losing again, promising revenge the next time.

"Let me know when," Leon said.

On the way out, the guys refused to allow Kim to pay the tab. They split the bill then headed for the Golden Corral restaurant.

The next morning before heading to church Kim did an online application to refinance her SUV. On Monday afternoon she was contacted by a loan specialist notifying her of two problems. Kim's debt-to-income ratio was too high and she owed two thousand dollars more than the truck was worth. She provided the HUD settlement statement showing her home had sold to rectify the debt problem, then she took two thousand dollars from the money in Darius' briefcase to pay off the negative balance. After being approved, she was grateful for a $250 monthly savings. Kim's budget had gone from being overextended to completely manageable, including the luxuries of cable and home phone service. She thanked God for blessing her with a new beginning and a peace of mind.

On Thursday morning, while she was getting dressed for work, her phone rang. It was Lynn saying Kelvin had taken Michelle to the hospital around midnight because she was in labor. Kim didn't have enough time to visit that morning but during her lunch break she joined Angel in the waiting room. Then at 12:47 P.M. on July 19, Kelvin announced Michelle had given birth to a seven-pound, four-ounce baby boy.

They cheered, then hurried toward the room.

After work, Kim went back to check on Michelle and the baby. While holding him, she relived the same closeness she had when Derrick Jr. was born. It was at that moment Kim decided she wanted to be a mother. She yearned to feel the emotional bond with a child of her own like she'd experienced with her friends' children. Kim knew it was time to have a conversation with Leon about starting a family.

When she left the hospital, she drove to his house. Leon had just gotten out of the shower and answered the door in a bathrobe.

"I guess I should've called first, huh?" Kim said.

"No, come on in," Leon replied, closing the door. He kissed her on the lips.

"Okay. Well, I'll wait in the den while you get dressed. I don't want you to start nothing," Kim said.

"I would never put you in an uncomfortable position," Leon replied.

Kim smiled, then she watched him walk toward his bedroom. She wasn't sure if he'd meant his words to sound sexual, but they did. *This is the second time he's done that,* she thought.

She continued into the den and sat on the sofa, waiting for Leon to return. Minutes later, he appeared wearing a pair of shorts and a T-shirt. "How was your day?" he asked, sitting next to her.

"Great," Kim said, resting her hand on his thigh. "I need to ask you a question."

"Go for it," Leon replied, giving her his undivided attention.

"Would you consider having more children if we were married?" Kim questioned.

"Of course," Leon said.

"Are you sure?" Kim quizzed. "I mean, your kids are all grown."

"I'm positive. I told you, I love living a family life. When are we getting married?" Leon asked.

"You tell me," Kim replied.

"Soon, I hope," Leon said.

"Let's have our bloodwork done, get a marriage license and we'll go from there," Kim said.

Leon looked at her. "Are you serious?" he asked, blushing.

Kim nodded. "Who's going to perform the ceremony?" she questioned.

"My pastor can," Leon said.

"Okay, but I don't want a big wedding. Just you, me, a witness, and the pastor," Kim said.

"What about your friends?" Leon asked.

"No. I'm not going to tell them until after we're married," she replied.

"However you want to do it is fine with me," Leon said. He leaned over and kissed Kim.

As she enjoyed the touch of his lips, she avoided the fears of something terrible happening to destroy their relationship. For a brief moment she wanted to get the ceremony done and over with. Then suddenly, Kim refused to panic. She believed God would order her steps.

The next day, she took a long lunch break. She visited Michelle and the baby before rushing off to *Keepin' It Real* magazine company. Once inside, she approached the woman sitting behind the front desk. "Good afternoon," she said. "I'm here to see Keith Anderson."

"What's your name, ma'am?" she replied.

"Kim McKenzie."

"One moment please." The receptionist picked up the phone and buzzed Keith's phone line. "There's a Ms. McKenzie here to see you," she said.

Moments later, she gave Kim permission to go to his office.

"Excuse me," a female voice whispered as Kim started down the hallway.

She glanced in the direction the sound came from and saw a familiar face. "I know you," Kim said, walking toward her.

"Yes. I'm Derrick's cousin, Destini. I met you at his and Angel's engagement party," she said.

"Oh, yeah. I remember," Kim said. "How are you and your husband? And Brandi?"

"We're all doing well. Bran should be here any minute. We're going out for lunch," Destini said.

"Have you spoken to Derrick recently?" Kim asked.

"I have. We talked a couple of weeks ago," Destini said.

"Oh good. I'm happy to hear y'all are keeping in touch. Derrick is a busy guy," Kim said.

"Yes, he is. By the way, I like the article. You have a very interesting story," Destini said.

"Thank you," Kim replied. "I'm anxious to read it. I came by to pick up some copies Keith set aside for me."

Brandi interrupted the conversation when she entered the office. "Hello," she said.

"Hey, girl. Do you know who this is?" Destini asked Brandi as Kim turned to face her.

"I do. How are you doing, Kim?" Brandi asked.

"I'm fine. And you?"

"Great. I read your story. It's really good. I have an outreach center. If you'd like to speak to our youth, we'd love to have you," Brandi said.

"That's a good idea," Kim replied.

"I think so. From the article, I believe it would be interesting to share your perspective of Darius' life—you know, maybe tie in your perception of a drug dealer's mentality and how it affected you as his girlfriend. Perhaps give the angle of how the streets and money can alter the thought process and distort priorities, cause disrespect and destroy lives by infesting our communities with drugs. Maybe talk about life after Darius grew beyond the street mentality and allowed God to show him a better way, then show how someone who hadn't experienced that change ended his life. Think on it," Brandi said.

"I got you covered. Do you use volunteers at your center?" Kim asked.

"I do. Are you interested?" Brandi asked.

"Yes, actually I am. I'd love to get involved in some type of community organization. I'm happy I ran into you ladies," Kim said.

She and Brandi exchanged business cards. "Call me and let me know when you need me," Kim said.

"I'm gonna take you up on that. We'll talk soon," Brandi promised.

"Okay."

"Tell Angel we said hi," Destini told Kim as she prepared to leave. "Keith's office is two doors down on the right."

"I will. Thanks," she replied, waving.

Keith told Kim about the great response he'd already received about her story.

"That's awesome. I really appreciate this," Kim said, accepting the stack of magazines. Excitement was written all over his face. She shook Keith's hand before leaving.

During the drive, she called Leon, then Kim dialed Angel's number to tell her about running into Brandi and Destini.

"Derrick told me he'd spoken to Destini. I need to invite her and Brandi over," she said.

"Yes. I really enjoyed talking with them." Kim entered Michelle's room after lightly tapping on the door. "I'm back," she said. I brought you lunch, a Chick-fil-A combo with lemonade."

"Thank you," Michelle said.

"Tell her hello and I'm on my way to see her. I'll let you go now," Angel told Kim.

Kim relayed the message. "I need to get back to work. Read my article on page eighteen. I'll see you later," she said, handing Michelle a magazine before hurrying off.

When she returned after her shift, she and the girls stayed until nine o'clock that night. They enjoyed the baby and everyone read the article and gave feedback. Although the story was about her and Darius, it transcended love, highlighting mind-set, struggle, survival, and deliverance. She loved it.

The next morning, Leon treated Kim to a spa day. He wanted her to relax and unwind. She'd almost forgotten how good it felt to have a deep-tissue massage. She moaned softly as her masseuse worked the kinks out of her tense muscles.

Next she received a manicure and pedicure, selecting a dark red polish for her nails. Kim left the salon feeling fabulous. She hurried to a two o'clock hair appointment for the final touch.

Finally at around six-fifteen that evening she walked through her front door with less than two hours to get ready for her and Leon's dinner date.

She was standing in front of the mirror applying makeup when the doorbell rang. Kim greeted Leon with a kiss. "Have a seat, sweetie. I'll be ready in a sec," she said before disappearing into her bedroom.

Minutes later, she returned. "Okay, now I'm ready," she said.

"You look beautiful," Leon complimented, walking toward her.

"Thank you," Kim said, smiling. She couldn't believe her eyes as he got down on one knee.

"Oh, my God. Leon," Kim whined, "I thought we weren't doing the engagement thing."

"Fear is the opposite of faith. I will not live in fear," Leon insisted before revealing a one-carat round diamond ring. Will you marry me?"

Kim's smile lit up the room. "Yes, I'll marry you," she said.

Leon stood, and they embraced before sharing several short kisses, then Kim allowed him to slide the ring onto her finger. "It's gorgeous. Thank you," she said, extending her hand, blushing.

"My pleasure," Leon replied.

Kim wrapped her arms around his neck once more. “I love you,” she whispered.

“I love you, too,” Leon said. “Let’s go celebrate.”

They decided on Red Lobster. While waiting to be seated, Leon’s church friends Brother Mack and his wife, Sister Mack, walked out.

“Hi,” Leon said to them. “You remember Kim, don’t you?” he asked.

“Of course. It’s great to see you. How’ve you been?” Brother Mack asked.

“I’m doing well. Thanks for asking,” she replied, smiling.

Kim could tell by the way Sister Mack had turned up her nose that she’d already read the article about her and Darius.

“You’ve had a very interesting life, Kim,” she said, confirming the assumption. “I read your story in that magazine.”

“I have indeed,” Kim replied. “I tend to think I’m living the best phase of it now. Life is a process. We learn and grow as we go.”

“I agree,” Leon said, kissing the back of her hand.

Sister Mack nodded but didn’t respond. “Nice ring,” she complimented moments later. “Will we see you at church tomorrow morning?”

“Thanks. No, I’m afraid not. I’ll come to visit soon though,” Kim promised. “Leon would like for me to come back as well.”

“Yes, we’d love to have you,” Brother Mack added.

“I appreciate that,” Kim said.

“Are you attending church at all?” Sister Mack questioned.

“When I can,” Kim stated, looking her directly in the eye. “Although I feel it’s important to fellowship on Sunday, I feel it’s equally important to be loving and non-judgmental to those learning the spiritual walk. You wouldn’t want to run anybody off—the job of the church is to bring the lost out of darkness to the light—right?”

“Yes, that’s true,” Sister Mack replied. “There are lots of people playing church nowadays. I don’t have time for those kinds of folk.”

“Are you perfect?” Kim asked.

“No,” she replied.

“Honey,” Brother Mack said, “can we ever have an evening out without there being an issue?”

"You're in my prayers, Deacon Hardy," Sister Mack said, then she started to walk off.

Her husband apologized, then followed.

"She'd better be lucky you and Brother Mack were standing there. I really would've put her in her place," Kim said. "That's why I dread going back to your church. I already know I'm going to curse somebody out. I'm not backing down, Leon. All I can say is they'd better get ready."

Chapter 15

On Sunday afternoon, Wanda anxiously anticipated her next stakeout. She was desperate for leads but continued to find herself at a dead end. Both Friday and Saturday she'd witnessed Ron leave the bingo hall and drive through her neighborhood before she trailed him home. She had parked along the street several houses down in front of a vacant property. Wanda waited for more than an hour each night, concluding he was in to stay.

Since following Ron, the only thing appearing out of the ordinary was the property in Hilton Head and his rationale for going there versus being in Savannah. What, if anything, he was involved in seemed organized and well thought out. After weeks of snooping around, Wanda still had a lot of questions but no answers. Suddenly, it dawned on her that perhaps Ron was being careful because of the likelihood of Sheila's family hiring someone to investigate him. "That has to be it. You will slip up, Ron, and I'll be waiting," Wanda said. She was certain he was hiding something.

Later that evening her home telephone rang. She wasn't in the mood for talking but glanced at the ID screen anyway. It was her sister, Tina, so she answered figuring she had gossip to share about their mother.

"Hey, Tina. What's up? What's wrong?" Wanda asked, hearing her cry out on the other end.

When Tina babbled that their grandmother was in the intensive care unit at the Candler Hospital, Wanda fell to her knees. "What happened?" she asked, panicking.

"Granny had a stroke," Tina said.

"I'm on my way," Wanda replied. She pressed the end button and tossed the phone on the sofa, then she bent over with her eyes squeezed shut, fighting back tears, feeling she'd been cursed because of the bad things happening.

Finally, she pulled herself to her feet. After stepping in a pair of sandals, Wanda grabbed her purse and hurried out of the door. During the drive she wondered if Ron had cast a witchcraft or voodoo spell on her. Too many things had gone wrong, affecting her and family members. She quickly dismissed the thought, refusing to believe any superstitions would work.

Shortly after, she arrived at the hospital and rushed inside the building. When Wanda approached the door to her grandmother's room she was shaking like a leaf. She took in a deep breath, then cautiously entered, unsure of what to expect. She first noticed Tina standing by the window wiping tears. Wanda offered her an empathetic stare before zooming in on their grandmother. She paused, observing the tubes and wires connecting her to machines and monitors. Wanda became overwhelmed by emotions. It took every ounce of her strength to keep moving. She embraced Tina then stood at her grandmother's bedside heartbroken and sad. Wanda had never seen her so frail or helpless. She watched her sleep, taking in what was happening before leaving a kiss on her left cheek. "Hi, Granny," she said.

Her grandmother opened her eyes and smiled, but quickly drifted off again.

Wanda pressed her lips against her forehead, then she stroked her hair, continuing to stare in disbelief. Minutes later, she pulled up a chair. As Wanda sat holding her grandmother's hand she studied the skin along her face, taking note of how she'd aged. Seeing her in such a vulnerable state forced Wanda to realize she was now an eighty-five-year-old woman. Although she'd lived a long, fulfilling life, the thought of her not being around was terrifying. Wanda didn't know if she could handle such a void. She closed her eyes and said a silent prayer, pleading to God like never before to renew her grandmother's health and her strength.

Tina rubbed Wanda's back. "Granny's going to be fine," she said in a comforting tone.

"She has to be," Wanda replied sadly. "This is the backbone of our family, Tina."

"Yes, and she's a fighter. Granny's not giving in easily. She's only resting. The medication is causing her to sleep," Tina said.

"You know what's so amazing? As long as she was up and moving around I never dwelled on her age. I only saw Granny's spirit, which has always been youthful, vibrant, and caring. Regardless of how often we've seen her, she greeted us with that big smile, a hug, and a kiss. Oh, and that sassy sense of humor, I love it," Wanda said smiling, thinking back.

Tina giggled. "Yeah, she's one of a kind. We have a lot of priceless memories because of Granny. She's such a great person."

"Indeed. Life wouldn't be the same without her. She has to recover," Wanda said.

The room fell silent. Meanwhile she thought back on how over the years despite her busy life and schedule she'd always make time to call or visit her grandmother. On Sunday evenings, they'd sit on the porch and eat apple pie with a scoop of vanilla ice cream on warm days and drink hot chocolate topping with whipped cream when it was cold. Wanda wished for those times again. After she'd begun dating Ron she was no longer consistent. She promised herself if blessed with another chance, not to miss Sunday dessert again and to spend as much time with her granny as possible.

"Where's Momma?" she whispered to Tina moments later.

Tina shrugged. "I have no clue," she said.

"Does she know Granny's here?" Wanda asked.

"No. I've left messages on her cell phone and at the house," Tina replied.

Wanda rolled her eyes. "She's probably somewhere with Michael."

Despite Wanda's disapproval, her mother continued to date Michael.

"That's what I'm thinking," Tina said. "Momma always answers her phone or she'll call right back, but I haven't heard from her in hours."

Wanda didn't respond. She rested her head against the bed until someone knocked on the door. She looked up as a tall, slender woman entered the room.

"Hello. I'm Stephanie, the nurse," she said.

They spoke, and Wanda moved her chair, giving Stephanie space to work. As she performed her duties, Wanda continued to think about her mother not being there. "Try Momma again," she told Tina.

Tina dialed the number once more. "Still not picking up," she said moments later.

Wanda shook her head. Then as the nurse prepared to leave, she approached her. "Is our granny going to be okay?" she questioned.

"Well, we've gotten her blood sugar under control and her vital signs are stable. The stroke affected her right side. Tomorrow morning she'll have more tests so the doctor can assess the extent of the damage. It's really important for her to rest right now."

"Thank you," Wanda said. After Stephanie left the room, Wanda walked toward Tina. "I'm staying here with Granny tonight. If you need to leave you can," she said as her cell phone rang. When she saw Ron's name across the screen she pressed ignore, sending his call to voicemail.

"Yeah, I'd better get going. I'll be back tomorrow after work," Tina said.

Wanda watched as Tina kissed their grandmother before grabbing her purse from the table.

"Keep me informed of any changes. When Momma calls, I'll be sure to let her know what's going on," Tina assured her.

"Okay," Wanda replied, hugging Tina before she left. Next, she dialed Malcolm's number. During their conversation, Ron beeped in twice. After hanging up, Wanda deleted his messages then sat watching her grandmother rest. Around 1:00 A.M., she attempted to get comfortable in the lounge chair and managed to get a few hours of sleep. She called off from work so she could stay at the hospital. While her granny was gone for testing, Wanda freshened up in the bathroom and went to the cafeteria for breakfast.

When she returned, her mother stood at her grandmother's bedside with tears streaming down her face.

"Good morning," Wanda said, making a trail to the chair she'd slept in. She sat down without making eye contact with her mother.

"Hi. How are you?" Joyce asked between sniffles.

"I'm fine. It's about time you made it," Wanda said.

"Don't start, Wanda," Joyce replied.

"Where were you?" Wanda asked, looking up at her.

"None of your business. I appreciate you being here with Momma, but I don't have to answer to you," Joyce said.

"You're right, you don't," Wanda replied nonchalantly.

"Why are you trying to pick a fight? I'm really hoping we can work on our relationship and be friends like we've always been. When I walked in this room and saw my mother lying here, it reminded me of how important family is."

"Does this mean you're breaking it off with Michael?" Wanda asked.

"No, it doesn't."

"I'll never accept him as your man, Momma—period. Hopefully, you won't wait until it's too late to reconnect with the ones who really care for you."

"If and when I stop seeing Michael, it'll be on my terms. You're not running anything."

Wanda smirked. "It's sad to say, Joyce, but you're not the woman I once admired so much."

"Joyce? Wanda Boyd, if you call me by my first name again, I'll knock your teeth out of your mouth—every one of them. Do you hear me? I don't care how you feel about how I live my life, you will respect me," Joyce said in a low but sharp tone.

Wanda yawned as she got up and walked away. She watched television in a waiting room down the hall until she spotted her mother leaving through a window.

Minutes later, Kim showed up for a brief visit during her lunch break. That evening, Tina returned as promised and their brother, Tony, stopped by. He entered and walked out in less than a minute. Wanda understood. Tony like most men she knew was a wimp when it came to the sick and elderly.

Soon after, the girls arrived with dinner for Wanda and flowers for her grandmother. Only two people were allowed to visit at once so they took turns until everyone had seen her. Afterward, they mingled in the waiting room.

Around nine o'clock Wanda walked them downstairs. On the way back up she sent Casey a text touching base with her. By the time she returned to the room, her grandmother was fast asleep. Wanda tucked her in, then she settled in the chair, watching television until she drifted off.

It was the next day when her mother returned. Wanda wasn't interested in being respectful because of her short stay the day before. "Can I talk to you for a minute?" she asked, clearly agitated.

"What is it, Wanda?" she replied.

"Let's go down the hall," Wanda suggested. She led her mother to the waiting room. "What's up with you? Can you tell me what's so important that you don't have time to visit with your ill mother? Granny needs you to be here for her."

"I am here. I don't have to hang around all day and night like you," her mother stated.

"No, you don't Momma, but why wouldn't you? This woman gave you life. If it was Michael lying in that bed instead of Granny, where would you be?"

Her mother stared at Wanda with resentment in her eyes, but she didn't respond to the question. Instead, she stormed out. After feeding her mother lunch, she kissed her on the cheek and told her she'd be back later.

Wanda spent the night again. The next morning she finally went home to shower and change clothes before going to the airport to pick up her aunt Vera who had flown in from Washington State. She rejoiced at the look on her granny's face when she woke up and laid eyes on her eldest daughter. Her expression said a thousand words.

"Hi, Momma," Vera whispered, returning her smile. She gave her a tight squeeze and several kisses.

Her mother tried to reply but couldn't form the words.

Wanda and Vera coached her to relax and to take her time so she wouldn't become frustrated.

"I came as soon as I could. Now I need you to get better so I can take you home," Vera said.

Wanda watched another big smile brighten her granny's face.

"I'm really glad you're here, Auntie," she said after her grandmother had fallen asleep again.

"There's no place I'd rather be. This is my mother, baby. I wanted to come as soon as I heard the news, but the last-minute flight prices were astronomical. I ended up with a much better deal by waiting an extra day. Where's your mother?" Vera asked. "I spoke with her earlier, and she said she'd be here."

"Yeah, she told Granny she'd come feed her lunch," Wanda said. She didn't go into details about her short visits on purpose. She'd choose to let Vera draw her own conclusion of what was going on.

Seconds later, Joyce walked through the door smiling. Wanda watched the sisters embrace. As they engaged in conversation she eased over to the window and stared outside, suppressing the resentment toward her mother. Suddenly, she missed the mom and friend she'd known for so many years. To witness Joyce act like an immature school girl and date someone she'd been intimate with simply disgusted Wanda. From her perspective the behavior was unjustifiable, and the only way to deal with the problem was for Joyce to end her relationship with Michael. Until she did, Wanda knew her frustration would continue to stir up anger, causing disrespect. She glanced at her mother and aunt as they rambled on.

While pondering the situation, she considered the possibility that Joyce may be afraid of being alone. *Is this why she refuses to break it off with Michael?* Wanda thought. *Dating him is an obvious mistake, but it seems she'd rather continue seeing him than to admit her flaw or be single. I can't believe she's ruined a long and healthy relationship for a short-term fling. Damn.*

The patient care tech interrupted Wanda's thoughts when she knocked on the door and entered the room with a lunch tray. Joyce fed her mother, then took off. Vera didn't mention her leaving so soon and neither did Wanda.

On the following Sunday her grandmother was relocated to a regular floor. The doctor informed Wanda and Vera that instead of going home from the hospital she needed to spend time at a rehabilitation facility. He stressed the importance of working with an occupational, physical, and speech therapist. Vera gave consent.

Wanda also agreed with whatever was deemed necessary to improve her grandmother's quality of life. Since she'd always been an independent person, Wanda was hopeful the therapy would restore her strength at least to the point of being semi-independent. Through the years, her granny had stressed not wanting to burden anyone in her old age, but Wanda viewed assisting her as a privilege.

The next day, she returned to work. Wanda sat thinking of how nice it had been with her aunt Vera at the hospital. The days went by much smoother having someone to talk to.

During her lunch break she dialed Casey's number, curious if she'd learned anything new about Ron. Once her grandmother became ill, Wanda had pushed everything aside. Her aunt Vera provided the leeway to follow through on unfinished business.

"Hey, Wanda. How's your grandmother?" Casey asked.

"She's doing better. Thanks for asking," she replied.

"I just pulled up at the Sonic on Montgomery Crossroads. Come have some ice cream with me," Casey said.

"I wish. I'm back at work," Wanda replied.

"Is it okay for me to come by your job? We need to talk. Face to face," Casey said.

"Naw, let's hook up after I get off. Good news or bad news?" Wanda asked.

"It's great news," Casey replied.

"Can you meet me in the lobby at the hospital around five-thirty?" Wanda asked.

"Sure. I'll let you go and we'll talk then," Casey said.

Wanda hung up the phone anticipating seeing her later that day. Then at five-thirty, she greeted Casey with a smile. "Thanks for coming," she said, embracing her.

"No problem," Casey replied.

Let's sit over here," Wanda said, pointing at a bench.

When they sat down, Casey looked at her, bursting with excitement. "I had to talk to you in person. Guess what?" she said.

"What?" Wanda asked, curious.

"I have a good friend who works at a car dealership. I told him I needed a huge favor without providing details. Girl, he hooked me up with a tracking device. I already put it underneath Ron's car bumper. Now you can find out where he is without following him around," Casey said barely taking a breath.

Wanda gave her a high five. "That's what I'm talking about. Thank you," she said.

"Please. You've got me feeling like a detective. I'm ready to make a bust," Casey said.

Wanda laughed. "We're trying to solve a kidnapping or possible murder, not a drug deal."

Casey giggled. "Let's do it," she said. "I'm ready."

Wanda shook her head. "I'll be in touch. My granny's going to rehab by the end of the week, and Friday is girls' night out. After that I'm free," she said.

"Cool. Just let me know what's up," Casey replied.

"I will. Again, I really appreciate what you've done," Wanda said, standing.

"You're my girl. I've got you," Casey replied.

Once upstairs, Wanda entered the room, happy to see her grandmother awake and bright-eyed. "Hi, Aunt Vera. Hi, Granny. Are you feeling okay today?" she asked.

She smiled and nodded.

Wanda kissed her on the cheek and squeezed her hand. "I love you," she said to her.

She smiled again.

Finally Wanda sat next to her aunt Vera. "How was your day?" she asked.

"Wonderful. Momma's doing so much better today. The doctor discontinued some of her medications. She's still not saying much, but she's alert," Vera said.

Wanda smiled, grateful for her progress.

Minutes later, dinner arrived. Afterward Wanda assisted Vera with bathing and getting her granny dressed for bed, then the three of them watched television until her grandmother began to snore.

"I was shocked when I met your mother's new guy friend today," Vera said, softly taking Wanda completely by surprise.

"I'm sure," she replied dryly. "I went to high school with him."

"How's your father?" Vera asked.

"He's okay. He came by to visit and brought Granny those flowers the other day," Wanda said, pointing, then she sighed.

"What's wrong?" Vera questioned.

"I have a lot going on, Auntie. My life is so out of order, it's ridiculous. Being here for Granny has actually been therapeutic for me. My concern for her hasn't allowed me to worry about my own problems."

"Do you want to talk about it?" Vera asked.

"Naw. It's too much drama. Just to give you an idea, I will say, besides what's going on with my parents, I stepped out on Malcolm. Now the man I cheated with is stalking me, and his wife has been missing for a few months."

"Damn, niece. Excuse my French. What have you gotten yourself into?" Vera whispered, peeking to make sure her mother was still asleep.

"A big mess," Wanda said. "Now, in addition to what I'm already dealing with, Granny is sick."

Wanda's phone interrupted the conversation. She glanced at the caller ID then she showed the screen to her aunt. "This is the guy I had the affair with. Although I've ignored his calls since I broke it off with him about a month ago he will not leave me alone. My patience is really wearing thin. I've tried to handle this confusion as quietly as possible for his sake as well as mine, but apparently he doesn't understand no means no."

Vera giggled.

"I'm serious, Auntie. Sometimes I wish he'd have a heart attack and die."

"That's not nice, Wanda," Vera said.

"I'm being honest. It seems like once things start going wrong in life, it gets worse before its gets better. I can't handle all of the pressure he's putting on me," Wanda said.

"You need to be careful. One good thing about your situation is there are no children involved," Vera said.

"Oh no. I've never wanted kids. I'm not the one," Wanda said. "A couple of my friends have babies. Now that we've approached thirty they're dreading their biological clock running out and I'm cheering. I can't wait for my childbearing years to be over."

"You're a trip, Wanda," Vera said.

She laughed. "If anything, I'm pondering my career. Time does seem to be running out in that aspect, so I've decided to return to college in the fall. I enjoy working at the courthouse, but I'm not doing what I love," Wanda said.

"What do you love?" Vera asked.

"I don't know," Wanda replied.

They both laughed.

Ron called again. Wanda pressed ignore. "I'm thinking of becoming a private investigator," she said. "Oh, how's retired life? We haven't talked about that."

"Fabulous," Vera replied, smiling.

"That's what I'm talk about," Wanda said.

Her phone began to ring again. She looked at the screen. "If I answer this phone, he's going to get cursed out like never before," she stressed, agitated.

"Honey, you have a fool on your hands," Vera said, shaking her head.

"I've had enough. I want this man out of my life. Damn," Wanda exclaimed. "Sorry, Auntie, but I swear I wish somebody would knock his ass off."

Chapter 16

Kim added the final touches to her makeup then stood in front of the large mirror feeling fabulous. She wore a Donna Ricco silk chiffon halter dress with one-inch sandals and was headed to the Outback Steakhouse for girls' night out. At the restaurant, she and her friends were seated then ordered drinks and dinner before starting the evening with concern for Wanda's grandmother.

"Oh, she's doing much better," Wanda assured them. "She was relocated to rehab this morning. The therapists are going to work with her so she can regain strength on her right side. She has a long way to go, but she's definitely in the recovery stage."

"That's a blessing," Kim said.

Angel agreed.

"It is," Lynn said. "How are your mom and aunt handling all of this?"

"Aunt Vera is fine. I'm pissed at Momma. She visits Granny once a day to feed her lunch, then in less than an hour she's gone. I don't understand her thinking, and it's weird because she's always been so reliable. Now, she's completely unpredictable," Wanda said.

"Maybe Mrs. Joyce can't tolerate seeing her mother in her condition," Kim said.

"No. That's just an excuse. I think being at the hospital is more of an inconvenience. The way I see it, if Momma can feed Granny lunch, she can do breakfast or dinner too. My argument isn't about the meal she serves. I'm upset at the measly amount of time she spends with her. If you truly love someone, wouldn't it be in your heart to do right by them? Especially, your mother—if you love her. I tell people all the time, love is action. It's what you do, not what you say," Wanda said.

"You're absolutely right, Wanda, but some people can't stomach caring for sick folks," Kim said.

"Momma doesn't have that phobia, trust me. She helped with my grandfather before he passed away. The timing is wrong, that's all. Am I asking too much by expecting her to support my granny and to show her love?" Wanda questioned.

"No. I'm with you, Wanda. I totally agree," Lynn said. "It's sad how sometimes we get caught up in our own lives and forget our elders. I made that mistake once with my favorite great-uncle. I grew up loving him immensely then let life get between us. When he became sick and died, oh my God, I thought I'd never stop crying. I regret not showing him my appreciation. I've vowed to let the people I love, especially my elders, know I care. It's amazing but something as simple as a one- or two-minute phone call or a short visit can have a powerful impact."

The waitress walked up and served the beverages before hurrying off.

"I hate to bring this up," Lynn said, "but look out for the vultures, Wanda. Although your grandmother is recovering, know that family members are lurking. They realize she's getting older. Trust me everybody's paying attention, trying to see what they can gain from the situation. Remember what I went through when my grandmother became ill? Our relatives stole things out of the house, spent her money, and used her identity to open new accounts, but when she was healthy and needed something to be done no one was around. I will never understand how we can abuse the ones who have been in our corner and loved us the most."

"Oh my God, you said a mouthful, Lynn. It's sad to say, but the truth is dealing with kinfolk is like people we meet in the streets. You need discernment—to separate the good from evil," Wanda said. "What gets me is those who should be setting an example are the crooks. Once the respect is gone, dealing with those kinds of people is hard. It's the same kinda thing with Momma. Like I told her, if that was Michael lying in that bed instead of Granny she'd be right by his side. I already know she would. Someone she's only known for a spell versus the woman who gave her life. Respect? Please?"

"Maybe she'll come around," Angel said. "I understand your frustration."

"So do I," Lynn said. "I hope y'all get it together soon. You and your mom were so close."

"We were. Now I'm hoping Michael hasn't introduced her to crack or some shit. Momma has done a one-eighty. I'm so disappointed in her."

"Why would you think your mom's on crack?" Kim asked.

"Something's wrong with her," Wanda stressed. "Oh, I never told y'all we couldn't find her the day Granny was admitted into the hospital. It was the next morning when she finally showed up. She's not the woman she used to be, that's for sure."

"Did she mention where she was or give any explanation?" Kim asked.

"Nope. She displayed the 'I'm doing what I want to and I don't care who likes it' attitude," Wanda replied.

"Let's say a prayer for her," Kim suggested.

"What's up with Michelle?" Wanda asked, ignoring Kim's offer.

"She's fine. Kelvin and the baby are doing well also. He's going to spoil that kid rotten," Lynn said.

"Who's next, Angel? Will it be Kim or Lynn?" Wanda asked.

"I don't know," Angel replied, glancing at Lynn, then Kim.

"Well, I've concluded I can't have children naturally. Chris and I have talked about our options, including adoption," Lynn said.

"Are you sure? It's risky enough bringing your own kid into your house, but a total stranger? I wouldn't do it, Lynn. I admire you, girl," Wanda said.

"If we adopt I'd want a newborn," she replied.

"Oh, okay. Yeah, I like that better," Wanda said.

"Kim, did you talk to Leon yet?" Angel asked.

"Yes. He's okay with having another child," she replied with a smile.

"That's great," Angel said.

"I told y'all, Leon is the man," Lynn said.

"Are y'all working on a baby now?" Wanda asked Kim.

"No. I just wanted to be sure that door would open if I chose to walk through it."

Wanda giggled. "I'm impressed. I thought you had given it up by now," she said to Kim.

"Would you tell us if you had?" Lynn questioned.

"Of course," Kim replied, blushing.

The waitress served the meals and refilled their drinks. She asked if everything was okay before walking away.

"So how's your little investigation going?" Lynn asked Wanda, changing the subject.

"It was stalled when Granny got sick. I dropped Ron like a bad habit. I have gathered some information. Now I need to figure out what it means. My girl Casey is helping me out," she said.

"Be careful. I'd hate for you or Casey to end up floating in a river somewhere or lying in the woods like the woman they just found," Lynn said.

"If something happens to me, I'm confident my girls will seek justice. Ain't that right?" Wanda questioned.

None of her friends responded.

"Do you think this is a joke? It's not," Lynn said, frowning.

"I know what I'm doing," Wanda replied. "At this point I really don't have a choice. Ron is stalking me. In order to get rid of his annoying ass, I need to prove he's a criminal so they can throw him in jail."

"Let the police handle it. You can talk to Chris and he'll get the ball rolling," Lynn insisted.

"Did he get the detective job he applied for?" Wanda asked.

"We'll know by the end of next week," Lynn replied.

"Maybe he can help me out without going through the police department. I have a reputation to uphold," Wanda said.

"No. That's not going to work. I can't believe you'd even ask him to put his job on the line when you can handle this situation the right way."

"Look, I'll keep doing what I'm doing. I didn't ask for your help Lynn—or Chris'."

"Don't," she replied.

"I think we need to pray for you and your mom, Wanda," Kim stated.

"Pray for Kim," Wanda snapped.

Lynn giggled. "I can see why you're so upset with Mrs. Joyce. From what you've told us you're behaving just like her—gotta have it your way. Recognize this, Wanda: As you insist there's a better way for her to handle Michael, we insist there's a better way for you to deal with Ron."

"That's right. File a restraining order against him," Kim suggested.

"You have already, right?" Angel asked.

"No. I said I was but never did. It was a bluff to keep him away from my house," Wanda admitted.

"Has it worked?" Lynn asked.

"Nope. Y'all have to understand, I don't want a paper trail connecting me to Ron. I don't want to be pulled into the drama when the mystery of his wife is revealed. There's a lot of ways this can play out if our relationship is made public. I don't like any of them," Wanda confessed.

"Honesty is always best," Angel said.

"Do you really believe that? When Derrick told you about his affair with Grant while they were stationed in Korea, do you agree that was the best way to handle the situation? Personally, I think he should've taken that shit to his grave," Wanda said.

Angel stared at her at a loss for words. She couldn't believe Wanda would bring up such a painful part of her past. She was crushed when Derrick came home on leave and told her he'd slept with another woman. The two of them were supposedly in a monogamous relationship, with plans of getting married. Derrick insisted they break it off and see other people because the long distance relationship was not working. He refused to hurt Angel more than he already had.

"Why would you go there, Wanda?" Lynn asked.

"I'm just saying," Wanda replied.

Angel held up her hand. "Regardless of how you feel, Derrick and I have gotten past that incident. Hypothetically speaking, even if he hadn't told me about the fling, I'm sure I would've learned the truth eventually. So looking back, yes, hearing the facts from Derrick was best. Had he not confessed, when he returned home and told me Grant was supposedly pregnant with his child, I'm positive the outcome would've been a lot different. That alone would've revealed to me that he was a liar.

"Instead of pretending or allowing me to believe he'd been faithful while in Korea, he chose to be honest. Yes, I felt betrayed and I was mad as hell, but in the end I forgave Derrick. What allowed me to get to that point was not being married at the time, our history, my love for him, and finally the realization that we all mess up. I'm not saying what Derrick did was right because it wasn't. Nor am I saying I'll forget it because I won't, but at the same time I made the decision to reconcile.

"Furthermore, while you're judging Derrick, if you really look at the situation, you're deceiving Malcolm the way you suggest he should've deceived me. You're deceiving him appearing loyal when in essence you're not. So like I said, honesty is always best. Tell Malcolm the truth and allow him to forgive you and move forward. Until then, Wanda, you're the liar."

"Derrick's a liar," Wanda rebutted.

"No, Derrick made a mistake, but he told the truth about it," Angel replied calmly.

"Hold up. Wanda, this conversation isn't about Derrick and Angel, it's about you," Lynn said defensively. "I don't know why it's so hard for you to confide in Malcolm. You're only making the situation worse. In my opinion, you couldn't care less about Malcolm's feelings. If you love him you'd find a way to deal with his imperfections rather than lying down with another man."

"Look, I'm not all mushy-mushy like y'all pretend to be. I don't want the truth to come out for Malcolm's sake. I really don't, but the bottom line is, if it does, it is what it is. I won't lose one night of sleep, I assure you," Wanda stated.

"You're finally in the hot seat," Kim said to Wanda, smirking.

"Yeah, and I'm about to get up and get out of here before I lose friendships," she replied.

"For someone who believes in saying what needs to be said, you surely don't receive it well," Lynn told Wanda.

Wanda paused. Lynn's words shattered her heart into tiny pieces. "Damn," she finally said, receiving her statement. "Wow. You're right, Lynn. Angel, I am so sorry. I guess holding in everything going on with my granny, Momma, the drama with Ron, and Malcolm…I guess I needed to blow off some steam."

"Why'd you pick me?" Angel asked.

"Because she already knows Kim will fight back and I'm ready to slap the hell out of her. You're the nice one, Angel," Lynn said.

Wanda laughed. "I apologize. You're right, Angel. Derrick slipped up, but he really is a good guy," she said.

"So is Malcolm," Angel replied.

"Yeah. You need to tell him about Ron, Wanda. He will find out, and it's better to hear it from you," Lynn said.

Kim sat quietly watching Wanda stare across the room. "I'll be praying for you, Malcolm, and your family," she said. "I have a bottle of oil in my purse if you—"

"No, thanks, Kim," Wanda interrupted. "I'm fine, really."

"Are you sure? Honey, you know I'll lay your burdens at Jesus' feet in a minute," she replied.

"That's what I'm afraid of. I'll pray for myself," Wanda said. "God is tired of you. Have you turned in that twenty-five grand, yet?"

"I don't want to talk about that money. It's none of your business," Kim said.

"Your response tells us you didn't. Look at you…you're a hypocrite. That's why God don't like you," Wanda teased.

The girls giggled.

"It's time to go," Lynn said.

After dinner, they hugged then went their separate ways on a good note.

Kim drove to Leon's house and stayed there overnight. The next morning after breakfast they met with his pastor about performing their wedding.

The reverend asked a series of questions ending with, "Have you set a date yet?"

Leon looked at Kim.

"How soon can we do it?" she asked.

"Anytime. Just let me know a few days ahead of time," he said.

"Is Friday a good day?" Kim asked Leon.

"This week?" he questioned.

"Yes. Is that too soon?"

"Of course not. Is Friday okay?" Leon asked the pastor.

"Let's see." He scanned his calendar. Will four o'clock work for you?" he asked.

Leon looked at Kim and she nodded.

"Yes. Four o'clock is fine," he replied, smiling.

* * *

During the ceremony, Kim faced Leon trembling like never before. When the pastor told Leon to kiss his bride, she blushed. She couldn't believe she'd finally done it. Kim was officially a married woman.

She hadn't told her friends about the wedding, so as soon as they left the church she called Lynn and asked her to initiate a five-line connection. "I have something to tell y'all," Kim said.

"Are you eloping?" Lynn asked.

"I'm not answering any questions until everyone is on the phone," she replied.

"Hold on. I already know you are. I have some news, too," Lynn said before clicking over.

Finally, they were all connected.

"Okay out with it, Kim McKenzie," Lynn said.

"Well, you're wrong, Lynn. I'm not eloping. I'm already married," Kim sang.

The girls cheered, congratulating her.

"Oh. My. God," Wanda said, emphasizing each word. "I can't believe you did it. I really can't, but I'm happy for you."

"Thanks. I appreciate it. I'll talk to y'all next week. Leon and I are headed to Myrtle Beach for a weekend honeymoon," Kim said.

"Now?" Lynn asked.

"Yep."

"Have fun," Angel said.

"Without getting pregnant," Wanda added. "That's why she's leaving town, ladies, so we can't hear Leon make her scream."

"Stop it, Wanda. Don't take me there. You know I'll get things started in the car. It's on," Kim said.

The girls laughed.

"Handle your business, Mrs. Hardy. Bang, bang, bang," Lynn sang.

"Let me get off this phone. Y'all are too crazy. Oh, Lynn what's your news?" Kim asked.

"Chris got the job," she squealed.

The girls were excited once more.

"Y'all already know this calls for a celebration," Lynn said. "We'll talk when you get back, Kim."

"Enjoy your weekend. We love you, Kim," Michelle slid in.

"I love y'all, too.

Kim hung up and glanced at Leon. He was shaking his head.

"What?" she questioned.

"Nothing. I can appreciate the relationship you ladies have. Sharing special moments with true friends is pretty nice and a blessing," Leon said.

"Yes, it is. We have our moments, but for the most part we have an awesome friendship."

Leon nodded, agreeing. "Do you want to grab a bite to eat or something to drink before we get on the interstate?" he asked.

"No, I'm good. I packed a few things in my bag," Kim said.

Four hours later, they were in Myrtle Beach. After checking into the hotel, Kim and Leon dined at Greg Norman's Australian Grille for dinner. Kim enjoyed a steak and Leon ate salmon while taking in the magnificent view of the Intracoastal Waterway.

Later they strolled along the beach, hand in hand under the dark sky. Once back at the suite Kim encouraged Leon to shower without her while she unpacked their things. Afterward, she bathed and slipped on her conservative but sexy soft pink nightgown. Kim wasn't sure of Leon's style when it came to lovemaking, but knowing he was a deacon she left the whips and chains at home. She enjoyed role playing, but instead of being her normal freaky self she portrayed the new Kim—classy and smooth.

"You look beautiful," Leon said, inhaling the soft fragrance along her neckline. He pressed his lips against her skin.

Kim closed her eyes. Thank you," she whispered, enjoying his touch.

Moments later, Leon initiated a powerful kiss. He removed her gown, massaged the small of Kim's back, and explored the curves of her hips and buttocks before leading her to the bed, lying her back. He undressed her and left kisses along her nude body. When he closed his lips around Kim's nipple she moaned.

She teased his earlobes with her fingertips and trailed her nails softly along his neck and shoulders, making her way down to his pants. As she removed his boxer shorts, their lips met once more. Kim's body heat grew more intense by the second. She wanted Leon inside of her. She pulled him on top, breathing heavily, grinding hungrily against him, then was devastated when he couldn't get an erection.

Oh, my God, Kim thought, shocked by what was happening and unsure of what to say.

"I'm sorry. I hoped this wouldn't happen. It's been a very long time since I've made love to a woman, Kim," Leon said in a low, sad tone.

"It's okay," she assured him calmly although her body begged for his affection. She didn't want Leon to feel bad about not being able to perform.

"I have backup," he said, reaching for his bag. "I'm not sure how long it'll take the pill to work, but I'm sure we'll find something to do to pass time."

Kim smiled. After Leon took the small blue tablet she climbed on top of him, layering steamy, wet kisses along his chest, then she paid special attention to his manhood until it began to grow. She gladly wrapped her fingers around Leon's erection and stroked it with finesse. Again, she was ready to become one. Leon rolled her onto her back and they kissed fervently. Next, he slowly and carefully penetrated her. "You're so warm," he whispered, tasting Kim's earlobe.

He fed her his tongue as their bodies moved together in a graceful rhythm. Afterward, Kim rested in his embrace, exhausted but satisfied. That moment confirmed she'd evolved to a different place in life. Although Leon's lovemaking wasn't as aggressive, he was gentle, passionate, and yielded the same result.

Kim and Leon showered, then lay in bed talking until he drifted off to sleep. A little later she was awakened by his touch as he explored her nakedness. When Kim felt Leon's erection, her juices instantly began to flow. Leon performed much more comfortably the second time around and so did she, following his lead, thrusting her hips to the rhythm of a perfect beat.

The next morning, Kim woke up in bed alone. She opened her eyes and smiled as Leon sang, "What a Friend We Have in Jesus," a hymn she absolutely loved. The lyrics were comforting, and she appreciated the old-time melody.

Kim rejoiced at how he'd blessed her by loving the Lord, ultimately winning her affection. She finally felt her life was right, and she enjoyed bonding with Leon on a different level. Although their initial sexual experience gave her a scare, Kim had hopes that with frequency Leon's penile muscle would regain strength. She said a silent prayer for her sexual desires to be fulfilled by her husband and for his impotence to be short lived, then she pulled back the covers and stepped out of bed, joining Leon out front. "Hi, husband?" Kim said, walking toward him.

"Good morning, wife," he replied.

They both blushed as she walked into his embrace, giving Leon a tight squeeze. "Did you sleep well?" he asked.

"I did. And you?" she questioned.

"Are you kidding? That was the best night I've had in years," Leon said.

Kim smiled and rested her head against his chest.

After eating they got dressed and toured Myrtle Beach. The next evening they returned to Savannah. Kim called Angel to let her know they were back in town.

Angel said she and the girls were visiting Michelle. "If you're up to it, come over for a little while and tell us about your weekend," she suggested.

"I think I will, but I can only stay for a short while," Kim replied.

After hanging up she looked at Leon. "Go ahead. Have a good time," he said, reclining in his chair.

"Okay, babe. I won't be gone for long." Kim walked over to Leon and kissed him on the lips.

Wanda answered the door when she arrived at Michelle's. "How was your trip?" she asked.

"It was lovely," Kim replied, stepping inside.

"Come on in. Have a seat," Michelle offered.

"Hey, girl. Where's the baby?" Kim asked, hugging her.

"He's in the bedroom with Kelvin."

"Can I see him?" Kim questioned after greeting everyone.

"Sure. Go knock on the door," Michelle said.

After talking to Kelvin and playing with his son for a few minutes, Kim rejoined the ladies in the living room.

"Sit down. Tell us about your weekend," Michelle said to Kim.

"It was great. I really enjoyed myself. The relaxation and peace of mind were heavenly."

"Did you give it up?" Wanda questioned, then laughed. "You don't even have to answer, I already know you did."

"Yes, I made love to my husband," Kim admitted.

"Was it good?" Wanda asked.

"After eleven months of abstinence, all he had to do was touch me and I would've exploded."

The girls giggled.

"Believe it or not, I've grown to appreciate my celibacy experience. Although I enjoy intercourse, I realized I don't have to have it. You couldn't have told me that a year ago," Kim said. "You know that reminds me of something I read in the Bible a while back."

"Oh, Lord. Here we go," Wanda said.

"Seriously. You know how it talks about a man having one wife and a woman one husband or if you can't be celibate, then you should marry. Now, everybody in the world is probably aware of this scripture, but I think we've been jaded by hearing people say it's impossible or unrealistic to live by certain biblical principles. For the first time, I digested Paul's message on a spiritual level.

"As I focused on why we're encouraged to live this way, I understood it's for our own good. Think about it, if we're faithful and abide by these instructions, not only can they protect us from the sins of fornication and adultery, but also disease or having children out of wedlock, thus allowing us a better opportunity to please God." Kim smiled. "I love it," she said. "Knowledge is power. I'm not saying there won't be temptation, but if our focus is on God and what he wants for our life, it can be done. It's a daily fight, but I'm ready."

No one commented.

Kim didn't know if her friends were processing what she'd just said or refusing to entertain a spiritual debate.

"Although the Bible is disputed by many, it's a powerful tool with great resources," Angel finally said.

Kim nodded.

"So how was it?" Wanda asked again, looking at Kim. "Did he do it right?"

"Well," she began, "Leon hadn't had sex in three years—"

"Damn," Wanda blurted, interrupting her.

"Be quiet, girl," Lynn told Wanda. "Keep talking, Kim."

"Honestly, we got off to a rough start. When we first tried to make love, Leon couldn't get it up."

The room fell silent for a few seconds.

"Oh, hell naw. I know you were mad as hell," Wanda finally said.

"Actually, I wasn't. Well, I guess I was disappointed because I was so horny, but then my compassion kicked in. I saw how hurt and sad he was about not being able to perform. However, he had backup in a bottle," Kim said, smiling.

The girls snickered.

"After the erection, did he make it up to you," Wanda asked.

"Yep. You know how it is when you need to feel the way only a man can make you feel?" Kim said.

"All too well," Wanda sang. "Ain't nothing like a big, strong…Lord, have mercy."

Chapter 17

On Monday, August 13 Wanda walked toward the courthouse exit behind the new criminal court judge, admiring how tall and sexy he was. She contemplated initiating a conversation but never said anything. Once at the door, he glanced back, noticing her.

"Hello," he said.

"Hi. How are you?" Wanda asked.

"Great. Thanks," he replied.

"How's it going so far? Do you like working here?" Wanda questioned.

"Yes. I love it," he said.

"Are you from Savannah?"

"No. I relocated here for the job. By the way, I'm Judge Thompson," he said, extending his hand.

"Wanda Boyd," she replied, attentive to his bare ring finger and the size of his hands. "Don't take this the wrong way, but you put me in the mind of an NBA player more so than a judge."

He smiled. "I played basketball in high school and attended college on a scholarship. During my fourth year, I was off the court a lot due to injuries, but I'm okay with not being in the NBA. I'm doing what I've always dreamed of doing," Judge Thompson said.

"Impressive," Wanda said. "I'm thinking of becoming a private investigator."

"Oh, really? That's a pretty interesting business. I have a PI friend in Atlanta. If you want, I can touch base with him and put you two in touch. I'm sure he can give you some pointers."

"I'd rather talk to you," Wanda replied, smiling.

Judge Thompson blushed. "Here's my business card. Call me," he said after writing his cell number on the back.

Wanda gave him a card as well. "When is the best time to contact you—evenings or weekends?"

"Whenever you get the urge," Judge Thompson replied.

"Are you sure?" Wanda asked.

"Yes. Right now it's just me, the computer, my television and books. A little conversation would be great," he said.

"Okay. I'll definitely take you up on the offer. I'm glad we had a chance to talk," Wanda said. "Have a good evening."

"You do the same. I'll see you tomorrow," he replied.

Wanda watched him walk away, shocked at how easy it was to get close and personal with him. After leaving the courthouse, she went to visit with her grandmother. As usual, her aunt Vera was there. Since Aunt Vera was staying with her mother, she rode to rehab with Joyce every morning then stayed until Wanda came in the evening. After visiting hours ended at eight o'clock, they'd have dinner together, then on her way home Wanda would drop Vera off. Once she made it in, she routinely tracked Ron's car to see where he was. The device seemed to be a good idea but hadn't produced any additional information. Whenever Wanda used it, Ron was either at the bingo hall, the club, his home in Savannah, or the one in Hilton Head. Still, she checked it faithfully, not knowing when she'd get a break and learn some valuable information.

On Thursday night, while at the Olive Garden restaurant with her aunt, Wanda received a call from a private number. She pressed ignore then continued eating. Once at home she remembered disregarding the beep alerting her of a new message. Wanda dialed her voicemail, surprised to hear Judge Thompson's voice asking her to give him a call.

She sat there for a few moments thinking about what she might be getting into. Wanda hadn't seen him after leaving work on Monday and didn't have an opportunity to call because of her already busy schedule. When she finally settled down at night, it was usually around ten o'clock, and she felt that was too late to bother him. Her weekends were a lot less congested, so she'd planned to contact him then.

Wanda looked at the time on her cell phone. It was nine-fifty-five. She located Judge Thompson's number on his business card and punched it in. When he answered, she identified herself then she began apologizing for calling so late.

"Don't worry about it," he said. "I looked forward to hearing from you sooner."

Wanda gave him the rundown of her daily routine. "I just walked in the door a few minutes ago," she said. "Instead of bothering you at this hour, I'd decided to wait until the weekend to call."

"I see. Well, take your shoes off and relax. We'll talk this weekend," Judge Thompson replied.

"Is Saturday morning okay? Let's say between ten and eleven o'clock?" Wanda asked.

"Sounds great. Have a good night, Wanda."

"You, too, Judge Thompson."

"Off duty it's Patrick," he said.

"Patrick it is. We'll chat later," Wanda said.

She fulfilled her promise to call on Saturday, and they talked for more than three hours, taking the conversation to a personal level. Patrick confided in her about his previous relationship. He complained his ex-girlfriend wasn't over her baby's father.

"Why do you think that?" Wanda asked him.

"She and I didn't live together, but I can't count the number of times while I was visiting that dude just popped up to see his kid—yeah, right," Patrick said.

"I'm with you. That's not cool," Wanda said, then she giggled a little.

"What's so funny?" Patrick asked.

"Life. Love is no joke. Let me guess—he's a deadbeat, right?" she questioned.

"Of course," Patrick said. "He doesn't even have a job. She tried to convince me that because the guy wasn't able to take care of their son financially, he needed to spend time with him so he'd know his father."

"She let an established man with a career go so her broke baby daddy can have a relationship with her son? She'll regret it because more then likely he was only coming by because he knew you were there," Wanda said.

"My thoughts exactly, but I don't have time for games. Not at this stage in my life. I had to mature early to pursue my career. I've learned to separate myself from nonsense," Patrick said.

"What drew you to Savannah? Did you look for a job here specifically, or did you put out résumés and ended up getting hired here?" Wanda asked.

"I sought out this city, mainly because of the high crime rate in the African-American communities. I plan to learn the area and mingle with the leaders so I can see where I fit in. I'd like to join or start some type of program to reach our young men. Prisons are being built for them, but we need to come up with alternatives. I'm tired of seeing so many of our babies enter the judicial system," Patrick said.

"Good luck. These kids want the thug life," Wanda replied. "Speaking of babies, do you have any?"

"I have a young man. He's seventeen and getting ready to start college on an academic and football scholarship," Patrick said proudly.

"Seventeen," Wanda questioned. "If you don't mind me asking, how old are you."

"I'm thirty-three," Patrick said.

"You didn't waste any time, did you?" Wanda commented.

"I was hard headed. Being a basketball player had its perks," Patrick said. "Do you mind me asking your age?"

"Wait, I'm not done with you yet," Wanda said. "What type of relationship do you have with your son and his mother?"

"He and I have a great relationship. I wasn't around as much as I would've liked while he was growing up because of college, but I visited often. I didn't miss birthdays, and we spent a lot of time together during the holidays. My parents are also very involved in my son's life. My mother babysat him until he turned three years old. As for his mom, we're friends," Patrick said. "I never loved her. The pregnancy wasn't planned of course. We were both young, doing what grown folks do, and ended up with a grown-up responsibility. She chose not to have an abortion because of religious beliefs."

"Wow, y'all were some young parents," Wanda said.

"Do you have children?" Patrick asked her.

"No, and I don't want any," she replied.

Patrick chuckled.

"I'm serious," Wanda continued. "Kids are a lot of work. I'm selfish—I like my time and space to myself. I may share it with another adult at some point but little people don't have a chance."

Patrick laughed. "Can I ask your age?" he threw in.

"Sure. I'm twenty-nine," she replied.

"Are you in a relationship?" Patrick asked.

"I am. Have been for nine years," Wanda said.

"Married?" he questioned.

"Not my style," Wanda replied. "I have a really nice guy but committing on that level is probably not going to happen. I'm single with no children on purpose."

"Why? I thought it was every woman's dream to be a wife and mother," Patrick said.

"No. That's not true. All women aren't meant to be mothers. I'd probably be a good parent but a child doesn't fit into my life right now. I told you, I'm selfish. "Do you want more kids?" Wanda asked.

"Not necessarily. With that said, if I marry someone who wants children, I'd consider it," Patrick said.

"That's fair," Wanda replied. "Relationships are tricky. Sometimes you think you're getting one thing and end up with another."

"What do you mean?" Patrick asked.

"For example, a friend of mine was dating this guy who appeared to be decent. Their relationship was great until she found out he was using drugs and tried to break it off with him. Now, the dude is stalking her," Wanda said.

"Tell your friend to call the police. Her best option is filing a report and taking out a restraining order against this guy. A lot of citizens make the mistake of taking the law into their own hands, putting themselves at risk of danger or doing jail time."

"Okay. Thank you," Wanda said.

"No problem," Patrick replied.

There was a brief silence.

"I've really enjoyed talking with you, Wanda," Patrick admitted.

"Same here. So what are you getting into today?" she asked.

"Nothing much. I need to run a few errands, but that's about it. What are you up to?" he questioned.

"I'm preparing to go visit my grandmother at the rehab center. Later tonight I'm going to a friend's birthday party," she said.

"Okay, well I'll let you start your day. I wish your grandmother a speedy recovery."

"Thank you. That really means a lot," Wanda said.

"You're welcome. Have fun, and be safe at the party," Patrick told her. "If you feel like talking later on or tomorrow, give me a ring. If not, I'll see you at work on Monday."

"Sounds good. Enjoy your day," Wanda said.

She hung up the phone, impressed. She liked Patrick because he was accomplished but accessible. She didn't detect a bit of arrogance.

Ten minutes later, she stepped outside into the blazing heat. During her drive to the rehabilitation center, she couldn't stop thinking of Patrick. Wanda entered the building in a great mood and felt even better when she walked into her grandmother's room and saw the big smile on her face.

"Hi, Granny. Hey, Aunt Vera. How are you doing today?" Wanda asked, hugging her grandmother.

"Where you been?" she mumbled.

Wanda laughed. "You know I'm usually here by now, don't you? I'm sorry. I was talking to a friend on the phone a little longer than I anticipated," she said.

"I told her you were coming," Vera said.

"Without a doubt. Granny, you know I'd be here sooner or later," Wanda replied, grateful for her grandmother's continued progress. Although her speech remained blotchy she'd regained strength on her weak side. "So what's up with you, Aunt Vera?"

"Nothing, darling. Momma and I just finished watching *Diary of a Mad Black Woman.* You know how much she loves watching Madea," Vera said.

"Yeah." Wanda picked up the deck of playing cards the therapist had left in the room to use as exercise. "Let's play I Declare War, Granny," she said, dealing the cards.

Her grandmother took a while but eventually picked up each card with her weak hand. "Okay. That's enough," she blurted twenty minutes later.

Wanda laughed. "Are you quitting on me? You knew I was about to win," she said, teasing her grandmother.

She nodded, then pointed at the TV.

"Granny, stop being lazy. Do you wanna go home? The sooner you get your strength back, the sooner you can," Wanda said.

Her grandmother made a silly face.

"I'm gonna keep bugging you," Wanda promised, leaning back in the chair, allowing her to watch television.

Throughout the day they did a couple more exercises, then at eight o'clock Wanda and Vera kissed her good night. After dropping Vera off at her mother's, she lounged around until it was time to get dressed for Casey's birthday party.

Wanda wore tight blue jeans with a back-out top and pumps. Soon after she entered the building she spotted Ron. "Damn," she complained underneath her breath. She tried to avoid him, but she felt by the end of the night he'd find a way to get close to her.

She roamed the room looking for Casey, but Casey spotted her first. "Hey, Wanda. I'm glad you came," she said, embracing her.

"Are you kidding? I'm always up for a party," Wanda replied, "especially with all of the drama going on in my life. I need this break."

"Yes, you do. Come on," Casey said, pulling her out on the dance floor. They sang, grooving to the beats of Beyonce's latest hit." Once the song ended they walked away.

"I have to find a place to sit. Just wanted to let you know I'm here," Wanda said.

"Okay. I'll catch up with you later," Casey replied, going in the opposite direction.

Wanda purchased a drink from the cash bar. As she scanned the room looking for a seat, she recognized familiar faces. Finally, she spotted two ladies who worked at the courthouse with her. They were in different departments but mingled during their lunch breaks. Wanda smiled and waved, making her way to their table. "Hey, ladies. Is this seat taken?" she asked.

"No, girl. Sit down," the petite one said.

"Did you just get here?" the other asked.

"Yeah. This place is packed," Wanda replied, settling in her chair. She took a sip of her amaretto sour, observing her surroundings, moving her head to the beats of Ludacris' number one hit.

Once she finished her drink, a server appeared with another round for her and the ladies at the table. They were surprised and happily accepted the free beverages. When Wanda asked who sent them, the server pointed out Ron. He lifted his cup in the air. Wanda nodded, then looked away.

About ten minutes later, she was distracted when a male voice said, "Wanda Boyd, is that you?"

Wanda looked up, surprised to see Mark Spencer, one of her high school classmates. She stood and greeted him with a smile. "How are you?" she asked.

"I'm great," he replied, embracing her. "I can't believe I finally ran into you."

"Where have you been?" Wanda asked.

After graduation I joined the Air Force. I've served for eleven years now," Mark said.

"That's wonderful. How long have you been in town?" Wanda asked.

"I came yesterday. I'm hanging out with my homeboy. Man, I'm happy to see you," Mark said. "Each time I've returned to Savannah, I had hopes that we'd cross paths. Let's dance."

"Sure," Wanda said. She led Mark to the dance floor. Throughout the song, she noticed the lust in his eyes.

Wanda thought back to their senior year of high school when she and Mark were homecoming king and queen. He had a major crush on her, but she was dating someone else at the time. Otherwise she would've entertained his advances. She had always thought Mark was cute and he'd grown more so with age.

"What are you drinking?" he asked.

"Amaretto sour," Wanda replied.

Not long after she had returned to her seat, Ron sent another round of drinks, then Casey appeared. "What's up? Are you having a good time," she asked, sitting next to Wanda.

"I am," she replied. "Would you like a drink?"

"Oh, I've reached my limit. I'm just chilling, enjoying my guests," Casey said.

"Okay. I was going to offer you one of these," Wanda said pointing at the cups. "Ron sent them. I don't trust him. He'll never spike my drink."

"I knew he'd be nice to you. He's been bugging me for the last couple of weeks trying to make sure you'd be here tonight. I kept telling him you were coming," Casey said.

"I don't know why. I'm done with Ron," Wanda said.

"He misses you. Every time we talk he asks about you," Casey said.

"Whatever. He'll hate me before long. He's going down," Wanda said.

Casey laughed. "I understand," she replied before being called away.

As soon as she left, Mark strolled over again, delivering Wanda's beverage. "I'll be right back," he said.

Ten minutes later, he took Wanda by the hand. "Let's have some more fun," he said.

Wanda followed his lead. They danced to four songs in a row before sitting down again. "You're wearing me out, Mark Spencer," Wanda told him.

He chuckled. "Are you enjoying yourself?" he asked.

"I am," Wanda replied.

"Good. Catch your breath. I'll be back," Mark said.

Not long after he walked away, Wanda picked up her amaretto sour and was about to take a sip when she remembered leaving the drink unattended. The ladies who'd been sitting with her were gone. Wanda set the cup down and pushed it aside.

As the crowd dwindled, Casey reappeared. "I had so much fun tonight," she said, flopping in the seat next to Wanda.

"So did I. The party turned out really nice," Wanda said. "I've been hanging out with my classmate, Mark. I haven't seen him in years."

Just as Wanda finished her statement Mark walked up.

"Him?" Casey asked, pointing.

"Yeah," Wanda said, smiling.

"What are y'all talking about?" Mark questioned.

"I was telling Casey that you and I hung out tonight."

"No doubt," Mark said.

"I didn't know you two were classmates," Casey said.

"Wanda and I go way back. Thanks to you I had the pleasure of seeing her again," Mark said to Casey.

He handed Wanda a piece of paper. "I'm getting ready to leave. Here's my number. Let's keep in touch."

Wanda stood and hugged him. "If I call you'd better answer the phone," she said.

"Why wouldn't I? I'm a single man. You can change that, you know," Mark said with a sly grin.

"Bye, Mark," Wanda replied.

He laughed. Just as he left, Ron and Pete showed up.

"Do you have a designated driver?" Ron asked Wanda.

"I don't need one," she replied.

"Just checking." Ron turned and walked away.

Wanda frowned. *I can't stand that man,* she thought.

She watched Pete sit next to Casey, giving her a set of keys. "Drive my car home. I'll catch a ride with Ron after we clean up the place," she heard him say.

"Okay, baby. Thanks for a wonderful evening. I had an awesome time tonight," Casey said, squeezing him.

"You're welcome. Would you like another drink?" Pete asked her.

"I guess I can handle one more," Casey replied. "I haven't had anything since earlier tonight. Come on Wanda, my treat."

Wanda stood as Pete kissed the side of Casey's face, then she followed her to the bar. Shortly after they returned, Ron walked up and sat next to her. "You look great. How have you been?" he asked Wanda.

"I'm well. Thanks for asking," she replied.

"I've been waiting all night for my chance to talk to you. I wanted to apologize that our relationship ended on such a bad note. It's clear now that I went overboard trying to hold on, but I didn't want to lose you, Wanda. Now I see my faults. Will you please forgive me?" Ron asked.

"It's done," Wanda replied, showing no emotion.

"I miss the good times we shared. If I can't have you as a lover, I'd settle for a friend," Ron said, lifting his drink. "Friends?"

"Friends," Wanda lied, tapping his glass before tasting her cocktail.

"Excuse us for a moment," Pete said. He and Casey held hands as they walked away from the table.

"You have no idea how happy I am that you came here tonight," Ron said.

"Why is that?" Wanda asked. She took another sip of her amaretto sour.

"Let me show you," Ron said. "Come with me for a minute."

"I don't think so." Wanda scanned the room. "Matter of fact, I'm getting ready to leave," she said, slurping down the rest of her drink. At that point she was uncomfortable being around Ron because the club was nearly empty. As she stood, Ron grabbed her arm.

"I asked you nicely. Now I'm telling you—come with me," he said. "If you don't, you'll regret it."

Wanda snatched away. "Get the hell away from me, Ron," she ordered.

He flipped open his cell phone and showed the screen to Wanda.

Her blood began to boil. She couldn't believe her eyes as Ron played a video of the two of them making love. Wanda looked at him with disgust. "You dirty dog," she bellowed.

Ron chuckled. "Let's go. If you don't, I swear I'll post this video all over the Internet. Not only will Malcolm know your little secret, the whole world will. Keep in mind, this bit of information could affect your job, which will affect your livelihood. Need I go on? You and I both know how much you love money and luxuries."

Wanda lowered her head, defeated. She grabbed her purse, then reluctantly followed Ron upstairs, livid for being in such an awkward position.

Once at the ladies' restroom, he turned to face her. "This is where it began for us, and this is where it ends," he said. Ron pushed the door open and shoved Wanda inside.

Chapter 18

Kim smiled as Leon laced her neckline with warm kisses, then she moaned as tingles spiraled from the top of her head down to the soles of her feet. "Mmm—Good morning," she whispered, reaching out for him.

"Morning," Leon replied, removing her spaghetti-strapped top. He pressed his lips against her breasts and tasted her nipples before flirting with her belly button. Kim slept without panties so when he positioned himself on top of her, she welcomed him into her love zone. He entered her, engaging with slow, passionate strokes. As the intensity grew, their bodies moved together in a complementary rhythm. Kim held Leon tightly, until finally, she released a squeal that pitched louder by the second and left her trembling. Turned on by the excitement, Leon exploded with her. Afterward, Kim lay in his arms breathing heavily. *I can work with this,* she thought. *Thank you, Jesus.*

Minutes later, she glanced at the clock. "You missed Sunday School, Deacon Hardy," she told Leon.

He chuckled. "We'll make the eleven o'clock service," he replied.

"For the record, I loved that wake-up call," Kim said, following him into the bathroom. They showered, got dressed then grabbed their Bibles before heading off to church.

"How did you convince me to come back to this place?" Kim asked as Leon parked.

"Don't make it sound so bad. You're with me. I'll protect you," he said.

"I'm sure you will, but that's not my concern. I don't want to embarrass you by cursing out one of the members," Kim said.

Leon took her by the hand. "Don't anticipate the worst. Isn't it easier to have a positive attitude?"

"I guess, but I already know who I'm dealing with. If somebody crosses me, it's on," Kim said.

To her surprise, during the service the pastor made an announcement congratulating her and Leon on their marriage, presenting them as Mr. and Mrs. Hardy. He asked them both to stand. When he applauded, the congregation joined in.

Kim smiled and waved. As she scanned the sanctuary she noticed stares as sharp as knives and others appearing genuinely happy for her and Leon.

Finally, everyone took a seat and the pastor proceeded with the sermon, "I Am What I Am because He Is Who He Is." Through the message he used an eloquent analogy of a caterpillar metamorphosing into a butterfly, teaching that a person's body is not his own, but the temple of the Holy Spirit and how abiding by the spirit, God transforms people into a new creation.

After the service had ended, Kim was humored by Sister Mack's gathering with a clique of friends pretending to be in conversation to avoid her. Kim wasn't fazed. She couldn't have cared less about associating herself with who she considered perfectionist wannabes.

Moments later, Leon walked up, and she followed him toward the exit, engaging in small talk along the way. Once inside of the car he looked at her and smiled. "See, it wasn't so bad after all," he said, starting the engine.

"I was a little uncomfortable," Kim admitted, "but it's all good."

Leon leaned over and kissed her. "Thank you," he said. "You're my wife and I want you here."

"You're welcome," Kim replied, winking at him.

Back at the house, they changed clothes and sat down for dinner. After eating, Kim listened to Leon talk to his children on the telephone. She stood in the background waiting to hear him explain why he'd gotten remarried again. Instead, he handed the phone to her. She spoke with his daughter, Christie, for a few minutes and encouraged her and her brother, Brian, to visit the following weekend before giving the receiver back to Leon. She was happy Christie didn't lecture him as she had during every conversation since their marriage.

"I think you've done an excellent job explaining your needs to them," Kim said after he'd hung up. "Some kids, regardless of age, have a difficult time when a surviving parent moves on."

"I agree. My children and I established a closer relationship after their mother passed away. I think they understand life comes without guarantees. We're here one minute and gone the next."

"That is so true," Kim said.

"After my ex-wife died, they were my sole focus. Now it's time for me to live again," Leon said. "I believe it's taking a little more effort on Christie's part, but Brian accepts my decision without question."

Kim nodded. "Yes, you sat on the sideline of a social life for far too long. I'm honored to be the woman you chose to move forward with," she said.

Leon kissed the back of her hand. "I'm the lucky one," he said. "I take my role as a husband very seriously. Rest assured that your needs will be met."

Kim smiled. "Well, I'm new at the wife thing, but I'm going to give it my best shot. I believe from the bottom of my heart I'm where I'm supposed to be," she said.

"Which reminds me, what are you going to do about the condo?" Leon asked, diverting the conversation.

"Um, I spoke with the property manager. She told me I'll lose the security deposit because I'm breaking the lease. Can you believe we have to move all of that stuff again? I have until the end of the month," Kim said.

"Okay," Leon replied.

"Since we're on the subject, we need to discuss what furniture is a must-have for you. I'd like to redecorate and add my style to the house," Kim said.

"Go for it. I'm not attached to anything," Leon replied.

"Are you sure?"

"Yes, I'm positive. Do your thing," he insisted.

"Okay. Good. What do you think about having a garage sale?" Kim asked.

Leon shrugged. "Just tell me what you need me to do," he said.

"We'll wait until your children get here to see if they need anything. If not, I'll work it out," Kim said. "What now? Bills. Are your monthly bills and debt the same?"

"Yes. I'll show you where I keep everything," Leon said, leading Kim to his office. He had all of his statements stacked neatly according to the due date with each day highlighted on the calendar so he wouldn't forget anything.

"Where's the mortgage payment?" Kim asked.

"Mortgage? The house is paid in full," Leon replied. "Our monthly bills are the utilities, phones, and Internet."

"That's it? That's great, Leon. My debt hasn't changed. I have a Visa card with a three-thousand-dollar balance that I used to stay afloat before I sold the house," Kim said.

"Are you current on everything?" Leon asked.

"Yes. I just refinanced my truck. My credit is still pretty good," Kim said.

"I'll pay the household bills and wipe out your credit card debt. You can focus on erasing the lien for your truck. How does that sound?" Leon asked.

"Are you serious?" Kim questioned.

"Of course," Leon told her.

"Thank you," Kim said. "Oh, my God. This is great."

"We can't allow bills or debt to run our life. How we avoid it is staying on top of it," Leon pointed out.

"I agree. I don't ever want to end up in the position I just got out of. Being overextended is no joke. It was really stressful," Kim admitted.

Leon put his arm around her neck as they headed toward the den. After he sat on the sofa Kim laid with her head resting on his lap. At that moment she decided to turn in the money she'd found, realizing Leon sincerely had her back.

"What's going on with your niece?" she asked as he turned on the television. "Is she still with my ex-fiancé, Troy?"

"Unfortunately, yes. I imagine she's hanging onto that guy because of the kids," Leon said.

"Possibly. Do you think she needs any of the furniture we're about to get rid of?" Kim questioned.

"I'm not sure, but I can ask," Leon said.

Kim began to wonder how often they visited. *I hope I don't have to deal with Troy and his baby mama too often,* she thought.

Rather than drag on a conversation about Troy and Leon's niece, Kim focused on Leon. His financial responsibility was impressive. Her heart fluttered as she acknowledged his maturity and spiritual dedication. Romantically, Leon didn't compare to Darius, but Kim was satisfied. She felt he was the balance she needed in her life, despite their eleven-year age difference.

Moments later, Kim had tuned in to the *CSI Miami* episode Leon was watching. While the show was on a commercial she went into the bedroom to get her cell phone from her purse.

"Oh, Lord. What's wrong?" Kim wondered, noticing several missed calls from her friends.

Angel had made the most recent attempt to reach her, so she dialed her number.

"Hey, Kim. Did you get my messages?" she asked.

"No. What's wrong?" Kim questioned, detecting anxiety in her voice.

"I have some bad new," Angel began. "Wanda was arrested last night for attempted murder."

Chapter 19

Anger and hatred clogged Wanda's mind like a thick fog. She felt humiliated and helpless, distracted by her parents' divorce, being at odds with her mother, her father and grandmother's illness—all complicated by the endless drama with Ron. Now, she was incarcerated.

Wanda lay on her bunk, staring at the ceiling, trying to pull facts from her memory bank. She recalled the details of Casey's party until the point when Ron had shoved her into the women's bathroom. Next, she remembered waking up on the floor with a killer headache. Once she'd gathered the strength to move, she rolled over preparing to get up. Wanda paused, revisiting the moment she laid eyes on Sheila's limp body lying beside her in a puddle of blood. She screamed as loud as she could, hopping off the floor. As she went to cover her mouth, she realized her hands and clothes were stained, then she focused on the knife near her feet. Wanda stood in shock trying to recall what had happened, drawing a complete blank.

Finally, it dawned on her to go and get help. She hurried to the bathroom door, opening it just as two Chatham County police officers arrived.

"Freeze," one of them said with his gun drawn.

Wanda didn't move. She watched the other officer race toward Sheila, kneeling at her side, checking for a pulse. "She's alive," he said, then radioed dispatch, requesting an ambulance.

"What happened, ma'am?" the police standing next to Wanda asked.

"No comment," she replied.

"You're looking at some serious charges. If I were you, I'd cooperate," the officer said.

"I am cooperating. I choose not to comment without my attorney being present," Wanda said.

Moments later, she experienced the lowest point of her life. She was read the Miranda rights and handcuffed. She asked the officer to get her purse which was lying on the floor before being led outside and taken to the county jail.

Wanda was baffled. She had no recollection of stabbing Sheila and because the details weren't clear, her confusion created doubt. Wanda continued to brainstorm, grasping for any bit of information to shed light on a dark situation. "How can I defend myself without facts?" she questioned.

The more she thought about her predicament, the more frustrated she became. Wanda badgered herself beyond measure, unable to digest being in such an awful position. She could hear her friends pleading, attempting to reach her, advising she walk away from Ron, but she'd refused to listen. Now, with him holding a sex tape over her head, Wanda had suddenly gone from being on offense to defense—praying he wouldn't post the video online, ruining her already smeared reputation. At last, Wanda admitted she'd underestimated Ron, and her life wouldn't be the same as a result of it.

"How in the hell did Sheila end up at Casey's birthday party?" she questioned. "Who brought the knife? And why?"

Wanda sighed then massaged her temples, exhausted by reality. Lying helpless led her to reflect on mistakes she'd made in life. For the first time, Wanda genuinely wished she could redo some things. The moments of humility caused her mind to drift. She relived the childhood days of sitting in church listening to the choir sing. The song pulling on her heart string at that moment was "Trouble in My Way." As the lyrics played in her mind, she held onto the part about Jesus fixing it. Wanda knew he was the only one able to get her out of the tangled mess.

She thought about Kim and how she'd always harassed her about leaning on God whenever the going got tough. "This is serious though," she said, justifying her own needs. "Kim leans on Him for stupid stuff."

Later that day, instead of eating dinner, Wanda used the telephone. She made an unsuccessful attempt to reach Casey before calling Angel again. She gave Angel Casey's number to try her a little later.

"Still can't remember what happened between you and Sheila?" Angel asked.

"Nope. I'm clueless. That's why I'm trying to contact Casey. Maybe she can add insight that will trigger my memory. Question her for me, Angel," Wanda stressed. "I'll call you back, if not tonight, tomorrow morning to see if you've learned anything new. I need answers."

"Yeah, this is major. Do you know you're being held without a bond? I looked up your information on the jail's website," Angel said.

"That's not surprising. Attempted murder is a serious charge," Wanda replied. "Not to mention, being a Chatham County Courthouse employee lands me in a more complicated situation than normal. Because I'm familiar with the judges and staff, an adjudicator from a different circuit has to preside over my arraignment hearing."

"Really? How long does this take?" Angel asked.

"I have to be arraigned within seventy-two hours," Wanda replied.

"So you're stuck in jail?" Angel asked.

"Unfortunately. For a couple of days at least," Wanda replied.

"Wow. I don't know what to say, Wanda," Angel stated.

"It won't help. Just know I appreciate you accepting my calls and being here for me. I'm looking forward to meeting with Attorney Blair tomorrow. I'm hopeful that between him and my supervisor, things can be pushed forward pretty quickly," Wanda said.

"Did you call any of the other girls, yet?" Angel asked.

"Naw. I haven't spoken to my family either. I'm going to touch base with my dad after I hang up with you. He has a spare key so I'll ask him to get my car from the club and park it at his apartment before Ron or Pete has it towed. In the morning I'll make more calls and probably give Lynn a buzz. I'm wondering if there's anything

Chris can do to help me out. I'd hate to put him in a bad situation with his new job," Wanda said.

"I'm sure he'll keep tabs of whoever investigates your case. It would've been cool if he could've taken this assignment," Angel said.

"Yeah, his first case as a detective—guaranteed victory. Realistically, that won't happen. We're too familiar," Wanda replied. "I have to go now. I'll holla at you later."

"Okay. Hold yourself together. Everything will be fine," Angel said.

Wanda ended the call. After a conversation with her father, she returned to her cell. She had gone the entire day without eating, so she climbed onto her bunk hungry, irritated, and desperate. She couldn't imagine being locked up for a long period of time. After one day of confinement, she was already fed up with hearing jailhouse talk. She and her roommate, Shauna, discussed their charges, but for the most part she'd kept to herself.

By the next morning Wanda was starving. Instead of having breakfast, she reached out to her family. She talked briefly with her siblings, Tina and Tony, then her aunt Vera. Wanda asked about her grandmother's well-being and if she knew what was going on with her.

"No, she doesn't, but she's asking about you," Vera whispered. "Momma's not crazy. She knows you didn't come by. I reminded her that you'd gone to a party on Saturday night and suggested you were probably resting yesterday. I'm sure she'll inquire again today."

"Thanks. I'm almost certain my arraignment will be held tomorrow. Once my bond is set, I'll be good to go. I should be out by the end of the day. Tell Granny I'm not feeling well and don't want to visit her while I'm sick but I'll come by as soon as I can," Wanda said.

"Okay. Have you spoken to your mother?" Vera asked.

"Nope. I don't want to talk to her," Wanda replied.

"You really should, Wanda. She's your mom, and I know she's worried," Vera said.

"Tell her I'm fine. I have to go, Auntie," Wanda said.

An hour later, a guard escorted her to the designated room for a professional visit. Wanda was overcome by embarrassment when she made eye contact with her friend and attorney, Nathaniel Blair. She sat across from him wearing jailhouse attire with her hair brushed back, feeling vulnerable and insecure, but relieved and anxious to start the process to reclaim her freedom. "Hey," Wanda said, softly.

"Please explain," he replied once she was settled.

Wanda shrugged. Seeing his disappointment made it difficult for her to speak. Finally, she began revealing details of the night she was arrested.

"Do you recall seeing Sheila at all," Attorney Blair asked.

"No, I do not," Wanda replied, shaking her head.

"Okay. Is there anything else of significance you can tell me that'll help our investigation? Not necessarily at the party but maybe leading up to it? Did you and Sheila ever have an altercation?" Attorney Blair quizzed.

"No. Well, one day while I was at Ron's bingo hall she sat next to me asking personal questions, but other than that encounter, nothing. I realized then she must've suspected something was going on with Ron and me, but we never engaged in another conversation.

"As far as Ron goes, I continued to see him even after Sheila was reported missing. Everything remained great with our relationship until I found out that he snorts cocaine. On that same night, I overheard him tell his best friend, Pete, that Sheila wasn't getting his money. He also said something about doing what he had to do. I wasn't sure what that meant, but it didn't sound positive. Anyway, Pete tried to persuade Ron to give Sheila whatever she was due and move on, but he was adamant about her having nothing. At that point, I felt he could've been involved or responsible for her disappearance. I started trailing him to gather more information. Although I didn't learn much, I found out he owns a home in Hilton Head, South Carolina. I followed Ron to the house. I drove back the next day and saw Ron's cousin and employee Sonya there," Wanda continued.

Attorney Blair scribbled notes on a pad. "Do you believe he purchased the house for her? Or maybe she's renting it from him?"

"Well, what's odd to me is Ron regularly traveling to Hilton Head after leaving the bingo hall at two o'clock in the morning. He has a home right here in Savannah," Wanda said.

"Good observation," Attorney Blair stated.

"Thanks. I'd hate to think he has a fling with his cousin, but why else would he drive that distance at that hour?"

"I'll look into it. Pretty interesting," Attorney Blair said. "I had no idea you had all of this going on, Wanda."

"Trust me, I didn't intend to. It's possible that Ron set this whole thing up to get back at me. Our breakup was kinda messy," she replied.

"Has he hurt you?" Attorney Blair asked.

"No, but he's been stalking me and making threats," Wanda said. "I can only image where he is now or what his next move will be."

"Have you called the police to report his harassment?" Attorney Blair questioned.

"No. I haven't. I tried not to link Ron and me to avoid a situation like we're dealing with now. Me, being pulled into him and his wife's drama."

"Well, it didn't work. Police reports would've been very beneficial in painting a picture of this guy's character. Nevertheless, I have more insight so it's time to rock-and-roll. You'll be arraigned tomorrow afternoon, and I'll ask for a bond to be set. Instead of going through the normal court proceeding I've requested a video arraignment so you won't have to stand before your colleagues," Attorney Blair said. "Once we've gotten past this appearance, your preliminary hearing should be within the next couple of weeks."

"Thanks, Attorney Blair. Tell your bail bondsman friend Kenny to be prepared to get me out of here. I'm predicting a ridiculous bond amount, but I'm prepared to use my house as collateral," Wanda said.

"You're welcome. In the meantime, take it easy. and don't cause more problems for yourself," he encouraged.

"I don't want trouble. I want freedom," Wanda said.

"That's the spirit. I'll get to work on your case right away. It's heartbreaking seeing you in here," Attorney Blair admitted, packing his briefcase.

"Tell me about it," Wanda replied.

They both stood. Attorney Blair embraced Wanda, concluding their session.

Once back at her cell, she became dizzy. Wanda held onto the bed for stability.

"Are you okay?" her roommate asked, reaching out to her.

"Get off me," Wanda yelled, snatching away.

"Fine. Fall the hell out then. I was trying to help yo' stupid ass," Shauna snapped.

Wanda rolled her eyes, irritated. Once the spell had passed, she climbed onto her bunk, mumbling, "Oh, my God. I have to get out of this place."

"It's too late to call God, playa."

"Will you shut the hell up?" Wanda blurted.

"I don't think so. This is my house. I'll whoop yo' li'l ass up in here," Shauna threatened, standing and looking at Wanda with her arms out to the side.

"Talk is cheap. Do what you gotta do," Wanda replied sternly, returning her stare. In the back of her mind she hoped Shauna didn't initiate a fight. She was weaker than ever. Wanda's last meal was finger foods at Casey's birthday party on Saturday night.

She watched Shauna lose her aggressive stance, then sit on her own bunk. Wanda closed her eyes and exhaled.

Before long, lunchtime had rolled around. Wanda ended her fast, eating a tasteless serving of baked chicken with runny mashed potatoes and bland mixed veggies. Afterward, she hurried to the phone and called Angel to see if she'd contacted Casey.

"No. She's not answering the phone," Angel replied.

"Keep trying for me, please," Wanda told her. "She may have spent yesterday recouping from the party, but by today she should be back on schedule, but then again it is a Monday."

"Don't worry. Eventually, I'll catch up with her," Angel promised.

"Okay. Thanks, girl," Wanda said. She went on to tell Angel she'd be arraigned and bonding out of jail on the following day.

"Really? That's great, Wanda," she replied, excited.

"Will you come get me?" Wanda questioned.

"Of course," Angel replied. "Just let me know when."

"I will. I can't wait," Wanda said. "Once I'm released I can figure out which direction I'm headed in. I really, really need to speak with Casey."

"Like I said, I'll continue to call. When I catch up with her, I'll question her for you. What time does she get off from work?" Angel asked.

"Five o'clock. I have to go now, Angel," Wanda said.

"Okay. Hit me up later," she replied.

"Hit you up? No you ain't trying to be hip," Wanda teased.

She and Angel both laughed before ending the call.

The next day, Wanda listened to the prosecutor read the charge against her. The judge asked for her plea.

"Not guilty," Wanda said.

Attorney Blair argued her case. "This is Miss Boyd's first offense, your honor," he began. "She's employed at the Chatham County Courthouse and has ties to her community. She's always been a law-abiding citizen, therefore, I'm requesting a bond be set at this time, allowing my client's freedom until more evidence can be obtained to prove her innocence."

Wanda looked directly at the judge to signal strength and sincerity. Meanwhile, she said a silent prayer asking for God's favor. She anticipated a high bond but remained hopeful it wouldn't be a ridiculous and unobtainable amount.

The room fell quiet while the judge looked over his notes. His expression didn't say much so Wanda remained optimistic, wanting him to weigh the positive aspects of her life and rule leniently.

"Ma'am, you appear to be a very nice person with a favorable job and history, however, it's imperative for you to avoid situations such as this. Do you understand that?" he said.

Wanda nodded in agreement. "Yes, your honor, I do," she replied.

"Bond request is denied. The defendant shall remain in the county jail until the preliminary hearing. Court's adjourned."

Chapter 20

Kim filed folders and cleaned off her desk to pass time, then she sat thinking about Wanda, reflecting on her stay behind bars. She picked up the receiver and dialed Angel's number, curious if she'd learned anything new.

"I'm still waiting to hear from her," Angel said. "We talked yesterday, and she told me she'd go to court this afternoon and bond out by tonight."

"She'll call," Kim said. Let me know when you leave to go and pick her up."

"I will. What's up with you?" Angel asked.

"Nothing much. I'm waiting on five o'clock so I can get out of here. Do you miss working?" Kim asked Angel, resting against the back of her chair.

"Sometimes, but for the most part I'm enjoying my son. It's discounted, but what I do around the house and taking care of him, it's a full-time job."

"I heard that. Leon's kids were supposed to drive over on Friday, but something came up. Now, they're planning to come the following weekend," Kim said.

"Are you looking forward to the visit? How does it feel being a thirty-year-old with adult stepchildren?" Angel asked.

"Great. I didn't have to raise them," Kim said, giggling. "If they were any younger I'm not sure this relationship would've worked. Taking on someone else's children is a bit much."

"I guess so, especially if you don't have any of your own," Angel replied.

"That's what I'm talking about. So, has Wanda mentioned going back to work, taking a leave of absence, or what?" Kim asked, changing the subject.

"I can't say. Honestly, we haven't discussed her job," Angel said. "Right now, she's focused on being released. I do believe she'll take a couple of days off. Maybe she'll return on Monday."

"Jail was embarrassing for me, but it has to be totally humiliating for Wanda considering she's somewhat a part of the judicial system," Kim said.

"I imagine so, but Wanda has thick skin. She'll be fine," Angel replied. "I can't wait until she gets out so we can discuss this situation."

"Yeah. Attempted murder is not a small crime. If Sheila dies, Wanda will be facing murder charges," Kim added.

As soon as those words escaped her lips a knot formed in the pit of Kim's stomach so tight she could hardly breathe. She had issues with Wanda, but she loved her. The thought of Wanda serving prison time for murder was frightening.

After ending the call with Angel, Kim gathered her things and clocked out. She couldn't help but giggle, visualizing Wanda being neat and prissy in a place that stripped every ounce of pride away.

During the drive, Kim stopped by the police department. She sat in her truck for thirty minutes thinking of things she could do with the cash in Darius' briefcase. In the end she made the right choice by giving the money to authorities, with the exception of what she'd taken to pay on her car loan, making good on the lie she'd told her husband. Then she repented for her sin.

Once at home, Kim read the note Leon had left on the kitchen counter saying he'd be back from church no later than nine-thirty. She threw the piece of paper into the trash then flipped through the envelopes of mail. Next, she continued into her bedroom, changing into a pair of shorts and a T-shirt, then she returned to the kitchen. After washing her hands, she removed the cover from the glass pan sitting on top of the stove. She prepared a small serving of lasagna and ate it along with a tossed salad, a side of broccoli, and she drank a glass of water.

Thirty minutes later, Kim made her way into the spare bedroom. Since Leon's children had rescheduled their trip, she and Leon had agreed to move forward with rearranging the house. Instead of waiting until the weekend and being overwhelmed with so many things to do, Kim decided to accomplish something every evening after work. Her job was to prep the area she wanted painted by removing photos and art from the walls.

By the time Leon made it home, Kim had finished both of the guest bedrooms, the master bedroom and the office. She greeted him with a hug and kiss, then showed off her work.

"Very good. I'll start painting first thing tomorrow morning," he said.

"Great. Are you ready to eat?" Kim asked.

"Sure. Just a bowl of salad, please," Leon requested.

While Kim was in the kitchen, he washed his hands in the hall bathroom.

"At this pace, we may have all of the painting done by Friday. If so, we can move this furniture out into the garage, then on Saturday we can bring in my things from storage so I can decorate," Kim said as they settled at the dinner table.

Leon agreed.

The appliances and flooring in the kitchen and baths had already been updated, and the carpet was less than a year old, so Kim was satisfied with that. She just wanted the décor to reflect her style and appeal.

Around ten o'clock, Kim's phone rang. It was Angel calling to initiate a four-line connection with her friends. Kim dialed Michelle, and Michelle connected Lynn.

"I didn't hear from Wanda, y'all," Angel said, starting the conversation. "She was supposed to call me to come and pick her up tonight."

"Hold on for a sec," Lynn said. "I'll call Chris. He'll find out what's going on for us."

The girls remained on the line while she contacted Chris and gave instructions to research Wanda's status, then she resumed the discussion with her friends. "I'm so pissed off at Wanda," Lynn fussed. "All she had to do was tell Chris about Ron and let the authorities handle him."

"We're talking about Wanda, Lynn. This may be a lesson learned for her. Jail is no joke," Kim stated.

"What freaks me out is Ron reminds me of Angel's psycho ex-boyfriend, Mike. We all know how his harassment landed her badly beaten and in the hospital," Michelle said.

Everyone agreed.

"Actually, I believe Ron is more dangerous that Mike," Lynn commented. "The more I talk about it, the madder I get. Wanda knows better."

"Yeah, but it's her call. There's no need of you beating yourself up about this, Lynn. I hate she ended up behind bars, too, but now that she has, the only thing we can do for her is be supportive," Kim continued.

"Maybe this will be her wake-up call," Angel said.

"Hold on, y'all. Chris is calling me back," Lynn said.

The girls listened in the background, learning Wanda had indeed gone to court earlier that afternoon and the judge had denied her bond request.

"Oh, my God," Michelle said, surprised at the outcome. "Angel, did she mention remembering anything else about the night she was arrested?"

"No—"

"I'm back," Lynn interrupted. "Did y'all hear that? Wanda has to sit in jail."

"We did," Michelle replied, speaking for everyone.

"This is not good. Apparently, things aren't leaning her way," Lynn said, concerned.

"Wow. Now, I understand why Wanda didn't call me. She's probably depressed," Angel said.

"That's an understatement. What do y'all think happened that night?" Kim inquired.

"I'm willing to bet, Ron used Casey to befriend Wanda in a plot against her. I wouldn't put it past either of them. Think about it, Casey's party was the perfect place for everything to go down. Wanda was alone, with none of us around and she was drinking," Lynn said.

"Well, we all know she has nothing to gain from Sheila's demise," Michelle said.

"Exactly. This could've been Ron's payback for Wanda breaking up with him. Or maybe something happened that she didn't tell us about," Lynn suggested.

"Do you really think he'd take it that far?" Michelle quizzed. "He had to. I refuse to believe Wanda's that stupid. My girl is innocent until proven guilty."

"Of course she is. Now her attorney has to prove it," Lynn said. "A seasoned prosecutor can easily make it appear as if she committed the crime, even if she didn't. We already know what the accusation will be—in a fatal attraction gone wrong, a woman attacks her lover's wife in an angry rage."

"True. Why can't Wanda remember the encounter?" Michelle asked.

"I don't know, but she seems to think Casey may have beneficial information. The problem is we haven't been able to reach her," Angel said.

"That's typical behavior for someone who's done something wrong. She's not answering on purpose—a sign of guilt if you ask me," Lynn said. "I knew she was bad news from the very beginning. I could feel it in my bones. If only Wanda would've listened when we tried to warn her."

"I can't figure out how Casey won her over so easily," Michelle said.

"Probably because she was supposedly helping Wanda spy on Ron," Angel said.

"All along she was setting her up. If our speculation is true, Casey is dirty," Lynn blurted.

"I'm not surprised by this. Casey knew Ron first. Of course her loyalty is with him," Michelle added. "Not to mention, she's dating his best friend. Hello?"

"I don't know. We can't prematurely convict Casey. Eventually, the truth will come out," Angel said.

"If Wanda finds out Casey has crossed her, she's gonna kill her," Michelle said

"No, she's not," Kim replied. "Wanda is a smart girl. The bottom line is she made her bed hard, now she has to lie in it."

Chapter 21

Wanda left the courtroom irate, furious at the judge's decision to deny her bond request. She couldn't believe how he'd discounted her work ethic and spotless record and kept her in jail. There was nothing anyone could say to calm her anger. She'd even refused to speak with Attorney Blair after the hearing was over. Wanda returned to her cell and had been there ever since, annoyed by the confinement and lack of control. She didn't know where Ron was or what he was up to, and it was driving her crazy.

Unable to channel her emotions in a positive direction, Wanda declined Attorney Blair's visits, and she didn't call friends or family members for days. The officers employed at the jail who knew her personally recommended she eat and make contact with the outside world to help her cope. Wanda refused to listen. She remained depressed, feeling the weight of the world on her shoulders.

On Sunday morning, she watched the guards lead inmates to the chapel for church. Wanda chose not to participate but felt awkward the entire time the ladies, including her cell mate, were gone. After the service was over she couldn't help but notice despite their issues and sentences, the women seemed joyful.

As the day went on, Wanda thought long and hard about how she'd taken life into her own hands, rejecting counsel or spiritual guidance. During dinner, while alone in the cell, she came to her senses. Wanda finally broke down and released tears she'd held back for years. Crying uncontrollably, she begged for God's forgiveness and direction, and asked him to replace her rage with humbleness.

Once settled, Wanda reflected on the night of her arrest, immediately zooming in on Casey. "I have to talk to her," she said, convinced Casey had helpful information. She went on to consider the possibility of Ron using Casey to conspire against her. "Maybe that's why she hasn't answered our phone calls," Wanda concluded.

Although aware of the possibility, she found it hard to believe Casey would deceive her, which landed her back at square one and the most frustrating aspect of the whole situation—a lack of physical evidence. Without proof, Wanda's thoughts and theories were futile. Ron's guilt of any crime had to be proven in court beyond a reasonable doubt.

Being back at that realization caused Wanda's mind to drift. She thought of her grandmother and said a silent prayer for her continued recovery. Wanda hadn't seen her in more than a week.

As the night grew old, she found it nearly impossible to fall asleep. The next thing she knew it was breakfast time. When lunch rolled around, Wanda attempted to reach Casey once again. She was shocked when she picked up and accepted the charges for her call. "Hey, Casey. Where have you been, girl? I've been trying to reach you," she began.

"Hi, Wanda," Casey replied. "How are you?"

"Not good. I have so many questions I'm not sure where to start. I'm being held in jail without a bond. Can you tell me anything, Casey? Do you know what happened between Sheila and me?" Wanda asked, almost desperate.

"No. After Pete and I left you and Ron sitting at the table, I never made it back inside the club," Casey said.

"Why? I came to the party to hang out with you, Casey. How could you leave me there, especially with Ron?" Wanda asked.

"I didn't mean to abandon you, Wanda, I promise," Casey said. "Pete and I left because he needed to get something out of the car. We ended up standing outside talking until some ladies ran toward us saying someone had a gun. Pete made me get in the car and told me to leave, so I got in and drove off. It all happened so fast, I didn't have time to think."

"Why didn't you call me?" Wanda questioned.

"I did. Check your voicemail. I left messages on your phone," Casey replied. "The only reason I was okay with being out in the parking lot in the first place was to give you and Ron an opportunity to talk. Because you were being sociable, I figured you'd pull some information out of him."

Wanda held the phone in silence. She didn't know what to believe. Casey's explanation sounded believable, but there was too much at stake for her to be persuaded so easily. "Do you realize I'm in jail for attempted murder?" she asked. "I don't even remember seeing Sheila, let alone stabbing her."

"I don't know what to tell you, Wanda," Casey replied.

"Did you know about the sex tape?" she questioned.

"Sex tape?" Casey repeated. "Of who, you and Ron?"

"Yes. After you and Pete left, he showed it to me and threatened to post the video on the Internet if I didn't go upstairs with him. I remember him pushing me inside the ladies' bathroom. When I woke up, Sheila was lying next to me, unconscious with stab wounds."

"I am so sorry, Wanda. I wish I could help you. I really do. I can put money on your books for canteen," Casey said.

"I don't need no damn money," Wanda exclaimed, frustrated. "Look—Casey, did you invite Sheila to your party? Yes or no?"

"No, I didn't, Wanda. I swear. When I learned about this situation, I assumed she showed up while you and Ron were talking and took things the wrong way," Casey said.

"How did she find out about your party? How did she know where to come, Casey?" Wanda asked.

"I can't answer that, Wanda," she replied.

"Damn. I was hoping to get answers from you. It's mind boggling that you weren't at your own party when all of this went down. You should've been there, Casey. Please don't let me find out you had something to do with this," Wanda warned.

"I'm telling you the truth, Wanda," Casey insisted.

"Where's Ron? Have you seen him," Wanda asked.

"No, I haven't. I don't know where he is," Casey replied.

Wanda shook her head. "Alright. Well, I have to go," she said.

"Take care. Call me anytime," Casey replied.

Wanda hung up the phone. She returned to her cell with more questions than prior to the conversation. She continued to brainstorm, trying to sort out the confusion. At four o'clock, the guard interrupted her thoughts. "Your attorney is here to see you," he said.

She stood and walked toward the door. Wanda was escorted to the professional room. She entered and sat across from Attorney Blair, lowering her head, embarrassed at how she'd acted. "Hi," she said softly.

"Hello. I wasn't sure you'd come," he replied.

"I need to apologize to you," Wanda said, making eye contact with him. "I admit, the way I've carried on is despicable. With this being my first charge, coupled with my history, record, and employment, I just knew the judge would set a bond."

"I was hoping he would. It's really unfortunate," Attorney Blair said.

"To say the least," Wanda replied. "Anyway, I'm sorry about how I've acted. Next time, I'll try to control my emotions better and not shut down."

Attorney Blair nodded, extending papers in her direction. One was a police report and the other a 911 transcript. "Read these," he said.

"Okay." Wanda took the documents. After reading them she looked at him, confused. "None of this makes sense to me. The transcript contradicts the police report," she said, shaking her head. "According to the transcript, the call reporting the incident was made from a location other than the club. The police report states the victim made the call, giving her exact position inside of the building. Something ain't right."

"No, it isn't," Attorney Blair agreed with a smirk. "We'll get our bond next time."

Wanda smiled. "Are you serious?"

"I believe so. When you followed Ron upstairs that night, do you recall seeing any familiar faces," he asked.

Wanda sat quietly for a few seconds. "No, I don't," she replied. "The only thing on my mind was that video. I wasn't paying attention to anything else."

"Okay. Well, I have some good news and bad news," Attorney Blair said.

"Bad news, first," Wanda replied.

"Your fingerprints were on the weapon. The good news is the discrepancies in these reports. I'll dissect them further to create reasonable doubt so you can go home. Also, thanks for the tip about the house in Hilton Head. We're working with the authorities in South Carolina. From what I've heard, they're gathering some incriminating evidence. We'll have to link it together and prove it's relevant to our case. We'll talk more about that later.

"Also, I've requested the bond hearing in conjunction with your preliminary hearing. Don't worry, Wanda. Just hang in there and sit it out. This should be over soon," Attorney Blair said.

"I will," Wanda assured him. Having hope and believing in the judicial system gave her the boost she needed. She tried not to be overly confident regarding the preliminary hearing or being released from jail as she had during the arraignment proceeding.

After concluding the meeting, Wanda returned to her cell. Later that evening, she reached out to her parents and siblings. They expressed how great it was hearing her voice and told Wanda to communicate with them so they'd know she was okay. She agreed. She also suggested they didn't bother to visit, insisting she'd be back at home soon. The truth was Wanda's pride wouldn't allow her to let them see her incarcerated. Her friends, on the other hand, were welcome. Wanda had a closeness with them that she shared with no one else—not even her relatives.

The next morning she was fortunate enough to speak with her grandmother during a conversation with her aunt Vera. Wanda couldn't bring herself to say why she hadn't been by, but assured her granny she'd visit as soon as possible. She blew her kisses before speaking with Vera again. Shortly after, they ended the call.

Later that day, Wanda chatted with Lynn and Angel on three-way. They told her how Malcolm had been calling everyone, trying to find out information about what was going on.

"What are y'all telling him?" she questioned.

"He needs to talk to you," Angel said.

"Great. I'll deal with Malcolm when I get home," Wanda said. Before ending the call, she told Angel and Lynn the visitation hours for that evening and asked if they'd come and see her. When they arrived, at first, she felt awkward talking to them from behind the large glass barrier, but she quickly got over it. She was happy to have them there.

"I finally talked to Casey," Wanda told Angel.

"You did?" she replied, excited. "What did she say? Did she help you out any?"

"Hell naw. Not really," Wanda complained. Lynn reached for the phone as she shared with Angel what Casey had told her.

"How well do you know Casey? I don't trust her, Wanda," Lynn confessed when she got a chance to talk.

"I have my doubts. I believe she's sincere, but at the same time I'm a little cautious," Wanda admitted.

"Do you know she has a criminal record for prostitution?" Lynn questioned.

"What? Casey? You're kidding me. I don't believe that," Wanda said.

Lynn and Angel both nodded.

"The Internet can be a valuable resource," Lynn said.

"How recently was she arrested?" Wanda asked.

"Almost four years ago," Lynn replied.

"That surprises me. How in the hell did she end up with Pete? He is so not her type. She appears to care a lot about him though. They are always together," Wanda said.

"Yeah, because he's trying to keep her off the streets," Lynn teased.

The girls shared a hearty laugh.

"That's dirty," Wanda replied. "Come to think of it, when we first started hanging out, she did say God had brought her a long way. Maybe that's what she was talking about."

"Probably so," Lynn agreed. "Your girl is a ho."

Chapter 22

Kim challenged Leon to a game of checkers while waiting for his children to arrive. When the doorbell finally rang, she followed him and watched as he greeted them with a big hug and a kiss. Kim embraced Brian and Christie as they walked inside. "How was the drive?" she asked.

"Long," Christie replied, scanning the room.

"Well I'm glad you had a safe trip. Are you hungry?" Leon questioned.

"No, sir. We're good. We ate a couple of hours ago," Brian said.

"What happened to our furniture?" Christie blurted with a frown.

"Oh, it's in the garage, sweetie. Kim stored it there just in case you or your brother wanted to keep any of it," Leon said.

"Dad, why are you getting rid of Mama's stuff," Christie complained.

Kim didn't comment. She looked at Leon, waiting to see how he would handle the situation.

"Calm down, Christie," Brian told her.

"Shut up, Brian," she replied.

"Hey, that's enough. Sit down," Leon ordered. "Let's talk."

Once everyone was seated, Kim listened as he continued.

"Both of you know how very much I love you and how much I loved your mother," Leon began. "Unfortunately, she's no longer with us. Although she'll always be a part of our life, I'm married to Kim now. I realize this may be difficult and will take time getting used to, but I ask that you try."

"It's okay, Dad. I'm happy you've found someone," Brian said, looking at Kim.

"Thank you," she said.

"I appreciate your blessings, son," Leon added.

Christie didn't comment.

"I can help you sort through the furniture, Christie. Whatever you decide to keep we can store until you graduate college or bring it to Florida, whichever you'd like," Kim said softly, attempting to engage her in the conversation.

She understood Christie was dealing with real emotions and was possibly unsure of how to handle her feelings. She hoped by being kind to her, she'd open up, making the situation easier for all of them.

"Deal?" Kim asked moments later.

Christie shrugged. She still didn't respond.

"I'm not trying to take your mother's place or get rid of her memories. I'm simply making this house my home," Kim told her.

"This isn't your home. It's my mom and dad's," Christie replied.

Leon took her by the hand. "Christie—"

"It's okay. Let her talk, honey," Kim told him.

"I don't approve of her staying here, Dad," Christie said.

"Sweetheart, where is all of this coming from? I thought you liked Kim," Leon said.

"No, sir. I was glad when you broke it off the first time. Well, I don't have anything against her," Christie clarified, "but you shouldn't have gotten married."

"Why?" Leon questioned.

"She's just not right for you," Christie said.

"Can you give me a reason, so I can better understand your thoughts?" he asked.

The room fell quiet. Minutes later, Kim left the room, allowing them time and space to talk without her being there.

An hour later, Leon joined her in their bedroom. "Are you okay?" he asked, sitting on the edge of the bed where Kim was lying.

"Yes, I'm fine," she replied.

Leon kissed her on the forehead. "I love you, Kim," he said, stroking her hair.

"I love you, too. Don't worry about me, Leon. I don't want you to feel torn between your wife and daughter. In time, all of this confusion will be a memory. I really don't believe Christie can hold a grudge against me for long. I haven't done anything to her."

"Yeah, but in the meantime I have to balance being a good husband and father," Leon said.

"You are. Don't stress over it. While she's here I can step aside—for now anyway," Kim said. "Our marriage is a big deal for her, and I understand that. Let's give her some time and not be forceful. It'll come together for her soon."

Leon nodded. "Will you join us? We're going to play softball on the Nintendo Wii," he said.

"Sure," Kim replied. She allowed him to help her out of bed. Leon hugged her really tight and they shared a short kiss.

"My niece Faye and Troy are bringing the girls over," he said as they left the room. "Christie agreed to baby-sit the kids tonight. Is that okay with you?"

Kim stopped in her tracks. "How did Faye know Christie was here?" she questioned.

"They keep in touch. Whenever she comes to town, Faye usually visits," Leon replied.

"Now I understand why Christie has a problem with our marriage. Perhaps Faye is feeding her misinformation, giving her a bad impression of me because of my past relationship with Troy," Kim said.

"That's possible. I was thinking the same thing. I also recall Christie being fond of you. I figured marriage versus dating made the difference. In either case, we must find a way to get along," Leon said.

Kim continued walking and he followed. *Wow. Dealing with Leon's church members is bad enough. Now, his daughter and niece are tripping. I really hope I can handle this situation like a Christian. One thing's for sure, I refuse to allow any of them to disrespect me,* she thought.

Once in the den, Kim played softball with Leon and his kids until Faye and Troy showed up with their children.

"I got it," Christie said, hopping off the sofa when the doorbell rang.

When they entered the room, Brian put the game on pause. Kim and Leon spoke, and Leon offered Troy and Faye a drink. They both accepted.

"I'll fix them, Dad," Christie said.

Kim watched Troy and Faye's daughters trail behind her. When Troy sat down, she caught a glimpse of a tattoo along the right side of his neck that spelled out Faye in cursive letters. She found it hard to believe he'd branded his body with her name.

"I heard you got married, Uncle Leon," Faye announced.

"Yes, I did," he replied.

"Congratulations," Faye said. "To you, too, Kim."

"Thanks. So, when's the big day for you?" Kim asked, putting her and Troy on the spot. She laughed within at both of their awkward expressions and how they looked at each other, Kim assumed, waiting for the other to respond. They never did.

"Where are y'all going tonight?" Leon asked, diffusing the awkward moment.

"Most likely we'll do dinner and a movie," Faye replied as Christie returned with two glasses of lemonade.

"Excuse me for a minute," Kim said, standing. She went into the kitchen just to get away from the soap opera. As she wiped down the countertop, Troy approached her from behind, pressing his manhood against her backside.

"What are you doing?" Kim asked, facing him.

"I'm returning the glass. Why did you marry that man? You know good and well Leon is too old for you," he scolded, taking her completely by surprise.

"You've got nerve," Kim said. "I'd rather have an older, faithful man than a young liar and cheater."

She walked past him, headed toward the den. Faye was leaving when she returned. Minutes later, Kim noticed Troy and Faye standing in the doorway, exchanging words. Shortly after, they were gone.

The next day, Troy stayed in the car while Faye came inside to get their daughters. Once they'd left, Leon drove Brian and Christie to the Oglethorpe Mall. Kim stayed at home, enjoying the peace and quiet.

Later that night, they all had dinner at the Olive Garden and ended up at the Galaxy Lanes Bowling Alley. Kim noticed as the evening went on how the barrier between her and Christie had began to crumble. While having dinner they talked about education. Kim applauded Christie's passion and anticipation of entering the medical field. While bowling, the ladies challenged the men, so Kim and Christie were a team. They encouraged each other to do well and celebrated together. Kim grew confident that before long they'd move beyond their differences.

The next morning, she and Leon went to church, allowing Brian and Christie to sleep in so they'd be rested for their drive back to Tallahassee. When they returned home Brian and Christie were packed up and ready for the road trip.

"I've decided what furniture I'd like to keep. Let me show you," Christie said to Kim.

"Okay," she replied, following her to the garage.

Christie pointed out almost everything.

Kim was surprised she elected to keep so much, but didn't question her. "Would you like for us to put it in storage or bring it to Florida?"

"I need to leave everything here for now," Christie said.

That isn't an option, Kim thought. "Why do you want the furniture to stay in the garage? If you chose not to take it to Florida we can put it in storage."

"No, I'd rather not. I haven't made up my mind if I'm staying in Tallahassee or moving back to Savannah. Once I decide, I'll let you know."

Kim sighed. "So in the meantime, you'll inconvenience me," she said underneath her breath. She understood forcing Christie to choose one of her options would only cause problems. She didn't want that. Progress had been made over the weekend and she refused to go backwards.

Why is this such a big deal anyway? Kim asked herself. *Am I being unreasonable? In my effort to obtain respect, am I being too territorial of what she's always known to be her parents' house?*

Suddenly Kim realized maybe she wasn't being fair. She'd already caused friction by replacing the furniture. Considering what she believed to be Christie's perspective allowed her to be more understanding.

"Whenever you make up your mind, let us know. The furniture will be here until you decide," Kim said.

"Okay. Cool," Christie replied.

"So, are you still going out with the same young man?" Kim asked, changing the subject.

"No. He cheated on me with one of my friends," Christie replied.

"She wasn't a friend if she slept with your boyfriend. Don't worry. You have plenty of time for love. Continue to focus on your education," Kim suggested.

"It's all good," Christie replied. "I've moved on."

"Are you in a relationship now?" Kim questioned.

"Yes, I am," Christie said, smiling.

"Who's the lucky guy?" Kim asked her.

"It's not a guy, it's a girl," she replied.

"Oh." Kim was shocked by her response. She didn't know what to say, so she said nothing.

"Don't tell my dad. I already know he won't approve," Christie said, breaking a brief silence.

"How long have you been a lesbian?" Kim asked, trying not to be judgmental.

"Well, it's complicated. I'm not really gay," Christie replied. "I'm just bisexual."

Kim wore a confused expression, thinking, *What the hell?*

Chapter 23

On Wednesday afternoon, Wanda listened as the prosecuting attorney portrayed her as a manipulative home wrecker who in a jealous rage attacked her lover's wife. "Your honor, the facts are clear," he said. "The defendant cornered Mrs. Phelps in the ladies' restroom and stabbed her multiple times with the intent of leaving her there to die. The defendant was fleeing the scene when the police arrived."

"I object," Attorney Blair said in Wanda's defense.

"Overruled," the judge responded.

"Your honor, we have a woman lying in the hospital fighting for her life. The defendant's fingerprints are on the weapon used in this vicious attack. Exhibit A," the prosecutor said, providing a copy of the knife receipt from Walmart addressed to Wanda's home. "The defendant purchased the weapon used in the attack online with a gift card via the Internet a week before she committed the crime. It's clear, her actions were premeditated. I have no further comments," the prosecutor continued.

"They are such liars. I didn't buy a knife from Walmart," Wanda complained.

Attorney Blair stood. "Your honor, my client is innocent. I have reason to believe there's been foul play in this case. The nine-one-one transcript indicates the call reporting this incident was initiated from a location different than the club where the crime was committed. The police report states the victim made the call, giving her exact position inside of the building, claiming to be hurt and unable to move before being disconnected. How could that be, your honor? It doesn't make sense. I'll tell you my theory: The victim didn't make the call. The victim didn't even know the call had been made. She showed up at the party with a knife and intentions to harm my client. In a fight for her life, my client knocked the weapon from the victim's hand and they struggled to recover it. It's clear that my client acted in self-defense."

"I object," the prosecutor blurted.

"Overruled," the judge said.

"Now, back to the nine-one-one call," Attorney Blair continued. "Your honor, we have technological proof that the call reporting this accident came from a phone booth down the street from the site where this incident actually occurred. This tells me, neither the victim nor the defendant could've made the call because they both were at the club. Therefore, it's evident, we have ourselves a witness. Someone saw the victim attack my client that night and did the right thing, notifying the police. We intend to find that person. As far as the Walmart receipt goes, the victim—or Mr. Phelps for that matter—could've ordered the weapon online and had it delivered to my client's address, then intercepted the package on the day it was delivered. Again, my client is innocent. I rest my case."

Wanda cheered within at her attorney's performance. She'd learned a few things, questioned some, but was overall impressed at how he'd pulled his defense together. In her opinion, he'd definitely created reasonable doubt.

"Your honor, I'd like to request a bond be set at this time," Attorney Blair said.

The room fell quiet as the judge rifled through papers. "The bond is set at one million dollars," he said minutes later without hesitation.

Wanda wasn't fazed by the amount. She didn't care what she had to do or who she needed to borrow money from, she was going home. She exhaled a big sigh of relief. "Oh, thank God. Thank you," she said, embracing Attorney Blair.

After court was adjourned, they did the necessary paperwork with the bail bondsmen for Wanda to be released. While waiting for the process to go through the system, she grew excited about regaining her freedom and finding evidence to clear her name.

Finally, around six o'clock the guard called for Wanda. She jumped up, rushing toward the doors. "You've made bail," he said.

"Yes," Wanda sang.

She was taken to a room where she received her belongings. She inventoried the clothing and jewelry she'd worn the night of the arrest and checked her purse making sure her wallet, keys, and cell phone were inside.

After getting dressed, she was free to go. When Wanda saw Angel, tears filled her eyes. She rushed towards her and gave Angel the tightest squeeze ever. "You have no idea how happy I am to see you," Wanda said.

Angel smiled. "I'm glad to see you, too. I didn't think the process would take so long," she said.

"Neither did I, but thank God it's finally over. I'm never going back in there. Now, I need something to eat. I'm hungry as hell," Wanda said.

"You sure do. You've lost weight," Angel said.

"If you only knew," Wanda replied.

"Where would you like to eat? My treat," Angel said.

"No, I'll have something quick. Wendy's is fine. Then take me to get my car so I can visit my granny. I can't wait to see her," Wanda said.

"What time do you think you'll be at home?" Angel asked.

"Probably around nine o'clock tonight. Visiting hours are over at eight, and since I'm getting ready to eat, I'll take Aunt Vera for carry-out before dropping her off at Momma's."

"Okay. Well, I'll meet you at your house," Angel said.

Wanda watched her initiate a call and listened as Angel told Lynn she'd been released from jail, but was going to spend time with her grandmother before heading home. "We can all meet up at Wanda's place around nine o'clock. Call Kim and Michelle and tell them what's going on and see if they'll come over, too," Angel said.

"I like your nerve. Who are you to coordinate a gathering at my house?" she asked. "Let me say hi to Lynn."

After hanging up, Wanda handed the phone to Angel. "Did I tell you I finally talked to Casey?" she asked.

"Yeah," Angel replied.

"I'm going to her job in the morning. I need to talk with her face-to-face so I can detect if she's lying to me. If she stutters or changes her story, I'm telling you, I'm gonna bust her in the face. I ain't lying," Wanda said.

"Girl, you'd better stop tripping. You just got out of lock up. The police wouldn't hesitate to throw your behind back in jail," Angel said.

"Oh, well that's not an option," Wanda replied as Angel whipped into the Wendy's drive-thru. Wanda placed her order and Angel paid the cashier. After receiving the meal she drove off.

Once at the Royals apartment complex, Wanda directed Angel to her father's unit and noticed his car wasn't there. "Darn. My dad's not at home. I wanted to surprise him," she said, gathering her things.

"You'll catch up with him later. Tell Granny hi and give her a kiss for me" Angel said.

"I will. I really appreciate you," Wanda replied, giving her another quick squeeze. "I'll see you guys later tonight."

Wanda got out and unlocked her car. After starting the engine, she took her phone out of her purse and connected it to the charger and plugged it in.

Refocused, she waved to Angel before driving off. Once her BlackBerry was charged, she checked the voicemail. Her mailbox was full. She retrieved five messages from Casey and the rest from frantic friends and family members trying to confirm or find out what was going on.

Casey did call, Wanda acknowledged, *but was she just covering up her tracks? Was it all a part of a plan?*

Wanda wasn't sure what to think. Reflecting on the ordeal she'd endured saddened her. It all seemed like a dream, but she knew the nightmare was reality. Wanda reminded herself that the worst was over, but she felt a strong sense of urgency to learn the truth. She dialed Casey's number and left a voicemail asking her to call at her earliest convenience, then she contacted her parents and sibling, telling them she'd been released and her plans for the evening. They all wanted to get together but Wanda insisted she'd be more up for visits in a couple of days.

Ten minutes later, she smiled, noticing the sparkle in her grandmother's eyes when she entered the room. "Hi, Granny," Wanda said, hugging and kissing her. "I'm so happy to see you. Are you feeling okay today?"

Her grandmother nodded, then shook a pointed finger. "You need to get down on your knees and pray," she said, clearly.

Wanda lowered her head, convicted and defeated. She felt horrible. "Okay, Granny. I will," she promised moments later, looking up at her.

Granny nodded again and extended her left arm. Wanda accepted the embrace.

"This is all a misunderstanding," she whispered, trying to make light of the situation, wondering how her granny knew what was going on. She didn't want her to worry because the doctor had already informed them of the likelihood she'd have more strokes.

Wanda sat next to the bed holding her grandmother's hand, rubbing the back of it. *I would never forgive myself if I caused her condition to get worse,* she thought.

"Hey, sweetie," Vera said, entering the room, startling her.

"Hey, Auntie," Wanda replied, standing.

"How are you? Come here," Vera ordered with open arms.

Wanda walked over to her, and they stood holding each other tightly. "I'll be fine," Wanda finally said. "How did Granny find out what happened?"

"She saw it on the news," Vera said.

"I really hoped she didn't find out about this," Wanda said.

"So did I, but the story came on while she was watching. What happened? Do you want to talk about it?" Vera asked.

Wanda shrugged. "Long story short, I went to the party and everything was fine until the end of the night when Ron showed me an inappropriate video of the two of us—one he'd recorded without my consent," Wanda noted. "He threatened to put it on the Internet if I didn't cooperate with him, so I did. He led me upstairs and shoved me in the bathroom. When I woke up, his wife was lying beside me in a pool of blood."

"When you woke up?" Vera questioned.

"Yes," Wanda replied.

"He spiked your drink," Vera stated.

"Why do you say that?" she asked.

"Why else would you lose your memory?" Vera asked. "Do you have a good attorney?"

"One of the best," Wanda said. "I think I remember stumbling when Ron pushed me. I could've hit my head."

"That's possible. I'm here if you need me," Vera assured her.

Wanda returned to her grandmother's bedside and held her hand until visitation was over. She kissed her and before leaving told her she'd be back the next day.

While dropping Vera off, Wanda was surprised to see her mother hurry out of the front door and rush over to her car.

"Are you okay?" she asked, opening the car door and embracing her.

"I'm fine, Momma," Wanda replied.

"Come in for a few minutes," Joyce insisted.

"No thanks. I may stay a little longer tomorrow," Wanda replied with no plan of following through.

"Are you sure?" Joyce asked.

"I am," Wanda said. "I'll talk to y'all later."

Soon after, she drove off. During the ride home, Wanda imagined how the night would've played out had she and her mother's relationship been the same as prior to her mother dating Michael. She figured not only would she have stayed overnight, she would've hung around for longer. Wanda loved having her father's protection and her mother to confide in. Now, she felt alone as far as her immediate family was concerned. Although she had a close relationship with Tina and Tony, Wanda didn't share much personal information with them.

As Wanda approached her house, she noticed Angel, Lynn, and Michelle's cars parked along the street. She whipped inside the garage then greeted her friends with hugs, thanking them for being there.

"I don't wanna hear nothing about my weight, heifers," she threatened.

"I was just about to ask if I needed to order a pizza or something," Lynn teased. "Are they serving crack in jail these days?"

They all laughed.

"Suck it up, Wanda. All that smack you're known for talking, you shouldn't have a sensitive bone in your body," Michelle added.

"Okay, but that's enough already," she replied.

Once inside, the four of them sat around the table, and questions poured in. The girls were puzzled to learn Wanda didn't have many answers. She relived the night of her arrest again and shared Attorney Blair's theory. "Have y'all been watching the news? What are the reporters saying?" Wanda asked.

"They're basically blaming you," Lynn said. "The speculation is Sheila returned to Savannah and confronted you about the affair with Ron, and you attacked her."

Wanda shook her head. "That is such a lie. I know it didn't go down like that," she said.

"Sheila's mom gave a touching interview. She's convinced you're innocent," Angel told Wanda. "Through heartache and tears, that woman was firm on her belief Ron was the perpetrator of her daughter's assault."

"Yes, she did," Lynn agreed. "She said it's been hell tolerating him as an in-law and labeled Ron verbally, emotionally, and physically abusive. She pointed out Sheila had left him several times, but he'd always persuaded her to come back home. That reminds me: Chris told me last night Sheila's family had enforced the restraining order she'd filed against Ron the day before her disappearance. The family has also requested around-the-clock security, fearing her safety."

"Man, this sounds like something out of the movies," Michelle said, joining the discussion. "Sheila filed a restraining order? The day before she vanished? Hmm. If Ron had something to do with her disappearance, why would she reappear all of a sudden?"

"That's a good question," Angel said.

"How in the hell did I allow myself to be entangled in this kind of drama? This is some serious shit—by far, the worst mistake of my life," Wanda admitted.

"You'll be okay. I wish there was more we could do to help," Lynn said.

"You're doing it now. Listening," Wanda replied. "I appreciate all of you."

"That's what friends are for," Lynn said.

Angel and Michelle smiled, nodding.

"What really gets me is how cool and calm Ron is. I've been involved with this man for more than two years and have only experienced fun and excitement until recently. It's amazing how people can hide their dark side," Wanda said.

"Has it been that long?" Michelle asked. "That's enough time to develop some real feelings, Wanda. Are you in love with Ron?"

"Hell naw. I love the way he made me feel," she said, "but that's about it."

"Would you do it all over again?" Angel asked.

"No. Honestly, I don't regret the relationship. I regret the ending. It wasn't worth the trouble. I thought about that a lot while I was in jail. Malcolm should've stepped up to the plate sooner," Wanda said.

"Have you spoken to him yet?" Angel quizzed.

"Nope. I know he's upset with me," Wanda confessed.

"I have to ask: Have you learned anything from this ordeal?" Lynn questioned.

"Yeah. There's some rough-looking females in jail," she said, masking her true feelings of total humiliation.

Moments later, the telephone rang. She looked at the ID. "Oh, hell, speak of the devil—it's Malcolm y'all," Wanda said. After the third ring, she took a deep breath, then answered.

"You have some explaining to do," Malcolm said in a somewhat calm tone.

"I have company. Can I call you later?" Wanda asked.

"What's going on, Wanda?" Malcolm insisted.

"I don't want to get into it over the phone. Just know my life has been turned upside down," she replied. "We'll discuss it later."

"No. We're going to talk right now. Either on this phone or I'm coming over," Malcolm yelled.

The girls were shocked to hear Malcolm's response blast through the receiver.

Wanda yanked the phone from her ear. "Okay. Come on over," she replied, then she put the phone on the base.

"Poor Malcolm," Angel said. "I know the heartache he's about to experience."

"Yeah, this is bad. I've never heard Malcolm raise his voice at you, Wanda," Michelle said.

"Well, I guess the sooner we have this conversation, the better," she replied.

"Do you need one of us to hang around, just in case things get out of hand?" Lynn asked.

"No, I'll be fine. Malcolm wouldn't touch me if his life depended on it. He might blow a fuse by keeping his own rage bottled up on the inside, but that's about it."

"Remember, we're a phone call away. Don't be too cocky with Malcolm," Lynn warned Wanda.

"I won't," she replied.

As they stood in the foyer, the doorbell rang. The girls looked at one another and Wanda peeked through the peephole. It's Kim," she said, then opened the door.

"Hey. Where are y'all going?" she asked, hugging Wanda.

"Home," Lynn said, stepping out onto the porch. "Malcolm is on his way over."

"Oh. Well, I just left Bible study. I wanted to stop by and check on you, Wanda. You lost weight," Kim said.

"If you were being fed slop for breakfast, lunch, and dinner, you'd lose weight, too," Wanda replied, not admitting depression also contributed to her weight loss.

"Was it that bad?" Kim questioned.

"Yep. Where's Leon?" Wanda asked as they strolled along the walkway.

"He went to the house. We drove separately so I could come and hang out with you guys. Angel told me everybody would be here," Kim said.

"Thanks for coming over, but we'll have to get together a little later. There's Malcolm, y'all," Wanda whispered, watching him drive up.

The girls said their good-byes and greeted him on the way out.

"Hi," Wanda said when they made eye contact.

"What's up?" Malcolm replied, walking past her to go inside.

Wanda remained on the porch, waving to her friends as they drove off. Once inside the house she found Malcolm waiting in the living room.

"Come have a seat," he said.

"I'll stand," Wanda replied. "There's no easy way to say what I have to say, so I won't beat around the bush."

"I'm all ears," Malcolm told her.

"Do you remember the issue you and I had prior to our conversation about it?" Wanda asked.

"I do," Malcolm replied.

"That night you asked me if I was seeing someone else and I told you no. What I didn't share was the fact that I had just ended an affair," Wanda confessed.

"Oh, really?" Malcolm questioned, looking at her attentively.

"Yes, but I've been faithful to you since. The guy I was involved with has caused a lot of problems for me. First of all, he's a married man. In addition to that, his wife was the woman reported missing several months back. You remember her because it was all over the news. Well, when I broke it off with him—by the way his name is Ron—he began stalking me. Apparently, his wife returned from the unknown the night I went to Casey's birthday party and it appears that I stabbed her. She's in the hospital fighting for her life, and I've been charged with her attempted murder," Wanda said.

"What in the hell were you thinking? This is humiliating," Malcolm fussed.

"I wasn't thinking," Wanda admitted. "I tried to expose Ron because I believe he was connected to his wife's disappearance, then all of a sudden she shows up and I'm the criminal. I think Ron is behind the scheme, but I can't figure out how he pulled it off and I have no proof. I apologize, Malcolm. My intentions were to get past this mess without you finding out about it."

"By being deceitful?" he asked.

"You can use the word *deceit* but I like *concerned* better. I didn't want to hurt you," Wanda said.

"How considerate," Malcolm stated sarcastically.

"I'm serious. Normally a man who's been cheated on has a harder time loving and trusting again. I really don't want that for you, Malcolm. You're a great person. I'll be the first to admit I was wrong for allowing my physical needs to control my actions. Once I presented the problem to you effectively, you addressed it. I offer you a sincere apology. Will you forgive me?"

Malcolm didn't respond. Instead he approached Wanda and without saying a word landed a slap across her face that brought tears to her eyes.

Chapter 24

Kim walked through the door calling out for Leon. Have you seen my phone?" she asked.

"It's here, in the den," he replied.

"Oh good. Thanks," Kim said, entering the room. She picked up her cell and looked at the screen, noticing four missed calls.

"Did you go by Wanda's?" Leon asked.

"Yes, but everyone was leaving when I got there. Malcolm stopped by," Kim said.

"So, how is she? Leon questioned.

"Wanda's fine. It looks like she's lost at least ten pounds, but other than that she's okay," Kim continued.

"Great. She was probably stressing herself and skipping meals. That'll do it," Leon said.

"I agree. I'll check on her in a little while. Malcolm didn't look too happy when he showed up," Kim stated.

She dialed her voicemail. Kim was surprised to hear a message from a literary agent. The soft-spoken, proper woman introduced herself as Natalie Maxwell. She offered encouraging remarks about the article featured in *Keepin' It Real* magazine and praised Kim for sharing such a powerful story. Then she expressed her interest in putting Kim's life on paper and connecting her with major publishing houses. The agent assured her of the potential of landing a nice book deal and ended the call reciting her telephone number.

Taken aback, Kim remembered her own thoughts of writing. She jotted down the agent's name and number before hanging up, then she told Leon about the offer. "I didn't tell you this, but before I sold my house I read through some of my journals, and the idea of doing an autobiography actually crossed my mind. This could be a unique opportunity for me—having someone already in the literacy circle representing my work. Wow. I started journaling when I was a teenager. To see my words in print would be awesome," Kim continued, excited. "What do you think?"

"I don't know. There's no need to commit to anything, but if you're truly interested, call her back and see where the conversation goes," Leon suggested.

Kim smiled. "I just might," she said.

Minutes later, she sat distracted by other desires, trying to put them into perspective. What stuck with her the most was being a mother. Kim knew writing a book would be a lot of work and more difficult with a child.

"What's on your mind?" Leon asked, breaking her trance.

Kim sighed. "Having a baby," she said. "I wonder how this writing idea will affect our plans."

"What's more important?" Leon questioned.

Kim shrugged. "Getting pregnant was. If we're going to have a kid, I think now is the best time in regards to our chances of birthing a healthy baby. You're getting old," she teased.

Leon laughed. "You're right," he agreed.

"At the same time, I'm considering how hard it'll be working on a book while caring for a newborn," Kim said.

"Nothing comes easy," Leon said. "Don't underestimate yourself. You're not pregnant yet, so the first thing is conceiving, then you'll carry the baby for nine months. What you don't complete before he or she is born you can finish afterward."

"It's so simple, huh?" Kim asked.

"No, I didn't say that," Leon replied. "All I ask is that you think this idea through before investing a lot of time and energy. I'll support you with the book and the baby."

"I like that," Kim said, smiling. "I tell you, I have to get use to having a real man—someone who truly has my back."

"Yes, you do," Leon agreed. "Just be sure this is what you want. Completing a book is only one part of being an author. Once it's complete, you'll have to get the book sold. As long as we have a plan, I'm with you."

"You're right. I have a lot to think about," Kim replied.

She kissed Leon, then left the room. Within minutes, she returned carrying her purse. She emptied her birth control pill pack and flushed the pills down the toilet. "It's on," Kim said, dropping the pack in the trash.

Leon smiled. "I gotcha," he replied.

"There's no time like the present," she said, pulling him from his seat. Once in their bedroom, Leon laid back and Kim straddled him, taking his bottom lip between hers. She stirred her hips seductively, pressing against his manhood, then opened his bathrobe and laced his body with wet kisses.

Finally, Kim lowered herself onto Leon's erection. Their mouths engaged hungrily, and he squeezed her buttocks as she orchestrated a dynamic rhythm. Kim held Leon tightly, increasing speed and intensity until she trembled.

Leon moaned, squirming underneath her.

Breathing heavily, Kim leaned back, looking into his eyes. "I love you," she said.

"I love you, too," he replied.

After a warm shower, Kim cuddled in bed and dialed Wanda's number.

"Hey, Kim. What's up?" Wanda answered in a somber tone.

"Nothing much. I just wanted to check on you. How did the talk with Malcolm go? He didn't look happy," Kim said.

"It wasn't good. Our relationship is over," Wanda said.

"Are you serious?" Kim questioned.

"Yep. I told him about Ron and apologized, but he wasn't trying to hear it. You're not going to believe this—Malcolm slapped me and has lived to tell about it," Wanda said.

"What? No, not Malcolm," Kim replied.

"Yes, Malcolm. He shocked the hell out of me. I allowed him to get away with it though. I feel I deserved to be smacked. I've slipped up on so many levels, it's ridiculous," Wanda said.

"Are you going to be okay?" Kim asked.

"I'll be fine. Thanks. Did you hear that? Somebody's at my house," Wanda said.

"Call the police. Are they inside?" Kim asked.

"No, at the front door. Hold on," Wanda whispered. "Just stay on the phone until I see who it is. It better not be Ron."

"Oh, Lord, I hope not," Kim said, concerned for her friend.

"Girl, it's my parents. What are they doing here this time of night? Together at that," Wanda questioned. "I'll talk to you later, Kim."

"Okay. Take care. I love you, Wanda."

"Love you, too," she said.

Kim hung up the telephone, relieved someone was there with Wanda. She was hopeful her mom and dad would stay overnight because no one knew what Ron was up to. *And Malcolm,* Kim thought. *I can't believe he hit her. He had to be pissed.*

Chapter 25

The next morning, Wanda woke up and looked around the room, grateful for her parents' companionship. She was bundled on the loveseat, her mom on the sofa and her dad had slept in the recliner, but he was already in the kitchen preparing breakfast. Wanda could smell the delicious aroma.

Instead of joining him, she reflected on their conversations the night before, beginning with her mother's confession of bringing her father along so she'd let her in. Sadness overcame Wanda. *How in the world did we get here?* she wondered. She actually appreciated Joyce for making herself available. She was no longer confident in her motherly instincts.

They also talked about working through their differences and remaining connected as a family. Wanda was receptive, but she knew she couldn't tolerate Michael, and her mother expecting her to, was unacceptable. Her father was ignorant to her and Michael's past, and she agreed to teamwork, for his sake.

Lastly, before going to sleep, Wanda shared details of her and Ron's relationship. Confiding in her parents made her feel better, but seemed awkward considering their pending divorce. Infidelity and loyalty weren't easy discussions to have.

"Good morning," Joyce said, startling Wanda.

"Morning," she replied.

"Did you sleep well?' Joyce asked.

"Yes, ma'am. What about you?" Wanda questioned, sitting up.

"Yes. Is it okay for us to come back tonight? I don't think it's a good idea for you to be alone," Joyce said.

"Sure. I'll be fine, but if it'll make you feel better to be here, you're welcomed to stay," Wanda replied.

"Great. It's a new day, Wanda. I'm hoping you and I can move forward," Joyce said.

"Momma, I refuse to live in a fairytale. Are you still dating Michael?" she asked.

"This isn't about him, Wanda," Joyce replied.

"Yes, it is. My position is the same," she stated.

"I thought I heard voices," Travis said, entering the room. "Breakfast is ready."

"Thanks, Dad," Wanda said, smiling.

She went in her room to freshen up while her mother used the guest bath. After eating, her parents prepared to leave. Wanda gave them a hug on the way out.

"Are those news reporters?" she questioned, noticing a van and car parked on the street.

"I believe so. What in the hell are they doing? I'll go talk to them," Travis said.

"No, Dad. We don't need negative press," Wanda said. "Come back inside."

"You're right, but I'll stick around until you leave and make sure they don't bother you," Travis said.

"I'm fine. If I need you, I promise to call," Wanda assured him.

He shook his head. "No. Get dressed. We're leaving together," he insisted.

"Dad, listen. My car is in the garage. They can't get to me. When I back out, if anybody gets in my way, I'll run them over."

"No, that's not the way to handle it, Wanda. You two are too much alike," Joyce said.

"Wanda, I'm waiting," Travis said.

"Okay, Dad," she replied.

She put on a pair of Apple Bottom jeans with a matching T-shirt and white tennis shoes. She packed a small overnight bag just in case she decided to stay away from home to avoid being harassed by reporters.

After her parents went out of the front door, Wanda locked it then set the security alarm before entering the garage. Once settled in her car, she pressed the remote door opener, then she fought to be respectable as she backed out of her driveway, attempting to shield her face. Although her natural impulse was vulgarity, Wanda was mindful of the image she needed to portray in the public eye. As the media swarmed her car, shouting questions, reality set in. Wanda felt powerless. Her once cocky persona had been suppressed by total humiliation. She no longer displayed confidence or boldness, but feared a loss of respect from the people who knew and loved her. The news reporters were escalating the shame by violating her privacy and plastering her face across television screens.

Wanda couldn't believe it when one of the vehicles began to follow her. She had intended to go straight to Casey's job, but diverted to Lynn's day care, and her dad followed. Wanda parked, then she told him her plan before going inside the building. Next, she confided in Lynn.

Lynn gave Wanda a cap and vest from her office. Minutes later, Wanda left through the rear door, driving away in Lynn's SUV. She giggled as she added distance between her and the reporters still sitting out front.

Before long, she'd arrived at Casey's job, unannounced, searching for answers. Casey looked like she'd seen a ghost when Wanda walked through the door.

"Let's take a walk," she said.

"O-okay. Cover me," Casey told a coworker.

Once outside Wanda put her hands on her hips. "What's up, Casey? Anything new to tell me?" she asked.

"No. Why? What happened?" Casey questioned.

"Well, it appears we have a witness who could testify on my behalf. I'm just giving you an opportunity to tell me anything you know. I'd really hate to find out from someone else something you could have told me," Wanda said. "I'm really trying to give you the benefit of the doubt."

"Sorry, Wanda. I can't help you," Casey replied.

"Are you sure?" Wanda asked, staring into her eyes.

Casey nodded.

Wanda continued to stare until Casey turned her head. "Look, I like you, Casey. I really do," she said, "but I promise you, if I learn you've betrayed me, I am going to beat the hell out of you. Do you hear me? You'd better understand the words coming out of my mouth."

"Wanda," Casey said, grabbing her hand.

"What?" she replied, snatching away, hoping she'd scared Casey enough to come clean.

"I'm sorry, okay. I wish I could help you. I really do. Just know I would never, ever side with Ron or participate in a scheme against you. You're my girl, Wanda, and I like you, too. Ron is my fiancé's best friend. He's nothing to me," Casey said.

Wanda lowered her head. She was unsure of Casey's loyalty, but her believability was undeniable. "Okay. All I have is your word, Casey."

"Yes, you do have my word, Wanda," she replied. "Again, I didn't betray you. I had nothing to do with what happened that night."

Wanda took note of her sincere expression. "I'll let you get back to work," she said.

Just as they walked off, Pete showed up.

"Hey, sweetie. What's up, Wanda?" he said.

"Nothing," Wanda replied, detecting what appeared to be a problem with Casey and Pete. She noticed Casey didn't smile or give him the warm greeting she normally did.

"When did you get out?" Pete questioned.

"Y'all take care," Wanda said, stepping away, ignoring the question.

Once inside the truck, she sat there for a few seconds, baffled. Before driving off, she called Angel to share the details of her morning. When she mentioned the media, Angel relayed the information to Derrick, and they persuaded her to stay with them until the story died down. Wanda accepted the offer. She knew encountering the press daily wouldn't end up good for her, not to mention seeing Pete was Ron's confirmation that she'd been released.

Wanda gave her parents a courtesy call informing them of where she'd be staying. Joyce pleaded with her to come to her house, but Wanda chose to avoid being in a bad predicament. Her father offered her his place as well, but she respectfully declined, assuring him she'd selected her best option to avoid harassment from the press.

Later that evening, Wanda assisted Angel in storing leftovers after dinner. "I really appreciate you and Derrick letting me crash here," she said.

"Girl, please. It's no problem. I'm glad you're here. Oh, I talked to Lynn. Tomorrow is supposed to be our girls' night out. Since you're keeping a low profile, she invited us to come over for dinner on Saturday to hang out and celebrate Chris' promotion," Angel said.

"Yeah, I'd love that," Wanda replied.

"Great. I'll let her know. In the meantime, she's supposed to get with Kim and Michelle."

"Okay," Wanda said.

Once finished in the kitchen, Angel went to her bedroom, and Wanda settled in the guest room. After gathering her toiletries, she showered then lay in bed, absorbing her day. Suddenly, the criminal court judge Patrick crossed her mind. Wanda wanted to call but didn't know what she'd say. "What the heck?" she figured. She picked up her BlackBerry and dialed his number. "I'm innocent," she said when Patrick answered.

"Hey, you. How's it going, Wanda?" he asked.

"Pretty good," she replied, "and how are you?"

"I'm fine. I have a question, then we're going to change the subject because I shouldn't be talking to you about this," Patrick said.

"Of course," Wanda agreed.

"The information you shared with me, was that your situation or a friend's as you led me to believe?" Patrick asked.

"Mine," Wanda replied without hesitation. "I went to the party I told you about and ended up in jail, and it's because of the scenario I gave."

"So, what's happening now? Are you okay?" Patrick asked.

"Considering the circumstances, I'm fine. Malcolm walked out on me last night. That's the latest," Wanda said.

"Really? I was just thinking to advise you to have someone around when you two sat down to talk. I've seen too many instances where domestic disputes are a result of similar events," Patrick said.

"Too late, but I'm all right. I can handle Malcolm. I was the more dominant one in our relationship anyway," Wanda said.

"Oh, no. What's happening to our men?" Patrick questioned.

"You already know. You deal with them every day," Wanda said.

"True. Well, I'm used to the criminals, but the high number of feminine men is something new," Patrick replied.

Wanda laughed. "You've got that right, but let me clarify: Malcolm is a masculine guy, but he's just easygoing. My personality overshadows his, that's all."

"Would you date a dominate man?" Patrick said.

"Yes, I would. I'm bossy, but girly. I love men who know how to take charge. That was the main thing missing with Malcolm and me," Wanda confessed.

"Would you have allowed him to lead—or should I say, were you prepared to follow?" Patrick asked.

"I believe so," Wanda stated. "Malcolm stood his ground a few times, and I liked it. The problem was, over the years he'd accepted my ways and adapted to them. I thought it was cute at first, but as we got older I believe I would've appreciated him more had he demanded respect and not let me run over him."

"How long did you two date?" Patrick inquired.

"For nine years."

"He's invested a lot of time. He may come back," Patrick said.

"I doubt it, but I can't focus on Malcolm now. I need to get my life back on track," Wanda said.

"Touch base with me every now and then. I'd like to know how everything's going for you," Patrick said.

"I will. Take care," Wanda replied.

She hung up the phone with a smile. She liked talking to Patrick. He was clearly a smart guy and down to earth.

As Wanda lay awake, her mind jumped from one thing to the next, until she eventually fell asleep, then all of a sudden she woke up in a cold sweat. Wanda sat up and looked around the dark room, focusing on the red numbers displayed on the clock. It was 3:15 A.M. She remained in bed, but her nightmare wouldn't allow her to sleep.

During breakfast, she told Angel she'd dreamed about Sheila.

"Do you remember what happened?" Angel asked.

"Yes. It's really weird. For some reason I was at her and Ron's house. Sheila and I were fighting and she tried to stab me with a kitchen knife, but I stabbed her. How ironic, right? Anyway, as I called out for Ron, there was a knock at the door and a voice shouted it was the Savannah Police Department responding to a disturbance.

"I panicked. While an officer pleaded for someone to let him in, I scrambled around the room trying to find a place to hide and ended up squeezing in the kitchen cabinet. Eventually they kicked the door down. I heard somebody request an ambulance and things got really hectic. Then finally, everything had calmed down and I thought the police were leaving when out of nowhere there was a loud thump that startled me. I jumped, banging one pot against another and that did it. The cabinet doors flew open and the police pulled me out onto the floor. I was handcuffed and taken to jail. The emotions were real," Wanda said.

"I'll bet," Angel replied. "That's weird. It's amazing how sometimes when we're dealing with a situation and it's on our mind, we dream about it."

"I know and I hate that," Wanda said. "I couldn't go back to sleep afterward. What gets me is had we not been at Ron's house, I could've mistaken the dream as my memory."

"I agree with Michelle. This craziness seems like something out of a movie," Angel said.

"It really does," Wanda replied.

She napped that afternoon then lounged around, and before she knew it the day was over.

The next morning, Wanda was rejuvenated. She gleamed with excitement during the drive to visit her grandmother—at home. Her aunt Vera answered the door. Wanda entered, thrilled to see her granny relaxing in her favorite recliner next to the window, wearing a bright smile.

"Hi there," Wanda said, walking toward her.

"Good morning," she replied.

"How does it feel to be back at home?" Wanda asked.

"Great," her granny said.

Wanda shared a heartfelt hug and kiss, then she sat down, taking note of her progress. When she heard movement in the back of the house, she looked at Vera. "Is someone else here?" she questioned.

"Yes. It's your mother," Vera replied.

Wanda was shocked and her expression showed it. "How did that happen?" she wondered.

Moments later, Joyce appeared. "Good morning, Wanda. Can I talk to you for a second?" she asked.

"Hello. Sure," Wanda replied. She followed Joyce into the spare bedroom.

"First, I have to say how much I enjoyed being with you and your father the other night. I miss those times," Joyce said with a faint smile. "Since then, Travis and my relationship has changed for the better. He's serious about being connected with his family and I appreciate that. Matter of fact, his sincerity has helped me see what a horrible mistake I've made by allowing a small disagreement to derail my marriage."

Wanda's heart melted when she saw tears roll from her mother's eyes. "Momma," was all she could say.

"I'm okay. I just wanted to let you know I'm not with Michael anymore, and I'm ready to fight for my family—and my husband," Joyce said.

Remembering her father saying he wouldn't take her mother back added more sympathy to the situation. "Do you really think you and Dad can work this out?" Wanda asked.

"I do, because he still loves me," Joyce said. "While you were in jail, we talked a lot, and he came over quite often to check on me. Now that you're home, we still talk every day. After more than thirty years of marriage and dating, I know that man better than anyone. I want him at home with me, where he belongs."

"Good for you, Momma. I hope everything works out the way you want," Wanda said.

"Thank you. When your father moves back in we'll have a family dinner to celebrate," Joyce said.

"Sounds great," Wanda replied.

She was shocked by her mother's confidence and more so that her father would entertain reuniting with her. For some reason, Wanda was persuaded. Her father's actions, considering what Joyce had said, weren't aligning with his character. "I don't know," Wanda concluded. "Love is a powerful thing."

Chapter 26

During the drive to Lynn's house, Kim thought about Leon's daughter, Christie, and the secret she'd asked her to keep from her father. She was perplexed by her statement of being bisexual, not gay, trying to pinpoint the difference.

Kim shook her head.

"What are you thinking about?" Leon asked.

"Oh, Christie just crossed my mind. Can you believe she's keeping all of that furniture?" Kim asked, trying to lead the conversation in a different direction without lying about her thoughts.

He laughed. "Yeah. I'm sure it's her way of holding on to her mother."

"I agree," Kim said as her phone rang.

It was Lynn. "We're parking in your driveway," she said.

As they approached the door, Chris opened it with smile. "Congratulations," Kim and Leon said.

"Thank you, thank you," he replied. "Come on in."

After greeting everyone, Leon joined the guys and Kim consumed herself with Derrick Jr. and Li'l Kelvin. She didn't see them often, but when she did she fell in love all over again. Kim hoped to become pregnant soon.

Kelvin walked up and took a seat next to her. "How've you been, Kim?" he asked.

"I'm fine, Kelvin. How about you? I already know you're enjoying this little guy," she said, looking down at his son cradled in her arms.

"I really am. I need to ask you something. By any chance, have you or the girls noticed anything different about Michelle lately?" he inquired.

Kim was puzzled by his question. "No. Is something wrong?" she asked.

"I'm afraid my wife may have some issues she's not dealing with," Kelvin said.

"What are you talking about?" Kim asked, feeling uneasy.

"Well, she's been acting strange, and I'm wondering if anyone else has picked up on it. My son is almost two months old and I don't think she's bonded with him yet. The way you're cuddling with him, she never does that."

Kim thought back and realized she hadn't seen Michelle hold the baby much, but she didn't comment.

"Hopefully, if there is a problem she'll confide in us soon," Kelvin said.

"I understand your concern, and I'll definitely keep an eye out," Kim promised.

As soon as he walked away, Wanda arrived.

"Just the person I wanna see," Chris said.

"Don't start with me, Chris. Hey, family," Wanda sang.

Everyone said hello.

"Come on, have a seat. Talk to me, Wanda," Chris said.

"All I can say is I messed up," she confessed.

"Yeah, but I want to hear in your words what went down that night," Chris insisted.

"Okay." Once again, Wanda relived the story as she knew it.

"Casey's still not talking?" Angel asked.

"Nope. I spoke to her a couple of days ago," Wanda said.

"I don't trust that girl," Lynn said.

"I think you're being too hard on her, Lynn. This time I talked to Casey in person, and she seems sincere. I'm not an easy person to deceive," Wanda said.

"The truth will come out eventually," Chris assured them.

"What I can't figure out is how Sheila appeared out of the blue showing up at her birthday party. Another thing that baffles me is your memory loss. In my opinion, that's what really links Casey to this equation," Lynn said.

"Yeah. Everything was normal until I followed Ron upstairs," Wanda said.

"It appears he led you into the ladies' room on purpose. And what do you know? That's where the crime to take place," Angel said.

"You could be right. Casey told me Ron had asked her on several occasions if I'd be there."

"That was her way of getting your confirmation, Wanda. Why can't you accept the facts and admit that chick set you up. Instead of impersonating a private investigator, you should've hired one."

They shared a brief laugh.

"Do you recall seeing anyone upstairs?" Chris questioned.

Wanda shook her head. "After Ron pushed me in the bathroom, everything went blank."

"Did you hit your head on something?" he asked.

"I could have. I think I remember stumbling," Wanda said. "When I woke up, my whole body hurt. I may have hit my head. It was sore."

"Or maybe Ron put something in your drink and that's why you can't remember," Kim speculated.

"It happens all the time," Lynn cosigned.

"That's what my aunt Vera said," Wanda replied.

"Sitting here taking all of this in, it's clear to me Ron had to have a scheme. Stuff like this doesn't just happen," Michelle said, dipping in the conversation.

"Exactly—and Casey knew about it. With that said, what is a logical reason to ensure you have no memory of what occurred, Wanda?" Lynn questioned.

"I didn't stab Sheila."

"Now that we're past that," Lynn said, "who do you think is behind this mess?"

"Ron."

"My thoughts exactly. Still, there are a lot of unanswered questions," Lynn continued. "For starters, how involved were Casey and Pete? How did Sheila get to the club if Ron was already there? Hypothetically speaking, if it was a coincidence that she showed up and her intentions were to get back with him, why'd she come with a knife? Finally, if you and Sheila did get into an altercation, why didn't someone break it up?"

"I believe dude had a premeditated plot to frame you for murdering his wife, Wanda," Derrick said.

"Casey is the reason the plan worked," Lynn slid in. "She made sure you were at that party."

"Wait a minute. If Ron really wanted Sheila dead, why isn't she? With me being knocked out, I'm sure he had ample time to execute his plan," Wanda said.

"That's a good point. Unless he thought he'd finished the job. Wanda, I'm with Derrick. You were the scapegoat in a murder plot. There's no way Ron would go through so much trouble to frame you for attempted murder," Chris said.

"Damn. Is it that serious? Would he go that far?" Wanda wondered.

"Yes. Now we have to prove it," Chris said.

"That dirty bastard. I can't believe him. I wish I could kill his ass and get away with it. Is there anything I can do about the video?" Wanda asked.

"Did you mention it to Attorney Blair?" Chris asked.

"Yes—"

"That brings up another interesting point. Ron made the tape because he knew he needed something to threaten you with to get you upstairs," Lynn said.

Wanda sighed. "Discussing different motives with her friends opened her mind to the endless possibilities of what took place that night. She couldn't believe Ron had played her. She questioned Casey's part in his plan, and Sheila proved to be another mystery.

"Let's take a break from this and eat," Lynn said.

Everyone agreed, then gathered around the dining room table. After Leon said grace, Chris restarted the conversation. "Wanda, I have one last question: Why did you treat our boy Malcolm like that? He's a good dude. Malcolm would never disrespect you like this guy."

"I know, Chris. I wish I could turn back the hands of time. Ron is an asshole. He walked in my life and left that shit all messed up."

Laughter filled the room.

"Excuse me, Leon," Wanda said.

He nodded.

"Wanda, you know better. You should've told us someone was stalking you," Derrick said and the other men agreed.

"I couldn't. I didn't want y'all to know I was cheating on Malcolm," she replied.

"Do you think Malcolm will take you back?" Michelle asked.

"No. It's time for us to move on. I believe our courtship lasted as long as it did because of our friendship."

"What gets me about the whole ordeal is the secrecy. Y'all ladies kept this quiet. It makes me wonder. Is there anything I need know?" Chris asked Lynn.

"Yeah, I used your Visa card to book a trip to Italy."

"What? You didn't tell me you were planning a trip? How much was the ticket?" Chris continued.

"Look at your statement. Is there anything I need to know?" Lynn asked.

"Yeah. I'm canceling that damn trip. What are you going to Italy for? Your man is right here," Chris said, pounding his chest.

Lynn rolled her eyes at him. "Don't fool yourself," she said.

"What? What did you just say to me?" Chris asked, standing.

Lynn ignored him.

"That's what I thought. Now had you purchased two tickets to Hawaii, that would've been a conversation worth having," Chris said, smiling.

"Sit your behind down, Chris," Lynn ordered.

"Okay, baby. Did you really book a trip to Italy?" he asked.

"Naw. You were looking for entertainment, so—"

"In other words, you know better. End of conversation. Now, back to you, Wanda," Chris said.

"No, Chris. I don't wanna talk anymore," she said.

"Alright. Well, keep your head up. You have veteran detectives working your case," he said.

"I hope so. They need to find that witness," Wanda replied.

"Let's pray reward money is offered and it entices them to come forward," Chris said.

"Pray? God blocked my number a long time ago. I'm kidding. God has really been good to me. Let me tell y'all about my granny," Wanda said. "I'll start by saying she's talking much better. Anyway, the day I was released from jail I went to visit her. When I walked in the room she was happy to see me of course, but then she shook that pointed finger, fussing. Granny looked me in my eye and told me to get down on my knees and pray."

"Ah, that is so sweet," Kim sang.

"Yeah, and I have to admit, it touched me, so I prayed. I pray anyway. Well sometimes. Y'all just don't know it. What I have to say to God I say privately. I may go to somebody's church soon," Wanda said. "I have to do something different."

"Amen. We'd love for you to join us," Leon said.

"Noooo, Kim already told me about the members at your church," Wanda replied.

Kim laughed. "Wanda, stop tripping. We're newlyweds. Don't be starting trouble."

"I'm kidding," she said to Leon. "When I'm ready, I'll let you know. Whenever I do go, don't be surprised if the walls come tumbling down around us."

Chapter 27

Wanda replayed recent experiences in her mind—the sound of doors slamming shut while in jail, disgracing news footage with photos of her and Ron as the backdrop, the embarrassment of reporters posted outside of her home, and feeling like an intruder, knowing Derrick and Angel were forced to adjust their lifestyle having her around. Wanda couldn't deny from the moment she stepped through their door she felt welcomed and at home. Really, she expected nothing less. Derrick and Angel were great friends and hospitable hosts. Not only did residing with them give her privacy, it provided security and the chance for Wanda and Angel to talk, reminisce, and create new memories.

She also enjoyed bonding with Derrick Jr. They played patty cake and peek-a-boo often. When he'd fall asleep she'd steal his kisses.

Now, the day had come to learn her fate. Attorney Blair and his team had pressed for a speedy trial, convinced they'd collected sufficient evidence to prove Wanda's innocence.

She and her family and friends arrived at the courthouse early. Leon led a group prayer, then Wanda waited to be called for the closed session hearing. In the meantime, she separated herself and paced the hallway, trying to calm her nerves. She couldn't help but notice her mom clinging to her dad. He clearly wasn't interested in the relationship she was trying to rebuild. When Wanda saw him pull away when she attempted to hold his hand, she wanted to sympathize with her but couldn't because she had caused his bitterness. Her reality was her fault.

While looking their way, Wanda made eye contact with her dad and he walked toward her. "Hang in there, sweetheart," he said.

"Yes, sir. Can I ask you something?" Wanda said.

"Sure. Anything," he replied.

"Are you and Mom reconciling?" Wanda questioned.

"No," he said bluntly. "I think she's confusing kindness with affection. Our divorce will be final any day now. Once it's done, I'll introduce you to my new lady friend."

Wanda's mouth fell open. "Dad, you've move on?"

"Yes, I have," he said.

"Oh, boy. Momma is going to be crushed," Wanda said.

"You and I both know she has no one to blame but herself," he replied.

Attorney Blair interrupted their conversation when he called out for Wanda. She hugged her dad before disappearing behind the double doors. Wanda sat shaking like a leaf, with sweaty palms depending on his experience and expertise.

The prosecutor showed no mercy. He sought a guilty plea, refusing to be defeated. He pounded on the facts that Wanda's fingerprints were on the weapon and she was the only other person at the crime scene when the police arrived.

"I object, your honor," Attorney Blair called out.

"Objection overruled," the judge replied.

"The defendant had motive and opportunity," the prosecutor said, reminding Wanda of the conversation with her friends saying the same about Ron.

"She's a woman scorned," he said, "because the victim's husband had ended their affair to reconcile with his wife. By attacking the victim—actually attempting to kill her, your honor—the defendant had an illusion it would allow her to resume the courtship with the man she loves."

"That's a lie," Wanda blurted.

Attorney Blair grabbed her hand.

"Order in the court," the judge yelled, banging his gavel against a wooden block. "Another outburst, and I'll hold your client in contempt of court, Counsel."

"It won't happen again, your honor," Attorney Blair replied. "Calm down, Wanda. You can't speak out like that. Let me handle this."

"He's lying," she rebutted.

"Look. Don't worry. I'm representing you. We'll get our chance to speak," Attorney Blair assured her.

Wanda took a deep breath as the prosecutor called Ron as a witness. She wanted to scream as he sat under oath fabricating. He told the judge she'd stalked him and made threats against his wife on several occasions.

Wanda fidgeted in her chair, fighting the urge to charge Ron and beat him with her fists. When she felt Attorney Blair watching her, she returned his stare, enraged.

"Not one word," he ordered.

Ron went on to say that Sheila had arrived at Casey's birthday party with him but stayed in the VIP area the entire night to avoid a confrontation with Wanda."

She shook her head.

"Your honor, I believe the defendant, Wanda Boyd, followed my wife into the women's restroom and attacked her."

Wanda tuned Ron out as he continued to lie. She fought the urge to break down, identifying with people wrongfully accused, convicted, and serving time for crimes they didn't commit. Although hard, she batted away tears, denying Ron the opportunity to see her weak. Wanda made up her mind, even if he won the first round, he wouldn't win the fight. She vowed not to quit until he was proven guilt of a premeditated offense.

Attorney Blair interrupted her thoughts when he stood. Wanda watched him approach Ron. "Sir, you've said your wife arrived at the club with you. Am I correct?"

"Yes," Ron replied.

"Can you explain why she didn't leave with you, Mr. Phelps?" Attorney Blair asked.

"I couldn't find her. I thought maybe she'd left without me," he said.

Attorney Blair smirked. "Even though you came together? Did you bother to look for her," he quizzed.

"Yes, I did," Ron said.

"It never dawned on you to have someone check the ladies' room?" Attorney Blair questioned. "Did you call and make sure your wife was okay?"

"My wife doesn't have a phone," Ron replied.

"No phone. Okay. I have no further questions for the witness, your honor."

"You may step down," the judge told Ron.

Ron took a seat with a smirk Wanda wished she could slap off his face. At that point she didn't feel very confident. Attorney Blair hadn't badgered him enough for her, but she felt better when he called Sheila's mother to the stand. She told the judge her daughter was conscious but unable to attend court, then she told Sheila's story, saying Ron had kidnapped her and she'd been confined to a small room with only a toilet, sink, and mattress since her abduction, which the South Carolina authorities later identified as a locked and separate area of a detached garage behind his house in Hilton Head. Ron's cousin Sonya lived there along with her best friend and Ron's lover Sylvia who was also subpoenaed and testified. She denied having knowledge of Sheila being bound by chains in her backyard for months, but confessed to a romantic relationship with Ron and plans of marriage.

"You may step down," the judge informed her.

Meanwhile Attorney Blair's assistant approached him and whispered something in his ear. "Your honor, it appears a witness has come forward to testify on my client's behalf."

"Call your witness," he replied.

Wanda looked around to see who it was. Then sat in utter disbelief as Casey walked toward the witness stand.

She glimpsed in Ron's direction and could've sworn steam was coming from his ears.

"Raise your right hand," the bailiff instructed Casey, grabbing Wanda's attention. "Do you solemnly swear to tell the truth, the whole truth, and nothing but the truth, so help you God?"

"Yes, I do," Casey said in a soft voice.

Attorney Blair proceeded to question Casey. "For the record, will you state your first and last name please?

"Casey Howard," she replied.

"Casey, will you tell the court what happened on the night of Saturday, August 18 during your birthday party, starting at the point when you left my client Miss Boyd sitting at the table with Mr. Phelps?"

"Yes, sir. Um, it was at the end of the night. My fiancé, Pete, and I exited the building to get something he'd left in his car, leaving Wanda and Ron inside the club. While in the parking lot a group of women came toward Pete and me, saying someone had a gun. Pete told me to get in the car, then ordered me to leave. I did, not thinking at the moment about Wanda still being inside the building with Ron. When it dawned on me, I called her several times but my calls went straight to her voicemail.

"Anyway, fifteen minutes later, I realized I'd left my purse on the seat of the booth where we were sitting, so I turned around and drove back to the club. When I pulled up no one was around so I assumed Pete had run off the stragglers because of the gun incident. Ron's car was still in the lot and so was Wanda's, which raised my suspicions. I parked, then tried to enter the club but the door was locked. I was driving Pete's car so I used the key on his ring to get into the building.

"When I walked inside I didn't see anyone, so I headed upstairs. About midway up, I noticed Pete entering the women's bathroom. There was no reasonable explanation that I could think of for him going in there so I eased to the top step then tiptoed over to the door and pushed it open just enough to peek inside. That's when I saw Sheila's body strapped to a dolly—the kind you use to carry heavy furniture or appliances. Her head was slumped to the side, almost like she was asleep in an upright position, and Pete was holding her steady. Then…"

Casey paused, lowering her head.

"Take your time," Attorney Blair told her.

"Um," she continued, "I took my cell phone from the holder and pressed record moments before Ron stabbed his wife, Sheila, in her stomach three times."

Tears rolled down Casey's cheeks, and she sniffed as she continued to tell the story.

"While Ron put Wanda's fingerprints on the knife, Pete lowered Sheila's body onto the floor next to her. Both Ron and Pete were wearing gloves and Wanda was lying on the floor unresponsive or unconscious or whatever.

"I carefully closed the bathroom door, eased down stairs, and ran out of the building as fast as I could. I'm the woman who made the nine-one-one call. I disguised my voice and pretended to be the victim because I knew Ron and Pete would be gone before the police arrived. I told the operator I was in the building in the bathroom on the second floor so the police would enter the club. It was clear to me, for Sheila to have any chance of survival she had to be taken to the hospital pretty fast," Casey said, wiping tears away. "I believe Ron had planned for her to die that night. It's apparent he wanted Wanda to take the fall for his crime."

"Objection," the prosecutor yelled.

"Overruled," the judge replied.

Wanda was in awe. When the prosecutor stood to cross examine Casey, things became more intense as he attacked her character.

"Will you tell the court how you know Ron Phelps," he said.

Casey hesitated for a moment. "Yes. I met him at Jazzy's strip club."

"Can you elaborate on your relationship with Mr. Phelps after that meeting," he asked.

Casey looked at Wanda, then lowered head. "Um, I was his call girl. I did private parties for Ron a few years back," she finally said.

Wanda shook her head, disappointed by Casey's confession. Although her friends had told her she was a prostitute it didn't seem real. "Oh, my God. She slept with him," she said, reflecting on the day Casey cosigned her statement about Ron being good in bed. "I had a feeling it was more to that comment than she led me to believe. I should've known."

Wanda didn't know what to feel.

"Why did you stop servicing Mr. Phelps?" the prosecutor asked Casey, regaining Wanda's attention.

"He hired me to dance at his best friend, Pete's birthday bash, which I did, and I also provided intimate services for him. Pete and I hit it off pretty well, ended up friends, then lovers," Casey admitted. "This is the reason it has taken me so long to come forward. My loyalty was with Pete because he helped me take my life in a better direction. I felt I owed him—until recently anyway. After the incident at the club Pete demanded I cut all ties with Wanda. One day, she stopped by my job unexpectedly and he showed up while she was there. Pete has been verbally and mentally abusive since. I can't take it anymore."

"So, is telling this story your way of getting rid of Pete?" the prosecutor asked.

"No, sir. I'm doing what I should have weeks ago. Here's the video," Casey said, lifting her cellular in the air.

The bailiff handed the phone to the judge. Approach the bench please," he told both attorneys. They watched the video in awe.

The moment the judge said all charges were dropped, Wanda leaped from her chair and hugged Attorney Blair as hard as she could.

When Casey walked up, her smile faded. Wanda was happy she came forward and told the truth, but she felt betrayed.

"I'm so sorry, Wanda," Casey told her.

"Thanks for doing the right thing. I understand you were in a tough position, but letting me sit in jail when you knew I was innocent…That's not cool."

"Wanda, you have no idea how afraid I was. What Ron and Pete did to Sheila, they could've done to me," Casey said.

"That's true, but my question is…If Pete hadn't been abusive, were you going to allow me to serve prison time for a crime I didn't commit?"

Casey stood speechless.

"That's what I thought," Wanda said.

When she walked off her eyes met Judge Patrick Thompson's. Wanda's heart raced. She was surprised and happy to see him.

"Congratulations. We'll talk later," he whispered.

Wanda smiled. When she stepped outside the courtroom, she looked at her dad and announced the verdict. Her family and friends surrounded her, jumping for joy.

Book Club Questions

1. Was it wise for Wanda to take the law into her own hands? Should she have gone to the police or consulted Chris about her suspicions of Ron? Was her rationale for not involving the authorities, understandable?

2. Do you think going to jail gave Wanda a reality check?

3. How do you feel about Wanda's mother? Did she get what she deserved?

4. Did Kim do the right thing by turning in the money she'd found? Would it have been smarter for her to keep it?

5. Was Kim's financial hardship a lesson learned? Why or why not?

6. Is Kim's relationship with Leon a quick fix or does she sincerely care for him? Will their marriage last? Why or why not?

7. Should Wanda forgive Casey and continue their friendship?

8. Is Wanda compatible with Judge Thompson? Why or why not?

9. Why are men more likely to walk away from a relationship because of infidelity? Why are women more likely to stay?

About the Author

Lisa Dumas Harris was born July 9 in Fort Myers, Florida and raised in Charleston Park, Alva, Florida. In 1988, Lisa graduated from Riverdale High School. A year later, she joined the U.S. Army.

After four years of active duty, Lisa was honorably discharged and returned to hometown, Fort Myers, Florida where she enrolled at Edison Community College. It was there she received an Associate of Arts Degree. Lisa then pursued to fulfill her objective of becoming a nurse. She attended Lorenzo Walker Institute of Technology. While in the nursing program, she was a member of the honor society. Upon receiving her nursing license, Lisa was employed by the Fort Myers, Veterans Affairs Department, Outpatient Clinic. She practiced nursing for two years before venturing into a real estate career.

Lisa is a real estate investor and co-owner of ALH Rentals, LLC and finds herself once again welcoming new experiences and embracing greater challenges. She co-authored the novel *A Collage of Life,* published in December 2004; however, her most recent project and accomplishment are establishing a small privately owned publishing company, Independent Visions of Richmond Hill, Georgia. Lisa's novels, *Only Time Can Tell, Finding My Way, It Ain't Easy* and *Trouble In My Way* are realistic fiction with Christian roots. Through these works she hopes to inspire many to understand the gift of life. Lisa understands, relates, and focuses on the importance of wisdom and wise counsel, dealing with challenges, and the power of choice.

Novels by Lisa Dumas Harris

Finding My Way Series

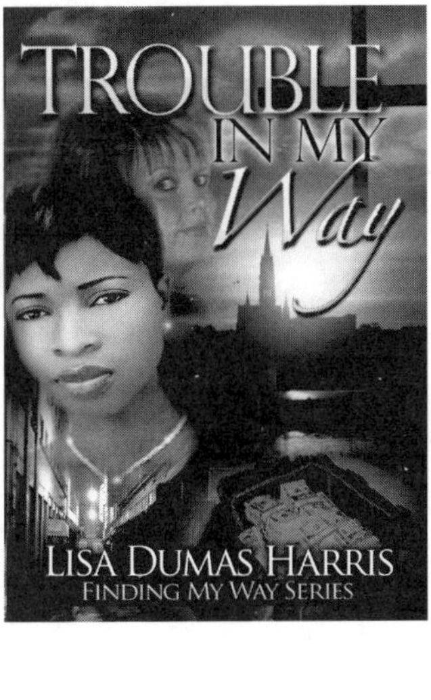

ORDER FORM

Name:____

Address:____

City:________________________ State:______ Zip:________

Telephone:___________ Email Address:__________________________

______ ***Only Time Can Tell*** **$14.00 each**

______***Finding My Way*** **$14.99**

______***It Ain't Easy*** **$14.00**

______***Trouble In My Way*** **$14.99**

Buy 2 or more books for $10 each plus $3.99 shipping.

To order by fax, send completed form to (912) 756-7615

Order Online: www.LisaDumasHarris.com
All debit or credit card purchases are handled through Paypal.

Mail order: Make check or money order payable to:

Independent Visions
Attn: Lisa Harris
PO Box 2991
Richmond Hill, GA 31324-4120

Payment:_____ Check ____Visa ____MasterCard _____Discover

Card Number:__________________________

Name as it appears on card:____________________________

Expiration Date: ____________________